CAPTIVA SISTERS

CAPTIVA ISLAND
BOOK FIFTEEN

ANNIE CABOT

CABOT PUBLISHING GROUP

CHAPTER 1

*B*ecca shifted uncomfortably on the deck chair, trying to find a position that didn't make her back scream in protest. At thirty-two weeks pregnant, discomfort had become her constant companion, but this morning felt different—worse somehow. The usually calming view of their Massachusetts backyard did little to ease her growing unease.

"You okay?" Christopher asked, glancing up from his coffee. The worry lines around his eyes had deepened over the past few months.

"Just the usual," she lied, forcing a smile. The dull ache that had started in her lower back during the night had gradually spread around to her abdomen. She'd been timing the twinges: seventeen minutes apart. Too irregular to be contractions, she told herself. Too early.

She pressed her palms against the small of her back and straightened, wincing at the sharp pain that shot through her side. The baby gave a forceful kick in response as if protesting the compression of its already cramped quarters.

"I think I'm going to lie down for a bit before we head to

Beth's," she said, pushing herself carefully to her feet. The world tilted slightly, and she gripped the edge of the table.

Christopher was beside her instantly, one hand on her elbow, the other at her waist. "That's it. I'm calling Dr. Winters."

"It's nothing," she insisted, but even to her ears, the words sounded hollow. "I just need to rest."

"Your appointment isn't for another week. I think we should —" Christopher stopped mid-sentence, his eyes fixed on the deck beneath her. "Becca, you're bleeding."

She looked down and saw the small dark spots on the wooden planks. Fear gripped her chest, making it hard to breathe. "It's too early," she whispered.

"I'm calling 911," Christopher said, reaching for his phone.

The ride to the hospital passed in a blur of sirens and urgent voices. Becca lay on the stretcher, one hand pressed protectively over her swollen belly, the other clutching Christopher's fingers so tightly her knuckles were white.

"BP is 150 over 95," the paramedic reported on his radio. "Patient is thirty-two weeks pregnant with vaginal bleeding and abdominal pain."

"The baby," Becca murmured, tears sliding down her temples and into her hair. "Please, my baby..."

"We're almost there," Christopher promised, his voice steady despite the fear in his eyes. "Everything's going to be fine."

But even as he spoke, another pain tore through her abdomen, this one so intense that she cried out.

"Contractions are now eight minutes apart," the paramedic said, his tone carefully neutral. "And increasing in intensity."

Dr. Winters met them at the emergency entrance, her face composed but serious as she helped transfer Becca to a hospital bed.

"Let's get her to Maternal Assessment right away," she instructed the nurses. "I want continuous fetal monitoring and a complete blood workup. And page Dr. Patel from neonatal."

"What's happening?" Christopher asked, jogging alongside the bed as they wheeled Becca through the corridors.

"We need to rule out placental abruption," Dr. Winters replied, her voice low but audible to Becca. "That's when the placenta separates from the uterine wall before delivery. The bleeding and the pain are concerning."

"But the baby—" Becca started.

"We're going to do everything we can," Dr. Winters assured her, squeezing her hand briefly. "Thirty-two weeks is early, but it's also late enough that we have good outcomes. First, let's see what we're dealing with."

The next hour was a flurry of activity. Blood draws, an ultrasound, and monitoring belts were strapped across Becca's belly, capturing the baby's heartbeat and her contractions.

"Heart rate is stable," a nurse reported, adjusting one of the monitors. "Strong and regular."

Becca closed her eyes in momentary relief, but another contraction seized her, stronger than before.

Dr. Winters studied the ultrasound screen, and her expression was grave. "There's a partial abruption," she confirmed. "About twenty percent separation from the uterine wall." She looked at Becca directly. "We need to control your blood pressure immediately. It's putting additional stress on the placenta."

"Will I lose the baby?" Becca asked the question she'd been afraid to voice.

"Absolutely not," Dr. Winters said firmly. "We'll start you on magnesium sulfate to stop the contractions and medication to lower your blood pressure. You'll also need steroid injections to help your baby's lungs mature faster, just in case we need to deliver early."

"And if that doesn't work?" Christopher asked, his voice rough with emotion.

"Then we'll need to perform an emergency C-section," Dr. Winters replied. "But let's take this one step at a time. The baby's vitals are strong, which is excellent news."

As the medical team worked around her, inserting IVs and administering medications, Becca felt oddly detached, as if watching herself from a distance. The beeping of the fetal monitor became her lifeline, each steady pulse a reminder that her child was still fighting.

"I should call Beth," Christopher murmured, his phone already in his hand. "She's expecting us for dinner. And then I'll call your dad."

Becca nodded, grateful he was handling the logistics while she focused on staying calm for the baby's sake. Amid the crisis, she couldn't help thinking of her mother, Julia, who had died years earlier. How much Becca wished she could call her now, hear her reassuring voice telling her everything would be all right. So many years had passed, and still, in moments of crisis, her mother was the first person Becca wanted.

Christopher stepped into the hallway to make the calls, and Becca could see him through the partially open door. His shoulders were tense, his free hand raking through his hair in that way he did when he was deeply worried. She saw him press his forehead against the wall momentarily after ending the first call, collecting himself before dialing another number.

When he returned, his expression was carefully composed, but he couldn't fool her.

"I can't lose this baby," she whispered when they were briefly alone. "We've come too far."

He brought her hand to his lips. "You won't. You're both fighters." His eyes were red-rimmed but determined. "Remember what we went through to get here? This kid is stubborn, just like you."

She managed a tremulous smile, then grimaced as another contraction gripped her. The monitor beside the bed showed a peak higher than the last.

"The contractions are getting stronger."

Christopher pressed the call button, and almost immediately, Dr. Winters returned.

"The magnesium needs time," she explained after checking the monitors. "But you're right; the contractions are intensifying." She hesitated, then continued, "We need to prepare for possible delivery. Your blood pressure is still dangerous, and the abruption could worsen."

"But it's too early," Becca protested weakly.

"Eight weeks early is concerning, yes," Dr. Winters acknowledged. "But we have an excellent NICU, and Dr. Patel is one of the best neonatologists in the state." She smiled reassuringly. "Thirty-two weekers generally do very well with the right care."

As if summoned by her name, Dr. Patel entered the room. She was a petite woman with kind eyes behind stylish glasses.

"I understand we might be meeting your little one sooner than expected," she said, approaching Becca's bedside. "I wanted to introduce myself and explain what would happen if we need to deliver today."

For the next few minutes, Dr. Patel outlined the specialized care their premature baby would receive, the challenges they might face, and the reasons for optimism.

"The most important thing," she concluded, "is that we're prepared. Your baby will be in good hands; I promise you that."

Becca nodded, strangely comforted by the doctor's straight-forward approach: there were no false assurances, just competence and compassion.

Another hour passed with intense vigilance. The contractions continued despite the medication, though their intensity seemed to plateau. Becca's blood pressure, however, remained stubbornly elevated.

Christopher had been making more calls—to his brother Michael, Becca's father and brothers in Florida, and their friends. He was building their support network and preparing everyone for what might come, and Becca was grateful for his steadiness.

"Beth and Lauren are on their way," he reported, returning to her bedside. "And your dad is trying to get a flight out tonight, but there's a storm system moving in over Florida. He might be delayed."

"Did you call your mom?" Becca asked, suddenly realizing they hadn't contacted the Wheeler matriarch.

Christopher's expression tightened slightly. "Not yet. I wanted to have more information first. You know how she gets—she'll be on the first plane here if I tell her what's happening, and with the inn fully booked..."

"Call her," Becca insisted gently. "She'd want to know, even if she can't come immediately."

Before Christopher could respond, Dr. Winters returned with a fresh ultrasound report. "The abruption hasn't worsened, which is good news. And the baby's showing no signs of distress." She studied the monitor readings. "But your blood pressure is still too high, and these contractions aren't stopping despite maximum doses of the tocolytics."

She pulled up a chair and sat beside the bed, her expression serious. "Becca, Christopher, I think we've reached a decision point. We can continue trying to manage conservatively, but I'm concerned about the risks of waiting—to both of you."

"You're saying we should do the C-section," Christopher stated, his hand tightening around Becca's.

"I believe it's the safest option," Dr. Winters confirmed. "The longer we wait with an unstable placenta and uncontrolled hypertension, the greater the risk of a complete abruption or seizures."

Becca looked up at the monitor, which displayed her baby's heartbeat, which was strong and regular despite the chaos surrounding it. Eight weeks early. Not ideal, but not impossible. This baby was a fighter—their fighter.

"Okay," she said finally, her voice steadier than expected. "Let's do it."

The preparations moved swiftly after that. Consent forms, surgical briefings, and a flurry of activity as the doctors prepared the operating room.

"I'll be with you the whole time," Christopher promised as they wheeled her bed toward the elevator.

"And I'll be waiting in the OR to take care of your baby as soon as she arrives," Dr. Patel added, walking alongside them.

As the operating room doors swung open, Becca felt a strange calm settle over her. Whatever happened next, they wouldn't face it alone.

"Ready?" Dr. Winters asked, already gowned and masked.

Becca nodded, reaching for Christopher's hand. "We talked about this, so don't forget. Call her Eloise," she whispered to him. "Eloise Julia. If anything happens to me—"

"Nothing's going to happen to you," Christopher interrupted fiercely.

In the sterile brightness of the operating room, surrounded by beeping machines and medical staff, Becca closed her eyes. She pictured the sun-drenched beaches of Captiva Island, where she'd grown up. The waves lapped at the shore, the salty breeze, the feel of the warm sand between her toes, her mother's voice on the wind.

Whether we watch it or not, the sun sets, and it's a shame to miss the show.

Becca opened her eyes, determination replacing fear. She wasn't going to miss any shows—not her daughter's birth, not her first smile, not her first steps—nothing.

"Ready," she said firmly, squeezing Christopher's hand.

Beth and Lauren arrived in the corridor outside, breathless. They had rushed from their homes as soon as Christopher called. They found themselves standing outside a set of imposing double doors, unable to go further.

"What happened?" Beth asked, looking at the nurse.

"Placental abruption and high blood pressure," one of the nurses explained. "They're performing an emergency C-section."

Lauren pressed a hand to her mouth, her eyes wide with concern. "The baby—will it be okay?"

"Dr. Patel is the best neonatologist in the state," the nurse assured them. "If anyone can ensure that baby thrives, it's her."

Beth wrapped an arm around Lauren's shoulders, drawing strength from her sister even as she provided it. "They're going to be fine," she said, with more conviction than she felt. "All three of them."

Lauren pulled out her phone as they settled into the uncomfortable waiting room chairs. "I should let Jeff know. And we should try to reach Mom again," she said.

Beth nodded, staring at the wall clock as if she could force it to move faster by sheer will. "A storm in Florida, a crisis here... when it rains, it pours."

"Literally, in Mom's case," Lauren replied, attempting a weak smile.

Neither mentioned the obvious—that the joyful family dinner they'd planned for tonight, celebrating Becca's pregnancy as she entered her third trimester, had transformed into a vigil for mother and child. Instead, they did what the Wheeler women had always done in times of crisis: they prepared for whatever might come, gathering their strength for the battle ahead.

In the operating room, behind the sterile drape across Becca's chest, a team of medical professionals worked with focused intensity, racing against time to bring Eloise Julia Wheeler safely into the world.

CHAPTER 2

The surgical procedure felt surreal—the blue drape erected across Becca's chest, the strange sensations of pressure without pain, Christopher's steady presence beside her head, whispering encouragement, and then a flurry of activity on the other side of the drape.

"The baby's out," Dr. Winters announced. "Your baby girl has arrived!"

A brief, startled cry filled the operating room—smaller than a full-term newborn's wail but determined, nonetheless. Becca felt tears streaming down her face as Christopher squeezed her hand.

"Is she okay?" Becca asked, straining to see beyond the drape.

"We're checking her now," Dr. Patel replied, her team already surrounding the tiny infant. "She's breathing on her own, which is excellent. Four pounds—normal for thirty-two weeks."

Christopher moved to peek at their daughter while the neonatal team worked, his face transforming with wonder. "She's beautiful, Becca," he said, his voice thick with emotion. "So tiny, but perfect."

After a few minutes of assessment, Dr. Patel said, "We need to get her to the NICU. Her oxygen levels are slightly lower than we'd like, and we want to monitor her closely. Would you like to see her before we go?"

The team brought the tiny bundle, now swaddled tight, close to Becca's face. For a brief, precious moment, she gazed at her daughter—dark wisps of hair, tiny features scrunched in concentration, impossibly small fingers—before they whisked her away.

"Christopher, go with her," Becca urged, though it broke her heart to be separated from them.

"Are you sure?" he asked, torn.

"I'm in good hands," she assured him, smiling. "She needs you more right now."

After a quick kiss on her forehead, Christopher followed the medical team out, leaving Becca with Dr. Winters, who continued working to deliver the placenta and close the incision.

"You've got a fighter there," Dr. Winters commented as she worked. That's a good, strong cry for a preemie."

"She gets that from both sides," Becca said, suddenly feeling very tired, the adrenaline of the crisis beginning to ebb.

"We'll need to keep you here for at least three days," Dr. Winters explained. "Longer if there are any complications. And we'll need to monitor your blood pressure closely—it's still elevated."

Becca nodded, only half listening. Her thoughts were with her tiny daughter and with Christopher. She hadn't even been able to hold her baby.

"I believe a few of your family members are already in the waiting area. I know you'll want to see them, but for now, let's focus on getting you stabilized."

As they wheeled her to recovery, Becca felt a strange mixture of joy and grief—joy at the birth of her daughter, grief at the loss of the final weeks of pregnancy, the birth she had planned, the immediate bonding she had imagined. Everything had happened so quickly, with barely a moment to absorb, that she was now a mother to a premature baby fighting her own battles in the NICU.

In the waiting room, Beth paced back and forth, unable to sit still. Lauren had stepped outside to make more calls, coordinating with Jeff and Michael, trying to reach their mother in Florida, and providing updates to Becca's father and brothers.

When Christopher finally appeared, his face was a complex mixture of emotions—joy, fear, exhaustion, and a fierce protectiveness that had never existed before.

"She's here," he announced, his voice cracking slightly. "Eloise Julia Wheeler. Four pounds exactly. They've taken her to the NICU, but she's breathing mostly on her own."

Beth rushed forward to embrace her brother. "And Becca?"

"Still in recovery. Becca's blood pressure is concerning them." He scrubbed a hand over his face. "It's been... intense."

"Eloise Julia," Beth repeated softly, her eyes filling with tears. "After Becca's mom."

Christopher nodded, emotion finally overtaking him. He leaned into his sister's embrace, his shoulders shaking slightly. "She's so tiny, Beth. So fragile. But she's fighting."

"Of course she is," Beth said firmly, pulling back to look him in the eye. "She's a Wheeler and a Powell. Fighting is in her blood."

Lauren returned, tucking her phone away. "Jeff's on his way with coffee and food. Michael's coming straight from work. I left messages for Mom and Crawford, but that storm is causing havoc with the cell service down there."

Christopher nodded gratefully, too overwhelmed to fully process the logistics. "Yeah, I tried earlier. I've got to get back.

They're letting me back into the NICU in a few minutes. I just wanted to update you first."

"Go," Beth urged. "Be with your daughter. We'll handle everything else."

As Christopher disappeared through the double doors, Lauren and Beth exchanged a glance that spoke volumes—concern, determination, and the unspoken acknowledgment that their family had just dramatically changed.

"I need to call Gabriel," Beth said.

Lauren nodded. "And I should check on the kids. My neighbor, Sherry, is with them, but I want to make sure they're okay. Jeff says they're fine, but I want to let them know they've got another little cousin. They've been so excited for another girl in the family."

They parted ways momentarily, each handling their rapidly expanding crisis management piece. When they reconvened fifteen minutes later, Lauren had a notepad covered in lists.

"Okay, we need a plan," she said, her organizational skills kicking in. Depending on how long Eloise is in the NICU, we're looking at weeks of support needed: meals, childcare for my three, house cleaning, hospital visits, rotations..."

Beth smiled despite the tension. "You and your lists."

"Lists keep me sane," Lauren replied without apology. "And right now, they need us to be the sane ones, handling the details while they focus on Eloise and Becca's recovery."

"You're right," Beth agreed, sinking into a chair. "It's just... not how any of us imagined today going."

Lauren squeezed her hand. "I know. But we'll get through it. We always do."

Beth nodded. "Whatever you do, don't call a Code Red," referring to their mother's usual response to family emergencies.

Lauren laughed. "I know I'm a lot like Mom, but I'm not that much like her."

Christopher stood beside the incubator in the NICU, looking wonderfully at his daughter. He wore a blue hospital gown and hospital gloves. The baby was impossibly small, her tiny body connected to monitors that beeped rhythmically, a miniature oxygen cannula in her nose. Her skin was slightly translucent, with a delicate network of veins visible beneath the surface. Dark wisps of hair peeked out from under the knitted cap that seemed too large for her head.

"You can touch her," a nurse said gently, opening one of the portholes in the incubator. "Just place your hand on her. She'll know you're there."

Hesitantly, Christopher reached through the opening, his large hand hovering over his daughter's tiny form before gently settling on her stomach. He could feel her heartbeat, surprisingly strong for someone so small.

"Hello, Eloise," he whispered, his voice catching. "I'm your dad."

She stirred slightly at his voice, her tiny fingers flexing.

"She recognizes you already," the nurse observed with a smile. "Talk to her more. It helps."

Christopher nodded, unable to take his eyes off his daughter. "Your mom's going to be here soon," he continued, his voice low and soothing. "She's resting now but can't wait to meet you properly. We've been waiting for you for so long."

As he spoke, memories of the past few months washed over him—the morning sickness, heavy school/work schedules, cravings, mood swings, all of it worth every minute knowing it would lead to this special moment.

"You're early to the party, sweetheart," he said, stroking her stomach gently. "But that's okay. We're ready for you anyway. We've been ready for you since your mother and I fell in love."

At that moment, in the hushed, high-tech environment of the NICU, Christopher transformed. The abstract concept of fatherhood, which he'd been preparing for intellectually for months, suddenly became viscerally real. This tiny being, this perfect, fragile daughter, was now the center of his universe.

And she was fighting for her life.

He felt a surge of powerful protectiveness that nearly took his breath away. "I'm right here," he promised her. "I'm not going anywhere."

The nurse worked around him, checking monitors, adjusting settings, and recording numbers on a chart. "She's doing remarkably well," she informed him. "Her oxygen saturation is steady at 93%, which is good for her gestational age."

Christopher absorbed this information like a lifeline. "And her lungs? Dr. Patel mentioned concerns..."

"The steroid injections they gave your wife before delivery have helped. We're supporting her with minimal oxygen, and she's handling it well." The nurse smiled reassuringly. "Dr. Patel will be back to check on her in an hour, but Eloise is showing us she's quite the little fighter."

Christopher managed a smile. "Her mother's stubbornness and my determination. Poor kid never stood a chance of being anything else."

After spending nearly an hour with Eloise, Christopher reluctantly left the NICU to check on Becca, who had been moved to a recovery room. He found her pale but alert, her eyes lighting up when she saw him.

"How is she?" Becca asked immediately, reaching for his hand.

"Beautiful," Christopher replied, sitting on the edge of the bed. "Strong. The nurses are impressed with her. She's on a little oxygen but breathing mostly on her own."

Becca's eyes filled with tears. "I want to see her."

"As soon as you're stable," he promised. "Dr. Winters says they need to get your blood pressure under control first."

Becca nodded, disappointment evident in her face despite her understanding. "Did you call my dad?"

"Left messages. There's a storm hitting Captiva right now, and the cell service is spotty. But he'll call as soon as he can." Christopher stroked her hair back from her forehead. "Beth and Lauren are here. Michael's on his way. And I finally reached my sister, Sarah when I couldn't get Mom."

Before she could respond, a nurse entered to check Becca's vitals. Her expression grew concerned as she noted the blood pressure reading.

"Still climbing," she murmured, adjusting an IV drip. "I'm going to page Dr. Winters."

Christopher's worry returned full force. "What's happening?"

"Her blood pressure continues to rise despite the medication," the nurse explained. "It could be the beginning of postpartum preeclampsia. Not uncommon after a placental abruption, but we must address it quickly."

Just as they'd weathered one crisis, another loomed. Becca closed her eyes, exhaustion threatening to overwhelm her. How much more could they handle in one day?

"One step at a time," Christopher murmured, seeming to read her thoughts. "We got through the first part. We'll get through this, too."

As the medical team again acted around her, Becca held on to that promise. Their daughter—tiny Eloise Julia—was fighting her battle in the NICU. Becca would fight hers here. Together, apart but connected by invisible bonds of love and determination, the Wheeler family would face whatever came next.

Beth and Lauren had set up camp in the family waiting area, their phones constantly in use as they coordinated the rapidly expanding support network. Jeff had arrived with food and coffee, and Michael had joined them straight from work, still in his police uniform.

"Any updates?" Michael asked, loosening his tie as he accepted a coffee from Jeff.

"Christopher texted a few minutes ago," Beth reported. "Eloise is stable in the NICU. Becca's blood pressure concerns them, though. They're monitoring her closely."

Michael nodded, his expression serious. "And Mom? Any luck reaching her?"

Lauren shook her head. "The storm's messing with communications. I got through briefly to Sarah, but then we got cut off. She knows the basics, though, and promised to tell Mom. I think Chris finally reached her."

"What about Crawford and the boys?" Jeff asked.

"Christopher said he left messages," Beth replied. "But the same issue with the storm."

Michael leaned back, concern etched on his features. "Of all the times for a weather crisis..."

Beth's phone chimed with a text, and she quickly read it. "It's from Chris. They've diagnosed Becca with postpartum preeclampsia. They're starting her on magnesium sulfate to prevent seizures."

The group fell silent, the seriousness of the situation sinking in. Finally, Michael spoke, his voice steady.

"Okay, here's what we do. Jeff and Lauren, you head home to the kids. They need stability right now, and Lauren, you can coordinate the meal train and support schedule from there. Beth and I will stay here tonight, trading off between checking on Becca and being with Chris." He looked around the circle. "Sound good?"

Everyone nodded, appearing grateful for the clear direction.

"I'll come back first thing tomorrow morning," Lauren promised. "After I get the kids off to school."

Jeff stood, helping Lauren gather her things. "Call us if anything changes overnight. Anything at all."

As they were preparing to leave, a nurse approached. "Are you Eloise Wheeler's family?"

They all nodded.

"Dr. Patel asked me to update you. She's doing very well—maintaining her oxygen levels, good color, and responding to stimuli appropriately. She's one of our stronger thirty-two weekers."

The collective relief was palpable. "Can we see her?" Beth asked.

"Family visits are restricted to parents for the first twenty-four hours," the nurse explained apologetically. "But after that, we can arrange brief visits for immediate family, two at a time."

"Thank you," Michael said, speaking for all of them.

As Lauren and Jeff departed, promising to return the next day, Beth and Michael settled in for what would likely be a long night. Neither said it aloud, but both thought the same thing: their family had just experienced a seismic shift. Nothing would be quite the same again.

"You should call Gabriel," Michael suggested. "Let him know you'll be staying."

Beth nodded, already dialing. "I wish Mom could be here," she said quietly. "She'd know exactly what to do."

Michael smiled wryly. "She'd be running the place by now, organizing the nurses, and probably redecorating the waiting room."

That drew a laugh from Beth. "True. But still..."

"I know," Michael agreed, understanding her unspoken thought. In times of crisis, they instinctively turned to Maggie Wheeler Moretti, the indomitable force at the center of their family. Her absence now, forced by distance and weather, was keenly felt.

"She'll be here as soon as she can," Michael said with certainty. "Storm or no storm, wild horses couldn't keep her from her new granddaughter."

Beth nodded, drawing comfort from the truth of his words. "And in the meantime, we step up."

"Exactly," Michael confirmed. "That's what Wheelers do."

CHAPTER 3

*W*hen Maggie Wheeler Moretti crossed the driveway to the Key Lime Garden Inn, the wind had picked up, sending a salty breeze through the lush gardens surrounding the property.

The early morning sun was already burning off what little coolness the night had left behind, but the air felt different now—thicker, more restless. The storm out over the Gulf was getting closer.

She stepped onto the back porch, the old wood creaking beneath her feet. A few of the wicker chairs shifted slightly in the wind, their cushions lifting just enough to hint at trouble to come. She made a mental note to have Paolo bring them in before they spread across the lawn.

Inside, the scent of coffee and warm pastries filled the air. Iris and Oliver, the inn's chefs, were already at work in the kitchen.

The inn was already stirring—guests shuffling in for breakfast, the distant hum of conversation blending with the clatter of dishes from the kitchen. She spotted Millie, the inn's housekeeper, already moving through the lobby with a basket of fresh towels.

"Morning, Millie," Maggie greeted.

"Morning, Maggie. That storm looks like it's heading this way. I'll check the guest rooms; everyone is up now. I should make sure the windows are latched tight."

Maggie nodded, moving toward the nearest set of French doors and pulling them closed. "Good idea. Let's go ahead and shut all the windows now before the rain starts blowing in."

"On it," Millie said, already heading toward the hallway.

Maggie filled a coffee cup and then returned to her seat at the kitchen island. Iris was busy pulling a tray of freshly baked croissants from the oven, replacing them with a tray of Maggie's scones.

Oliver, the other chef, was standing at the counter, slicing strawberries with a focus that suggested he wasn't just thinking about fruit. Maggie caught the glance he sent in Iris's direction—quick, almost cautious—but she didn't miss its warmth.

She didn't lose sight of how close they'd become in the last few months, and it was lovely to watch.

"Iris," Maggie said, "Can you help Millie with the windows? That storm looks like it will be here any minute."

Iris wiped her hands on her apron and peered out the window above the sink. "Wow. Look at that sky."

"Yep. And I don't want our guests dealing with wet floors and soaked curtains."

"Of course." Iris set down her towel. "I'll do it right away."

Maggie turned and nearly collided with Paolo as he entered through the back door. He had a crate of fresh oranges in his arms, his dark, wavy hair slightly windblown from being outside.

"Did you see that wind?" he said, setting the crate down. "It's kicking up hard. We should bring in the porch furniture before it ends up in the mangroves."

"I was just about to tell you that." Maggie pressed a quick kiss to his cheek. "Think it's going to be a big one?"

Paolo glanced back out the window, studying the sky like one of the local fishermen. "That's what they say. It's got that feel to it. Fortunately, they're not predicting a hurricane."

Before Maggie could respond, the front door swung open with a burst of warm air, and Maggie's best friend, Chelsea, strolled in, sunglasses perched on her head, her hair slightly windblown. She didn't even glance at the guests milling about—she walked straight toward the kitchen like she owned the place.

"Boy, do you see the wind out there?" Chelsea announced, pulling off her sunglasses and tucking them into her bag. "The tide brought the water right up to my back door."

As her best friend made a beeline for the coffee pot, Maggie arched a brow. "Good morning to you, too, and why do you have sunglasses on top of your head when the sun is nowhere to be found?"

Chelsea poured herself a cup, taking a long sip before sighing satisfactorily. "That's better. Now I can be social." She set the mug down and gave Maggie a pointed look. "Because, Maggie dear, it keeps my hair from blowing all over the place. Did you make scones?"

Maggie smirked. "Iris just put them in the oven, but croissants just came out."

"Bless you." Chelsea grabbed a stool at the island, leaning elbows on the cool surface. "So, what's on the agenda today? Other than storm prep, of course."

Maggie glanced at Paolo, who was already heading out to move the porch furniture. "Right now? Keeping this place from blowing away."

Chelsea huffed, stealing a piece of fruit from Oliver's cutting board. "You're no fun. But fine. I'll stay and help you batten down the hatches."

Maggie chuckled, shaking her head as she placed the croissants on a cooling rack. Chelsea might complain, but she would stay. She always did.

"Where is your husband? I thought you'd be having breakfast with Steven," Maggie asked.

Chelsea shrugged, "Is that your way of saying you'd rather I eat breakfast at home?"

Maggie laughed. "Not at all. I just wondered where he was, that's all."

"Well, if you must know, Steven is in Chicago now. Some conferences about building materials. I forget the details except to say that your son-in-law, Trevor, is with him."

Maggie nodded. "Oh, right. Sarah did tell me he was going on a business trip to Chicago."

Smiling, Chelsea added, "So, you get to see my beautiful face for the next three days."

Maggie chuckled, "And a beautiful face it is."

As they continued their friendly banter, Maggie's cell phone rang from where she'd left it on the counter. She glanced at it, planning to let it go to voicemail—the inn was too busy this morning for personal calls—but something made her check the caller ID.

"It's Sarah," she said, surprised. Her youngest daughter rarely called this early. "Let me just make sure everything's okay."

She picked up the phone. "Hi, sweetheart. Is everything—"

"Mom," Sarah's voice was breathless, urgent, "I've been trying to reach you. The cell service is terrible with this storm."

Maggie's maternal instincts immediately went on high alert. "What's wrong?"

"It's Becca. She went into premature labor. Chris has been trying to reach you."

Maggie's heart dropped. "What? She's only—"

"Thirty-two weeks," Sarah finished. "Chris finally got through to me. They had to do an emergency C-section. The baby's in the NICU."

Maggie gripped the counter, her knuckles going white. "And Becca?"

"Stable, but they're worried about her blood pressure. It's some postpartum complication. Chris didn't share more details than that."

"I need to be there," Maggie said immediately, already mentally packing a bag. "Are there any flights still going out?"

"That's the problem. The airport's shut down because of the storm. Nothing's flying until at least tomorrow, maybe longer."

Maggie closed her eyes, fighting a wave of helplessness. Her son needed her. Her daughter-in-law needed her. Her grandchild had arrived eight weeks early and was fighting in the NICU. And she was trapped on an island hundreds of miles away.

"I'm going to find a way," she said firmly. Thanks, Sarah, I'll call you back."

Maggie ended the call and dialed Christopher's number, but the call went nowhere.

Paolo returned from the porch and stood in the doorway, watching Maggie with worried eyes.

"What is it?" he asked as soon as she ended the call.

"Becca went into premature labor. They had to do an emergency C-section. The baby's in the NICU." The words tumbled out, each making the situation more real and frightening.

"Oh, Maggie," Chelsea breathed, immediately moving to embrace her friend.

Paolo stepped closer, his hand finding Maggie's shoulder. "And how is Becca?"

"They're worried about her blood pressure. Some postpartum complication." Maggie looked up at her husband, determination replacing shock. "We need to get to Massachusetts. Now."

Paolo nodded, already thinking through the logistics. "The Fort Myers airport is closed. Maybe we could drive to Tampa and see if they're still operating flights?"

"I'll check," Chelsea offered, pulling out her phone.

Maggie nodded, grateful for their immediate support. "I'll

keep trying to reach Chris. Sarah said he's been trying to call me, but I don't see anything on my phone."

She stepped away from the kitchen, finding a quiet corner in the now empty dining room. Her hands were shaking slightly as she dialed her son's number. It rang several times before connecting, the signal struggling against the storm.

"Mom?" Christopher's voice was distant, fading in and out.

"Chris! I just heard from Sarah. How's Becca? How's the baby?"

The line crackled, his response fragmenting before strengthening again. "—stable for now. They've got her on medication to prevent seizures."

"And the baby?" Maggie pressed, straining to hear through the static.

"She's doing better than they expected. She's four pounds, on some oxygen but breathing mostly on her own."

Even though Maggie knew Becca and Christopher were having a girl, she still needed to hear her son say it again.

"She?" Maggie's voice caught. "A granddaughter?"

"Yes." The pride in Christopher's voice was unmistakable, even through the poor connection. "Eloise Julia Wheeler."

Tears sprang to Maggie's eyes. "Julia. After Becca's mother."

"It was always the plan," Christopher confirmed. "But now that she's here... it feels even more right."

"It's perfect," Maggie said softly. "Perfect."

The line crackled again, Christopher's voice fading before returning. "—trying to get here?"

"The airport's closed because of the storm," Maggie explained, frustration evident in her voice. "But we're looking at options. Tampa might still be operating."

"Don't take risks, Mom. The roads will be dangerous if—"

The call dropped completely, the storm finally severing their tenuous connection. Maggie stared at her phone, willing to reconnect, but the signal was gone.

She returned to the kitchen, where Chelsea and Paolo were huddled over their phones.

"Fort Myers is grounding all flights," Chelsea said.

"Tampa's still operating, but they're expecting to close within the hour," Paolo added. "We'd never get a flight at this point."

Maggie took a deep breath, forcing herself to think logically despite the emotional turmoil. "So we wait it out. The storm should pass by tomorrow. We'll be on the first flight available."

Paolo nodded, wrapping an arm around his wife. "I'll call the airline now; see what I can book."

"And I'll handle the inn while you're gone," Chelsea volunteered. "You two focus on getting ready to leave."

Maggie squeezed her friend's hand gratefully. "Thank you."

As she turned to head to the carriage house to pack, Maggie nearly collided with her mother, who was making her way into the kitchen.

"What's all the commotion?" she asked, her keen eyes missing nothing despite her eighty years. "I could hear the urgency even upstairs."

Maggie quickly explained the situation, watching her mother's weathered face shift through the same emotions she had just experienced—shock, concern, and determination.

"Another great-grandbaby," Grandma Sarah murmured, her eyes misty. "Eight weeks early but fighting. That's the Wheeler spirit."

"And Powell," Maggie added. "They named her Eloise Julia."

Something in Grandma Sarah's expression softened. "Julia would be so proud. That girl of hers becoming a mother..."

"I need to be there," Maggie said, the words tight with emotion. "Chris needs me. Becca needs me. That baby—"

"And you will be," her mother interrupted, her voice firm. "As soon as this blasted storm passes. In the meantime, they have Beth, Michael, and Lauren. They're not alone, Maggie."

Maggie nodded, taking comfort in that truth. Her children

had always been there for each other. They wouldn't fail now, in this most critical moment.

"I should call Crawford," Maggie suddenly realized. "He'll want to be there too."

"I imagine Chris already has," her mother pointed out. "But yes, check. That man loves his daughter something fierce."

As Maggie ran out the back door, the wind outside intensified, rattling the windows and sending a potted plant Paolo forgot to move, crashing from the porch railing. The storm that had seemed merely inconvenient an hour ago now felt like a malevolent force, keeping her from where she most needed to be.

But storms passed. They always did. And when this one cleared, nothing would stop Maggie Wheeler Moretti from reaching her family.

At Powell Water Sports on Captiva Island, Crawford Powell stared out the window at the angry waves battering the shoreline. The shop was closed for the day—no sane person would be renting kayaks or booking fishing charters in this weather—but he'd come downstairs to the shop, needing something to do with his restless energy.

He'd tried his son-in-law's number for the past hour, but the cell service was patchy at best. The landline at the shop was more reliable, but so far, Chris hadn't answered his cellphone. All he had was the brief, terrifying message Christopher had left hours ago: *Becca was in premature labor. Complications. Heading to the hospital now.*

The not knowing was torture.

The shop's door burst open, letting in a gust of wind and rain, along with Crawford's wife, Ciara. Her dark hair was plastered to her head despite the rain slicker she wore, and her expression was grim.

"Any word?" she asked.

Crawford shook his head. "Nothing new. Cell service is garbage."

Ciara shed her rain gear, hanging it on the hook by the door, immediately forming a puddle on the wooden floor. "The boys are going crazy. Luke's talking about driving to Tampa to catch a flight."

"In this?" Crawford gestured to the window, where the palm trees were bending at alarming angles in the wind. "No one's driving anywhere right now. And even if they could, I don't think anything is flying out there any more than they are in Fort Myers. The saving grace is it's a fast moving storm, at least that's what the weather report says."

Ciara sighed, moving behind the counter to start a pot of coffee. It was a familiar routine they'd enacted hundreds of times since their marriage. In times of stress, Ciara made coffee. Strong, Italian-style coffee that could strip paint but always helped clear Crawford's head.

"I know," she agreed. "I told him that. Doesn't make the waiting any easier."

Crawford nodded, understanding completely. His sons— Luke, Joshua, and Finn—fiercely protected their only sister. The idea of Becca in danger and their inability to reach her undoubtedly drove them to distraction.

"What about you?" Ciara asked, studying her husband's face. "How are you holding up?"

Crawford ran a hand through his salt-and-pepper hair, not bothering to pretend. "Terrified," he admitted. "She's my little girl, Ciara. And now she's having a baby eight weeks early, with complications, and I can't even get to her."

Ciara nodded, reaching across the counter to squeeze his hand. "She's strong, Crawford. Just like Julia was, and she has Christopher, who adores her. She's not alone."

Crawford nodded, drawing strength from his wife's support.

The shop phone rang, startling them both. Crawford lunged for it, nearly knocking over a display of fishing lures in his haste.

"Powell Water Sports," he answered, his voice tense.

"Crawford? It's Maggie Moretti."

"Maggie," Crawford breathed, relief and fear mingling in his chest. "Do you have news?"

"Yes, but the connection wasn't great. I just spoke with Chris briefly. Becca had to have an emergency C-section. The baby's in the NICU but doing better than expected."

Crawford closed his eyes, absorbing this information. "And Becca?"

"Stable for now, but they're concerned about her blood pressure. Some postpartum complication." There was a pause, and then Maggie's voice softened. "They've named the baby Eloise Julia Wheeler."

Crawford's throat tightened. "Julia," he repeated, his voice barely audible.

"Yes," Maggie confirmed. "After her mother."

For a moment, Crawford couldn't speak, overcome by a wave of powerful emotion that threatened to knock him off his feet. Ciara moved closer, her hand on his arm providing silent support.

"Are you trying to get there?" Crawford finally managed to ask.

"Yes, but the airports are closed because of the storm. We're looking at options, but it might be tomorrow at the earliest."

Crawford nodded, even though she couldn't see him. "Same here. The boys are anxious, but there's little we can do until this weather clears."

"I'll keep trying, Crawford," Maggie promised. "If I get through again, I'll call you immediately with any updates."

"Thank you, Maggie, and vice versa."

After ending the call, Crawford relayed the news to Ciara, who listened with tears in her eyes.

"Eloise Julia," she repeated softly. "Oh, Crawford. Julia would be so proud."

"She would," he agreed, memories of his late wife washing over him—her smile, her laugh, how she'd loved their children with a fierceness that had sometimes taken his breath away. I just wish she could be here to see it."

Ciara wrapped her arms around her husband, hugging him tightly. "She is," she said with certainty. "In her way, she is."

As the storm raged outside, two families separated by distance but united by love gathered their strength, preparing for the journey ahead. Through it all, the newest member of both families fought her own battle in the NICU, unaware of the love and concern surrounding her from hundreds of miles away.

CHAPTER 4

The next twenty-four hours brought new challenges. Becca's blood pressure continued to climb despite medication, and Dr. Winters diagnosed postpartum preeclampsia. They began a magnesium sulfate infusion to prevent seizures, confining Becca to her bed just as she longed to be with her daughter.

"Chris, you have to go back to her," Becca insisted, fighting the fog the medication created. "She needs to know we're near."

"I will. I'll be happy when your family gets here," he countered, reluctant to leave her side with her condition unstable. "I hate leaving you even for a minute. At least when they get here they'll be with you when I'm with Ellie."

There was a soft knock at the door. Beth peeked in.

"Hey, Mama," she said softly, entering with Lauren close behind. "We brought reinforcements."

Michael and Jeff followed, arms laden with flowers, balloons, and stuffed animals.

"The gifts are mostly symbolic," Lauren explained. "Since I understand our niece is still in the NICU."

"How is she?" Michael asked.

"Stable," Christopher replied. "She's on oxygen but still breathing mostly on her own. They say that's good for thirty-two weeks."

"I love the name Eloise," Beth said, moving to Becca's bedside and taking her hand.

Becca nodded, tears threatening again. "Eloise Julia Wheeler."

Beth's eyes filled at the middle name. "After your mom," she whispered. "Oh, Becca, that's lovely."

"I finally reached my father," Becca said. "He's trying to get a flight out as soon as possible, but everything's delayed with the storm system over Florida. He and my brothers might not make it until tomorrow or the day after."

"And Mom and Grandma are calling constantly," Michael added. "They're organizing the prayer chain by calling everyone they know on the island, including people in Sanibel."

Despite everything, Becca felt a bubble of laughter rise in her chest. The thought of her mother-in-law and Grandma Sarah mobilizing inn guests in spiritual support was perfectly in character for both of them.

"Chris," she said, squeezing his hand. "Go see our daughter. Tell her... tell her I love her. That I'll be there as soon as I can."

With his siblings present to support Becca, Christopher finally agreed, pressing a gentle kiss to her forehead before departing for the NICU.

"Now," Lauren said, settling into the chair Christopher had vacated, "tell us everything. And don't you dare downplay how scary this has been."

For the first time since the crisis began, Becca let her guard down completely, tears flowing freely as she recounted the terrifying events of the delivery. The trauma of the emergency, the fear that still lingered, and the guilt she couldn't quite shake.

"I feel like my body failed her," Becca admitted in a small voice.

"Your body did not fail," Beth said firmly. "Your body recognized a dangerous situation and sounded the alarm. Your bleeding saved her life, Becca. If you hadn't noticed it when you did..."

She didn't need to finish the thought. The possibilities were too frightening to voice.

"Besides," Lauren added, "from what I hear, she's quite the fighter. Takes after her mother."

"And her father," Michael chimed in. "Remember when Chris broke his arm in high school and insisted on finishing the sailing regatta?"

"Or when he had that terrible flu during the state championships?" Jeff recalled, shaking his head. "Stubborn doesn't begin to describe it."

Becca smiled weakly, comforted by their attempts to distract her. "Between the Wheelers and the Powells, she didn't stand a chance of being anything but determined, did she?"

"Not a chance in the world," Beth agreed with a grin.

The conversation flowed around Becca, but the medication made it hard to focus. She felt herself drifting, the voices of her family becoming distant. The last thing she remembered clearly was Beth noticing her fatigue and shooing the others from the room, promising they'd be nearby if needed.

Sleep claimed her, deep and dreamless, her body desperately needing rest to heal.

The next day, Lauren Phillips stood in her kitchen, her hands wrapped around a mug of tea she hadn't touched. The steam curled up in lazy tendrils, disappearing before they reached her face. She barely noticed.

The house was quiet for the moment—too quiet. Jeff had taken Olivia to her tennis lesson, Lily was at a friend's house, and

Daniel was napping upstairs. It should have been a moment of peace, but instead, she felt the weight of something she couldn't quite name pressing on her chest.

She wasn't drowning, not exactly, but she was floating just under the surface, watching the world move above her while she tried to reach for it.

She didn't think it was postpartum depression, but something wasn't right. Daniel was nine months old, a grinning, wiggling force of energy who adored his big sisters and had just started pulling himself up to stand. She loved him, loved all of them, but lately, something had felt... off. Frustration? Exhaustion? A bone-deep longing that she couldn't seem to shake?

She missed them: her mother, Maggie, Grandma Sarah, and her sister, Sarah. These three women had been a guiding force and a touchstone when she felt untethered and alone.

It had started as a quiet ache months ago, something she could reason with and explain away. But now, it was louder, settling in her ribs like a dull throb.

No amount of FaceTime calls could make up for her mother not being here to wrap her arms around her or Grandma Sarah's knowing look that always said, *You're stronger than you think, sweetheart.*

And Sarah—Sarah, who had been her partner in everything growing up—was raising her babies just a few miles from their mother in Florida. Their lives had moved forward without her, and though she knew it wasn't intentional, she felt the distance more acutely than ever.

A sharp cry from the baby monitor startled her. Daniel.

She took a breath and set down her tea, untouched, like so many other cups before it. By the time she reached his room, he was already pulling himself up on the crib rail, his round cheeks red with frustration.

"Hey, buddy," she murmured, lifting him into her arms. He

immediately nuzzled against her shoulder, warm and soft, his tiny hands gripping her shirt.

Lauren closed her eyes briefly, inhaling his scent—baby shampoo and something purely *him*. This was the part she loved, the part that made the exhaustion worth it. But even as she rocked him gently, her thoughts drifted back to Captiva Island.

She needed to be there with them.

A lump formed in her throat. It may be time to stop pushing it away and pretending everything was fine. She'd finally accepted that it didn't matter how old she was; needing to drop in to talk to her mother over a cup of tea was as necessary as breathing.

Everyone said Lauren was just like her mother, and even though she'd fought the idea growing up, she embraced it now and longed for more of what made her who she was.

After her father died, the urge to stay as close to her mother became stronger and eventually the only way she could define home. Being connected to the women in her family made her stronger; without them, she struggled to find stability.

She shifted Daniel on her hip and returned downstairs, absently bouncing him as she paced the house. She could call someone. She needed to talk to *someone*. But who?

Becca? Not. Not now. Her sister-in-law was still recovering from serious complications and premature delivery. Little Eloise was fighting in the NICU, and Becca herself had only just been stabilized after that terrifying postpartum preeclampsia scare. The family rallied around them, as they should have been. This wasn't the time for Lauren to dump her emotional struggles on anyone, especially not Becca.

Beth? Lauren sighed. Beth and Gabriel had their hands full with the orchard. They worked constantly, getting things off the ground, dealing with suppliers, planting schedules, pest control— everything. Now, Beth was driving back and forth to the hospital to support Christopher and Becca. The timing couldn't be worse.

Michael? He'd listen, too, in his way. But her brother had

always been more pragmatic than sentimental. He'd tell her to make a pros and cons list and remind her that she and Jeff had built a solid life in Massachusetts, and since their mother lived in Florida, he'd renamed her the family's Massachusetts Matriarch.

She laughed at her new title, but it did little to remove her worries.

And Jeff—her sweet, supportive husband. She didn't want to worry him. She knew he'd support her no matter her choices.

Lauren let out a slow breath.

She was out of people.

But she still needed to talk to someone.

Her gaze drifted to her purse on the kitchen counter, where her phone sat. It wasn't right to burden anyone in the family right now, not with the crisis they were all weathering. But there could be something she could *do* instead.

A thought struck her. She adjusted Daniel's weight in her arms and opened the refrigerator to survey the contents. It was well-stocked—she'd done a big grocery run just yesterday. Opening the pantry revealed the same abundance.

Christopher and Becca wouldn't have had time to cook or shop, spending every possible moment at the hospital with Eloise. And the rest of the family was so focused on supporting them that they'd probably been living on vending machine snacks and hospital cafeteria food.

"What do you think, buddy?" she asked Daniel, who blinked up at her with curious eyes. "Should we make some meals for everyone? Give them one less thing to worry about?"

It wasn't the heart-to-heart conversation she'd been craving, but something tangible she could do—a way to channel her restlessness into something useful. And keeping her hands busy would quiet her mind a little.

She grabbed her phone and quickly texted Beth: *Is Christopher home from the hospital, or are they both staying there 24/7?*

Beth's response came quickly: *He went home to shower and change. He is heading there now to bring fresh clothes for Becca. Why?*

Lauren typed back: *I'm making meals. I will drop them off at their place and at the hospital. Let me know if they have preferences/restrictions.*

You're an angel, Beth replied. *They're living on coffee and whatever the cafeteria serves. Will let them know. Their spare key is under the ceramic frog on the back porch.*

Lauren smiled, already mentally planning the menu: hearty soups that could be easily reheated, casseroles that would keep well, nutritious muffins and energy bars for quick snacks at the hospital, food that would nourish and comfort a family in crisis, requiring minimal effort from a family in crisis.

"Come on, Daniel," she said, grabbing her grocery list pad. "We've got work to do."

Three hours later, Lauren's kitchen was a controlled chaos of delicious smells. A pot of chicken soup simmered on the stove. Two already-baked casseroles and one prepped for baking sat on the counter. Blueberry muffins cooled on a rack. Energy bars, packed with nuts and dried fruit, were being cut into squares.

Daniel watched from his high chair, occasionally being offered tastes of appropriate ingredients and banging his spoon in approval. The work had been therapeutic, keeping Lauren's hands busy while her mind slowly untangled itself.

Jeff had returned with Olivia, who immediately joined the cooking efforts, proud to do something for her baby cousin. Soon after, Lily was dropped off, and she, too, was enlisted, packing individual portions into containers with handwritten labels and heating instructions.

"This is nice of you, Mom," Olivia said as she carefully wrote "Becca & Chris" on a stack of containers.

"It's what families do," Lauren replied, stirring the soup once before turning off the heat. "When someone's going through a tough time, we step up."

"Is baby Eloise going to be okay?" Lily asked, her voice small.

Lauren set down her spoon and knelt to meet her daughter's worried gaze. "The doctors are taking excellent care of her. She's tiny because she was born early but strong—just like her mom and dad."

"Like Auntie Becca and Uncle Chris?"

"Exactly like them," Lauren confirmed, tucking a strand of hair behind Lily's ear. "And she has all of us rooting for her too."

Lily seemed satisfied with this answer and went back to her labeling task. Lauren stood, catching Jeff's eye across the kitchen. His gaze was warm and understanding. He knew something was bothering her—he always did—but he wasn't pushing. Instead, he'd simply stepped in, helping however he could, giving her the space to work through whatever was on her mind.

"I'll deliver these to the house," he offered, picking up a cooler they'd filled. "You want to take the hospital batch?"

Lauren nodded, grateful for his intuition. "I won't stay long. Just drop off the food and see if they need anything else."

"Take your time," Jeff said softly. He pressed a kiss to her temple. "I've got things covered here."

As Lauren packed the last of the meals into insulated bags, her phone chimed with a text. She expected it to be Beth with an update on timing, but instead, she saw her mother's name on the screen.

The storm has passed. Looking forward to seeing everyone soon. Love you, honey.

Lauren stared at the message, her throat suddenly tight. She texted back quickly: *We're all taking care of them. I'll send updates. Love you too, Mom.*

She hesitated, then added one more line: *I miss you.*

The simple admission felt like releasing a breath she'd held too long. It didn't solve anything, but it helped.

"Ready to go, Mom?" Olivia called, already holding the insulated bags by the door.

Lauren tucked her phone away, nodding as she picked up Daniel. "Ready."

CHAPTER 5

*B*ecca watched the stripes move across her bed from the filtered light through the hospital blinds. She'd been drifting in and out of consciousness for what felt like days, the magnesium sulfate creating a foggy barrier between her and the world. But this morning was different. The heaviness was lifted, her thoughts coming into sharper focus.

"Good morning," Dr. Winters said, entering the room with a tablet and Beth following close behind. "How are you feeling today?"

Becca took a moment to assess. "Less... underwater," she replied.

Dr. Winters smiled. "That's the medication clearing your system. Your blood pressure readings have been stable for the last twelve hours, which is excellent news." She checked the monitors and made a note on her tablet. "I think we can start weaning you off the magnesium today."

Becca's heart leapt. "Does that mean I can see Eloise? Hold her?"

"If your next few readings stay stable. We'll arrange for a wheelchair transport to the NICU this afternoon."

Tears sprang to Becca's eyes, overwhelming gratitude washing over her. It had been almost three days since her daughter's birth, and she had yet to hold her, to study her face, to feel her warm weight against her chest.

"Thank you," she whispered.

Beth stepped forward as Dr. Winters left, taking Becca's hand. "Just a few more hours," she encouraged. "Chris says she's doing wonderfully. Her oxygen levels have improved overnight, and she's taking fluids through the feeding tube."

Becca squeezed Beth's hand. "How is Chris? He must be exhausted."

"Managing," Beth replied with a small smile. "You know Chris —running on coffee and determination. Michael forced him to go home and shower a few hours ago."

"And my dad? Any word from Florida?"

Beth's smile widened. "The storm cleared overnight. Crawford and your brothers are on an early flight. They should land around noon. And Mom texted that she and Paolo got seats on a noon flight from Tampa."

Relief flooded through Becca. Her family was coming. As much as she appreciated the Wheeler siblings' support, she longed for her father's steady presence and her brothers' protective energy.

"Lauren brought enough food to feed a small army," Beth continued, gesturing to the mini-fridge in the corner of the room, now stocked with containers. "She stopped by your house and filled the fridge so you and Chris won't have to cook much. Gabriel's bringing your favorite blanket from home when he comes by later."

Becca nodded, grateful for these concrete expressions of love and support. But her mind kept circling back to one thing.

"I need to see my daughter," she said softly. "It doesn't feel real yet."

Beth nodded in understanding. "It won't, not completely until you hold her. But we have pictures." She pulled out her phone and opened a gallery of images Christopher had sent overnight. "Look."

Becca took the phone with trembling hands. The first image was of Eloise in her incubator, tiny fists raised beside her face, dark lashes fanned against pink cheeks. The next showed Christopher's finger being gripped by an impossibly small hand. Then Eloise stared directly at the camera with her eyes open, dark and alert.

"She has your eyes," Beth said gently. "And Christopher's chin, I think."

Becca studied each image hungrily, trying to memorize every detail. "She's beautiful," she whispered.

"She's perfect," Beth agreed.

The door opened again, and Christopher entered, looking rumpled despite the clean clothes. His face lit up when he saw Becca awake and alert.

"Hey," he said, crossing to her bedside and kissing her forehead, and then hugged Beth.

Holding Becca's hand, he said, "You look better."

"I feel better," she confirmed. "Dr. Winters says I might be able to see Eloise today."

Christopher's exhausted face broke into a genuine smile. "She's waiting for you. I told her this morning that her mom would be visiting soon."

"Tell me the truth. How is she?" Becca asked, searching his face for the complete truth.

"She's a fighter," Christopher said, sitting beside the bed. "Dr. Patel says she's exceeding expectations. Her oxygen requirement has decreased, and she's responding well to touch and sound." He reached for Becca's hand. "She turns her head when she hears my voice."

Fresh tears welled in Becca's eyes. "She knows you."

"She'll know you too," he assured her. "She's just waiting to meet you properly."

Beth slipped quietly from the room, giving them privacy. Christopher's face grew more serious as he studied his wife.

"How are you feeling?" he asked. "And don't say 'fine.'"

Becca attempted a smile. "Not fine," she admitted. "Scared. Relieved. Guilty."

"Guilty?" Christopher's brow furrowed.

"That my body couldn't keep her safe for just a few more weeks." Her voice caught. "That she has to fight so hard because I couldn't—"

"Stop," Christopher said firmly but gently. "Your body did exactly what it needed to. If we hadn't recognized something was wrong, if we hadn't gotten you to the hospital when we did..." He couldn't finish the thought. "We saved her life. And yours."

Becca nodded, not entirely convinced but too tired to argue.

"Our families are coming," she said instead. "Dad and the boys should be landing soon."

"I know. Michael's going to pick them up." Christopher's mouth quirked into a half-smile. "Your brothers have been texting me constantly for updates."

"That sounds like them," Becca said, fondness coloring her voice.

"And Mom and Paolo are on their way too. Mom called from the airport, practically vibrating with excitement even through the phone." He squeezed her hand. "They're all coming, Bec. Everyone who loves us, who loves Eloise."

Becca felt a wave of gratitude wash over her. For all the fear and trauma of the past two days, there was this, too—the absolute certainty that they were surrounded by love.

"I want to see her," she said again, her voice stronger. "I need to see our daughter."

Christopher nodded. "Let me check with the nurse. If your

blood pressure's still stable, we might not have to wait until this afternoon."

He pressed the call button, and a nurse checked Becca's vitals within minutes. The readings were good—better than they'd been since the delivery.

"I'll page Dr. Winters," the nurse promised. "If she approves, we can arrange the NICU visit sooner."

The next hour passed in a blur of preparations. Becca was helped to sit up fully, the movement sending dull pain through her abdomen where the incision was still healing. A shower was out of the question with her IV still in place, but the nurse helped her wash her face and brush her teeth, simple acts that made her feel more human.

Christopher brought her a clean nightgown and robe from home, the soft fabric a welcome relief from the stiff hospital gown. Beth helped brush Becca's hair, her fingers gentle as they worked through the tangles.

"Beautiful," Christopher murmured when they finished, and though Becca knew she was pale and drawn, his eyes held such sincerity that she almost believed him.

Dr. Winters arrived, checked her readings, and approved her. "Keep it short for this first visit," she cautioned. You're still recovering, but both of you need to have this connection."

The nurse brought a wheelchair close to the bed, and Christopher carefully helped Becca into it, mindful of her IV and the tenderness of her abdomen.

Waving, Beth said, "I'll be here when you get back."

The journey to the NICU felt both interminable and too short. Becca's heart pounded as they approached the entrance, a mixture of anticipation and fear making her light-headed.

"Ready?" Christopher asked as they paused outside the double doors.

Becca nodded, unable to speak.

The NICU was quieter than she expected, the hush broken only by the gentle beeping of monitors and the low murmur of nurses. They were required to wash their hands thoroughly at a scrub station before proceeding, and Christopher helped Becca through the process since standing was still difficult.

"Hi, Ms. Wheeler," the nurse greeted warmly. "I'm Natalie, one of Eloise's primary nurses. Your husband has been keeping us entertained with stories about you."

"All good ones, I hope," Becca managed, but her eyes were fixed on the clear plastic box where her daughter lay.

Eloise looked even smaller in person than in the pictures, her tiny body dwarfed by the monitoring equipment. A knitted cap covered her head, and she wore a diaper that seemed too large for her frame. Her skin was no longer the alarming translucent shade Becca had glimpsed right after birth; it was now a healthier pink tone. She had a feeding tube taped to her cheek and a small oxygen cannula in her nose, but her chest rose and fell with reassuring regularity.

"Can I...?" Becca began, reaching toward the portholes in the side of the incubator.

"Of course," Natalie encouraged. "She'd love to feel your touch."

With trembling hands, Becca reached through the opening. She hesitated momentarily, overwhelmed by the delicacy of her daughter's form. Then, gently, she placed her palm against Eloise's side. The warmth of her baby's skin, the subtle rise and fall of her breathing, the quicksilver flutter of her heartbeat—like touching a miracle.

"Hello, Eloise," she whispered, her voice breaking. "It's Mama. I love you more than anything in this world. You stay strong."

As if in response, Eloise stirred, her tiny face scrunching

momentarily before relaxing again. One small hand flexed, fingers spreading like a starfish before curling back into a fist.

"She knows your voice," Natalie said softly. "She's been hearing it for months, after all."

Tears slipped down Becca's cheeks, but she didn't bother to wipe them away. "She's so beautiful," she said, unable to take her eyes off her daughter. "So perfect."

Christopher's hand came to rest on her shoulder, a reassuring weight anchoring her to the moment. They stayed like that, a family circle not quite complete but connected for several minutes.

"Her oxygen levels are improving while you're here," Natalie observed, nodding toward one of the monitors. "That happens sometimes with contact, but hearing your voice helps, too."

"Mother-baby connection is powerful medicine," Christopher murmured, echoing what Dr. Patel told them.

Eventually, Becca's medical needs forced them to end the visit. The fatigue was setting in again, her body reminding her that it was still healing.

"I have to go now, sweetheart, but I'll be back soon," she whispered.

As they wheeled Becca back to her room, she felt something she hadn't since the crisis began: hope. Not just the desperate, clinging hope of survival but a brighter, more certain hope for the future.

Back in her room, she found a surprise waiting. Beth had turned the sterile hospital space into something approaching homey. Fresh flowers brightened the windowsill, a soft throw blanket was draped across the foot of the bed, and framed photos of the family had appeared on the bedside table.

"Beth says a healing environment matters," Christopher explained, helping her back into bed. "She might have gone a little overboard."

Beth laughed. "When have I ever gone overboard on anything? Besides, I had help. Lauren's here too."

"It's perfect," Becca said, settling against the pillows. "Thank you both so much."

As if summoned by her gratitude, a knock came at the door, and Lauren peeked in. "Is it a good time? I have reinforcements."

Without waiting for an answer, she pushed the door wider to reveal Jeff carrying a large thermal bag and Michael's wife, Brea, right behind them with what looked like more supplies.

"We come bearing lunch that doesn't taste like hospital food," Lauren announced.

"You guys are amazing," Becca said, looking at her sisters-in-law with amused disbelief.

Lauren began unpacking containers of what smelled like homemade soup. "Also, your father just texted. They have landed and are on their way," Brea added.

Becca's heart leaped at the news. "Dad's here?"

"Almost. Traffic from the airport is heavy, but Michael knows the back routes." Beth handed her a bowl of soup. "Eat something before they arrive. You need your strength."

Becca accepted the bowl, suddenly aware of the hollow feeling in her stomach. She hadn't had real food in days, subsisting on IV fluids and the occasional broth. The soup smelled heavenly.

"Lauren made it," Beth added. "She's been cooking enough to feed an army."

"It's what I do when I'm worried," Lauren said with a self-deprecating smile. "I got it from Mom."

"We're grateful," Christopher said, accepting his bowl.

The simple act of sharing food created a pocket of normalcy in the chaos of the past days. Before setting it aside, Becca managed half her bowl, her appetite still suppressed by medication and stress.

Just as they were finishing, Brea's phone chimed. She checked the screen and grinned. "They're here. Five minutes out."

Becca's heart raced in anticipation. She hadn't seen her father or brothers since Christmas. The thought of having them here now, when she needed them most, filled her with a complicated mixture of emotions—relief, gratitude, and a childlike desire to be comforted by her dad, to have him tell her everything would be okay.

Lauren quickly tidied up the lunch things, and Jeff excused himself to give the family space for their reunion. Beth fussed with Becca's blankets and helped her sit up straighter, quickly combing her hair.

"You look perfect," she assured Becca, who was suddenly self-conscious about her appearance.

"I look like I've been through the wringer," Becca countered.

"That's because you have," Christopher said, squeezing her hand. "And you're still beautiful."

CHAPTER 6

*W*ithin the hour, Becca's hospital room door swung open, and her father and brothers filled the room with more people than the hospital allowed.

Crawford's weathered face, deeply tanned from a lifetime on the water, was drawn with worry, but his eyes—like Becca's own —lit up at the sight of his daughter.

"Bec," he said, his voice rough with emotion.

"Dad," she whispered, as if she were a child again, reaching for him.

Crawford crossed the room in two long strides and wrapped her in his arms, careful of her IV but holding her as if she might disappear.

"You scared the hell out of me, sweetheart," he murmured into her hair.

"I'm okay," she assured him, though her voice wobbled. "We're both okay."

Crawford pulled back just enough to study her face.

"Of course you are," he said gruffly.

Luke, Joshua, and Finn Powell were variations on the same theme—all tall and broad-shouldered like their father, with the same sandy hair and easy physical confidence from lives spent in motion.

"Hey, Bec," Finn, said first. It's nice of you to give us all heart attacks."

"Yeah, couldn't you have waited until after tourist season?" Luke added, his attempt at humor betrayed by the worry lines around his eyes.

Joshua, the youngest at twenty-six and always the most emotionally transparent of the brothers, didn't bother with banter. He moved straight to the bed and wrapped his arms around his sister, nearly dislodging her IV in his enthusiasm.

"We were so scared," he admitted quietly.

Becca hugged him back fiercely. "I'm okay, Josh. Really."

"And our niece?" Finn asked, his gaze finding Christopher, who had stepped back to make room for the Powell invasion.

"Small but mighty," Christopher replied. "Growing stronger every day. Some respiratory support was needed, but she's doing well."

"Eloise Julia," Crawford said softly, still carrying an emotional weight.

Christopher nodded. "We've been calling her Ellie."

"Ellie," Crawford repeated, testing the nickname. A smile spread slowly across his face. "I love it."

"When can we see her?" Joshua asked.

"They're strict about NICU visitors," Beth explained. "Parents first, then grandparents, then others by arrangement. But they make exceptions for special circumstances. They'll make you sign in before you go in. They've got high security here."

"No one's going to steal our little Ellie," Lauren added with a wink at Becca.

The room felt crowded now, but in the best possible way— filled with family, love, and the reassurance of being surrounded by your people in a crisis. Becca leaned back against her pillows, suddenly overwhelmed by the sheer presence of everyone.

It didn't take long before a nurse came in and insisted everyone but Christopher leave.

Beth, Brea, and Lauren leaned down to hug Becca.

"Call us if you need anything," Lauren said.

Becca nodded. "I will. Thank you all for everything."

Crawford nodded. "We should let you rest," he said, ever attuned to his daughter's needs. "We'll be here when you wake up."

"The hotel's five minutes away," Finn added. "We've got rooms for a week."

"A week?" Becca questioned.

"At least," Joshua confirmed. "Ciara's got everything under control at the shop. She even enlisted the help from a couple of volunteers at the Outreach Center. Powell Water Sports is in good hands."

"You didn't have to—" Becca began.

"Yes, we did," Crawford interrupted gently. "Family first, Bec. Always."

The simple statement, delivered with his characteristic certainty. Of course, they were staying. Of course, they had rearranged their lives to be here. It was what Powells did—what her families did, the Powells and the Wheelers alike.

Christopher moved back to her side as if reading her thoughts, his hand finding hers. "I think we should let Becca rest before Mom and Paolo arrive," he said to Crawford. "It's been an emotional morning."

Everyone nodded in agreement. Crawford leaned down to kiss Becca's forehead once more. "Rest, sweetheart. We'll be back soon."

One by one, they filed out—her brothers squeezing her hand or kissing her cheek, Beth promising to return for the evening shift, Lauren assuring her there would be plenty of food. Only Christopher remained, settling into the chair beside her bed.

"Quite a family you've got there," he said with a tired smile.

"We've got," she corrected softly. "They're your family too."

"Get some sleep, Bec. Big day today."

She nodded, fatigue already pulling at her. But as she drifted toward sleep, her mind was full, not of the trauma of the past days but of the future—of Eloise growing stronger, of bringing their daughter home, of their families merged and expanded by this tiny new life.

For the first time since this ordeal began, Becca slept without fear, shadowing her dreams.

Crawford Powell stood at the window of the NICU, staring through the glass at his granddaughter. Eloise—Ellie—was impossibly small, her tiny body seeming almost lost amid the medical equipment surrounding her. And yet, even from a distance, he could see the determination in her—in the steady rise and fall of her chest, in the occasional flicker of movement as she shifted in sleep.

"She looks like Becca did," he said softly to Christopher, who stood beside him. "Same dark hair. Same serious little face."

Christopher nodded, his eyes never leaving his daughter. "That's what the nurse said when she first saw her. 'She's her mother's daughter.'"

"Poor kid," Crawford joked weakly. "Stubborn as hell, then."

That drew a genuine laugh from Christopher. "Between the Powell determination and the Wheeler stubbornness? We're in for it."

They lapsed into silence again, two men united by love for the same two women—one fighting her way back to health, the other fighting her way into life. Crawford studied his son-in-law's profile, noting the shadows under his eyes, the tension in his jaw, and how he stood as if braced against an invisible wind.

"You should get some rest," Crawford suggested. "I can stay here for a while."

Christopher shook his head. "I'm fine."

"Son," Crawford said, the term of address slipping out naturally, "you're running on fumes. Becca's stable. Ellie's stable. Your family is here now. Let us help."

For a moment, Christopher looked like he might argue. Then, abruptly, the fight seemed to drain out of him. His shoulders slumped, and he ran a hand over his face.

"I need to be here if anything changes," he said, but his voice held less conviction.

"And you will be," Crawford assured him. "The hospital's thirty minutes from your house. Go home, shower, and sleep in a real bed for a few hours. I promise I won't leave this spot until you're back."

Christopher looked torn, his gaze moving from Ellie to Crawford and back again.

"I give you my word," Crawford said quietly. "Father to father. Ellie's your little girl, and Becca's mine, and aren't we the luckiest two men in the world? We've been blessed."

Those last three words reached Christopher in a way nothing else had. He nodded slowly, acknowledging their shared status—as fathers, protectors, and men tasked with caring for these extraordinary humans—passing silently between them.

"Two hours," Christopher conceded finally. "I'll be back in two hours."

"Four," Crawford countered. "Minimum."

A ghost of a smile crossed Christopher's face. "Three. Final offer."

"Deal." Crawford clapped him on the shoulder. "Now go before you fall over."

With one last look at his daughter, Christopher turned and walked away, his steps heavy with exhaustion. Crawford watched him go, respect and empathy tangled in his chest. Then he turned back to the window, to the tiny granddaughter who, impossibly, already had his heart in her minuscule fist.

"Well, Ellie," he said softly to the glass, "it's just you and me for a while. Your grandpa's got some stories to tell you about your mama. And about your grandma Julia, who you're named after." His voice caught slightly. "She would have loved you something fierce, little one. Almost as much as I already do."

Ellie's tiny hand moved as if in response, fingers spreading in what looked remarkably like a wave. Crawford smiled and settled into the chair beside the window.

"That's right," he murmured. "I'm not going anywhere."

As the afternoon light slanted through the hospital windows, Crawford Powell began the first of many vigils he would keep for Eloise Julia Wheeler, the newest branch of his family tree.

CHAPTER 7

*L*eaves rustled in a light breeze, the scent of damp earth and pine rising from the packed dirt trail. Beth Walker walked along the worn path, her black lab, Charlie, trotting ahead, nose to the ground, tail wagging with each discovery. The woods had become her sanctuary over these past months, where the constant mental chatter of her former life as a prosecutor faded to whispers.

She wore mud-spattered jeans and work boots; her shirt sleeves rolled up to expose forearms that had grown strong from orchard work. Once manicured weekly for courthouse appearances, her hands now bore calluses and tiny scars—badges of her new life that she wore with quiet pride. Her sister Lauren had commented on them recently, concern in her eyes as she'd taken Beth's hands in hers. "Bethy, what happened to your beautiful hands?" Beth had just smiled, understanding that her sister couldn't see these marks the way she did—as symbols of life finally lived on her terms.

Charlie barked excitedly, bounding off the path to chase a squirrel that darted up a nearby maple tree.

"Don't go too far, buddy!" she called, smiling as he disappeared momentarily into the underbrush. The dog had been Gabriel's when they married—now, a companion for her long walks in the woods while he and his brother, James, worked on the structural renovations to the old farmhouse. Charlie had arrived as a trembling eight-week-old puppy and had grown into Gabriel's shadow, but now, her confidant, her witness to the transformation that had taken place within her over the past year.

Beth paused by an ancient oak tree, its trunk wider than her arms could encircle. She placed her palm against its rough bark, feeling the life pulsing beneath the surface. She closed her eyes and took a deep breath, filling her lungs with the earthy scent that had become as necessary to her as oxygen—decaying leaves, damp soil, pine, and something indefinable that she could only think of as a possibility.

In Boston, she'd spent hundreds on expensive perfumes, trying to cover herself in scents that announced her presence before she entered a room. Now, she preferred to carry the smell of the woods on her skin, in her hair. Gabriel often buried his face in her neck at night, inhaling deeply. "You smell like home," he'd whisper.

Finding an old, weathered stump, Beth sat down and pulled out her phone. The incongruity of the sleek technology against this primal backdrop wasn't lost on her. Two years ago, the phone had been an extension of her arm, constantly buzzing with emails, calls, and calendar alerts. Now, days would pass before she remembered to charge it.

She scrolled through recent photos her sister Sarah had sent. Sarah, on Captiva Island, cocktails in hand, waves lapping at her feet, her smile bright in the tropical sun. Having left Massachusetts to start an inn on the island, their mother, Maggie, was content in her new life, and Beth couldn't be happier for her. She missed her mother and sister but knew that island life was not for her.

She laughed at some of the images her mother sent. They brought a bittersweet ache to Beth's chest. She zoomed in on one photo—her mother sitting on a chair, gazing out at the ocean, a wistful expression on her face.

After her father's death almost five years ago, her mother had thrown herself into the plan to relocate permanently to Captiva, determined to create a new chapter in the place where she'd found happiness with her second husband. She wanted all her daughters with her to recreate the closeness they'd had growing up before careers and marriages had scattered them.

Her sister Lauren had more than once mentioned considering moving to Florida to be closer to Sarah and their mother. Even their grandmother had moved there two years ago. Like birds, all migrating south, except for Beth, who was more at home in the woods than anywhere else.

She set the phone down beside her. Charlie returned, panting happily, and flopped at her feet, a twig caught in his thick fur. Beth leaned forward to work it free, feeling the strength in his muscles beneath her hands.

"They think I'm crazy, you know," she said softly to Charlie, who tilted his head as if understanding every word. "Trading the corner office for... this."

She gestured to the woods around her, the rustling of the branches soothing her as she looked to the left and right, smiling at a large birch standing out among the evergreens. Two years ago, she wouldn't have been able to name a single tree species; now, she knew each one intimately and understood their needs, cycles, and silent strength.

A sudden memory surfaced: standing before Judge Harrington in a navy blue power suit, her closing argument memorized, adrenaline coursing through her veins as she fought for a conviction she believed in with her whole being. She'd been good at it—no, she'd been exceptional. The youngest senior prosecutor in her office, with a reputation for thoroughness, intimidated even veteran defense attorneys.

And yet, she'd walked away. Not because she'd failed but because success had begun to feel hollow, and the trauma of seeing the worst of society daily was too much for her. One morning, she'd looked in the mirror and hadn't recognized the woman staring back—someone hard-edged and exhausted, running on caffeine, ambition, and little else.

Beth pulled a small, smooth stone from her pocket—one she'd carried since childhood, a memento from a family vacation on Captiva when she was ten. The feel of it in her palm still took her back to those sunlit days when the Wheeler sisters had been inseparable. She'd found it on the beach after a storm, the three racing along the shore to collect treasures revealed by the churning waves. This stone had caught her eye—ordinary gray but with a perfect white circle running through it like a promise.

"Little Ellie is doing well in the NICU. Before you know it, she'll be home with her mommy and daddy," she told Charlie, turning the stone between her fingers. "You know what will happen after that? Eloise Julia Wheeler will be riding the surf on Captiva Island."

Suddenly sad, Beth knew it was only a matter of time before Becca and her brother Chris moved to Captiva Island. Beth could read the signs, even though she tried to ignore them. She couldn't blame Becca for wanting to be near her father and brothers. After all, she was born on the island, and only after falling in love with her brother, Christopher, did she move to Massachusetts.

"What do you think, Charlie? Do you think I'm right?"

Charlie was too busy chewing tree bark to answer.

"Mom would like nothing better than for us to move south. She doesn't understand," Beth murmured, slipping the stone back into her pocket. "I'm never leaving New England. This is who I am and where I belong."

She looked up at the canopy of trees swaying gently in the

breeze, sunlight refracting through the leaves in a kaleidoscope of green and gold, and a lump formed in her throat.

"I miss them. I do. Every day."

Charlie whined softly, sensing her emotion. He rested his head on her knee. Beth ran her fingers through his slick fur, grateful for his companionship.

The truth was, she'd tried to explain it to them—to her mother, to Sarah, to her grandmother. She'd tried to put into words how this place had saved her, how working with her hands in the soil had healed something she hadn't even known was broken, how Gabriel had seen in her, not the polished, ambitious attorney but the woman underneath who longed for something real and lasting.

"Sarah thinks we're playing farmer," she told Charlie with a sad smile. "She asked if we were 'still doing that orchard thing' when we spoke yesterday."

Two rabbits emerged from a thicket nearby when they spotted Beth and Charlie. The dog, trained not to chase the wildlife on their property, remained beside her, though his ears perked up with interest. Beth held her breath, watching as the rabbits deemed them unthreatening, and continued on their way, disappearing into the underbrush. Charlie jumped up and ran to the far end of the property, most likely to find something to chew or carry back to her.

These moments—these small glimpses into the secret life of the woods—were what she lived for now: the glorious slow surrender of autumn, the hush of snowfall in winter, the first tentative green shoots in spring, and now, the explosion of life in summer. The rhythm of the seasons had become her heartbeat.

A breeze picked up, sending a shower of whirligigs spiraling down around her. Beth tilted her face upward, letting them brush against her cheeks like gentle fingers. Her mother had always told her she was too serious, even as a child—the responsible one, the planner, the achiever. It wasn't until she left that life behind that she learned to play again and find joy in simple pleasures.

Pocketing the phone, she turned her attention to the eastern edge of their property, where a grove of sugar maples provided sap for the small-batch maple syrup they produced each spring. Next to it lay the cleared area where they planned to plant blueberry bushes—Gabriel's project, inspired by memories of picking berries with his grandmother as a child.

Beth kneeled, digging her fingers into the rich soil, bringing a handful to her nose, and inhaling deeply. The complex scent of it —minerals and microbes, decay, and renewal—grounded her in a way nothing in her former life ever had.

"This is who I am now," she whispered, opening her fingers and letting the soil sift back to the ground.

The realization wasn't new but settled into her with renewed certainty. Her sisters might find their paradise on Captiva's shores, but hers was here—on this property, in the farmhouse with Gabriel, in the connection to the land that had healed something broken inside her long before she'd known it needed mending.

Standing, she brushed the dirt from her hands and whistled for Charlie to follow. The dog bounded back to her side, and together, they continued deeper into the woods as the day's light faded. The invitation to join her sisters on Captiva would always tug at her heart, but the pull of this land—her land—was stronger.

Tomorrow, she'd go back to the hospital to see her niece, but she needed to take some time in the woods to regroup. She thought of how Gabriel would be waiting for her, probably with a tall glass of lemonade and questions about her walk, how they would sit together on the porch swing after dinner, planning tomorrow's work, next year's crops, and their shared future. How she would fall asleep tonight with his arm around her waist,

Charlie curled at their feet, the windows open to let in the sound of crickets.

Beth smiled, quickening her pace as the path began to curve back toward home. She belonged here now, roots grown deep as the apple trees they'd hoped to tend. And somehow, she hoped, her sisters would understand that one day. Until then, she would keep extending invitations and keep building bridges. Perhaps one day, they would cross them.

A lone cardinal flashed bright red against the sky, and Beth paused to watch its flight. In Boston, she'd gone weeks without noticing a single bird. Now, each one was a reminder of the life she'd chosen—vibrant, wild, and gloriously free.

CHAPTER 8

*L*auren balanced Daniel on her hip while scrolling through her phone, trying to respond simultaneously to three separate text conversations. The day's detritus covered the kitchen counter—mail, grocery bags waiting for unpacking, Lily's art project from summer camp, and a stack of forms for Olivia's tennis league that needed her signature yesterday.

"Mama! Mama!" Daniel squirmed in her arms, pointing insistently at the window where a blue jay was perched on the bird feeder.

"I see, buddy," Lauren said absently, focusing on Beth's latest update about Becca and Eloise. *Becca's blood pressure is fine, and Eloise's was up to 20ml per feeding. Discharge paperwork is in process.*

The microwave beeped, signaling that the pasta she was reheating for Lily's late dinner was ready. Lauren set Daniel in his high chair, handed him a teething biscuit, and moved to retrieve the food.

"Mom!" Lily called from the dining room. "Is dinner ready yet? I'm starving!"

"Coming," Lauren said, spooning the pasta into a bowl. "Did you set the table like I asked?"

Silence. Then, the hurried sound of drawers opening and silverware clattering.

Lauren sighed, fighting the familiar wave of exasperation. nine years old was undoubtedly enough to remember to set the table, especially when asked directly. But Lily operated on her timeline, in her dreamy world where practical concerns like dinnertime and chores were distant, uninteresting distractions.

As she carried the bowl to the dining room, Lauren caught sight of her reflection in the window—hair escaping from its hasty ponytail, yesterday's T-shirt sporting a suspicious stain that probably came from pureed carrots, and eyes shadowed from too many late nights and early mornings. She barely recognized herself.

"Here you go, sweetie," she said, setting the bowl in front of Lily, who had laid out a fork and napkin, if not a plate. "Sorry, it's so late."

Lily shrugged, already digging in. "It's okay. I was drawing a picture for Eloise. Do you think she can see colors yet? She's really little."

"I don't think so," Lauren admitted, touched by her daughter's thoughtfulness. "But even if she can't see the colors yet, I know she'll love knowing you made something special for her."

"I'm making a whole book," Lily explained between bites. "One picture for every day until she comes home. Then she'll know what she missed."

Lauren's heart squeezed. The Wheeler tendency toward gestures of love ran strong in her middle child.

The front door opened and closed, followed by Jeff's voice calling, "We're home!"

Lauren heard Olivia's voice, too, animated in a way it hadn't been in weeks. Then, she heard the thump of a tennis bag hitting the floor. She thought practice must have gone well, moving back to the kitchen to greet them.

Jeff entered first, his expression a curious mixture of excitement and caution. Behind him, Olivia fairly vibrated with contained energy, her face flushed with what looked like a triumph.

"What happened?" Lauren asked, instantly alert to the emotional current in the room.

"Show her," Jeff prompted, nudging Olivia forward.

Olivia pulled an envelope from her jacket pocket and held it out, practically bouncing on her toes. "I got in," she announced, her voice hushed with disbelief. "The Tampa Bay Elite Tennis Academy. I got in."

Lauren stared at the envelope, her mind racing to catch up. The Tampa Bay program—the long-shot application they'd submitted at Coach Reyes's insistence three months ago, the one even Olivia had tried not to hope for too much.

"Let me see," she said, reaching for the letter unsteady.

The letterhead was professional and embossed with the academy's logo. *Dear Olivia Phillips*, It began. *We are pleased to inform you that you have been accepted into our Junior Elite program, which begins September 1st.*

"Oh my Gosh," Lauren breathed, scanning the rest of the letter—details about the program structure, the coaching staff, and the remarkable opportunity it represented. "Olivia, this is...this is incredible."

"Coach Reyes cried," Olivia said, her voice still hushed with awe. "He said only two kids from Massachusetts have ever been accepted."

"They want her in the fourteen-and-under group, even though she's only twelve," Jeff added, his pride evident. "Coach Mendez—the head of the program—saw her play at the New England Juniors last month. He was scouting another player, but Olivia caught his attention."

Lauren looked at her daughter—tall for her age, with long limbs and focused energy—the opposite of dreamy Lily. Olivia had been playing tennis since she was seven, showing an early aptitude that had blossomed into genuine talent under Coach Reyes's dedicated mentorship. But this—national-level recognition and elite coaching—was beyond anything they'd dared hope for.

"I'm so proud of you," Lauren said, pulling Olivia into a hug. "So, so proud."

For once, her independence-seeking preteen didn't pull away, instead hugging back fiercely. "I can't believe it, Mom. It's like... it's everything."

Over Olivia's head, Lauren met Jeff's eyes, seeing in them the same swirl of emotions she was feeling—joy and pride, yes, but also the dawning realization of the practical implications. As the name suggested, the Tampa Bay Elite Tennis Academy was in Tampa Bay, Florida, not Massachusetts.

"Let's celebrate," she said, pushing aside the logistics. "This calls for ice cream."

"Can I have sprinkles?" Lily called from the dining room, apparently having overheard enough to understand that treats were forthcoming.

"You can have whatever you want," Jeff replied, scooping up Daniel from his high chair. "Your sister just did something amazing."

As they piled into the car for an impromptu trip to the ice cream parlor, Lauren watched Olivia—the confident tilt of her chin, the way she couldn't stop reading and re-reading the acceptance letter, the future unfurling in her eyes. Whatever complications this opportunity might bring, Lauren knew with absolute certainty that they would find a way to make it work. Her daughter's dream demanded nothing less.

Later that night, after the children were in bed, Lauren and Jeff sat at the kitchen table, the acceptance letter between them like a map to undiscovered territory.

"It requires relocation," Jeff said, stating the obvious. "The training schedule is too intense for commuting, even if we were closer than Massachusetts."

Lauren nodded, tracing the academy's logo with her fingertip. "I knew that when we applied. I just didn't think..."

"That she'd get in?" Jeff finished, a small smile playing on his lips. "I did. I've watched her play, Lauren. She's exceptional."

"I know she is," Lauren agreed, feeling a tug of guilt she hadn't fully believed. "But this is a world-class program. Olympians have trained there."

"And now our daughter will too." Jeff reached across the table, taking her hand. "If we let her."

The question hung between them, heavy with implications. They knew this wasn't just about moving for Olivia's tennis career. It was about all the things Lauren had been trying not to want too desperately—being closer to her mother and grandmother, to Sarah and her family, to the place that still felt like home despite her only having spent summers there.

"You've been thinking about moving south for a while now," Jeff said gently, reading her thoughts as he often did. "Even before this opportunity came up."

Lauren nodded, not trusting her voice. The longing for Captiva had been growing in her for years, intensifying in the months since Daniel's birth. But she'd pushed it down, not wanting to uproot their life here or disrupt the children's routines.

"I have," she admitted finally. "But it wasn't practical. The kids' schools, the house..."

"And now?"

"Now we have a reason that can't be dismissed as just my

missing my mother," she said, the words coming out more bitterly than she'd intended.

Jeff's expression softened. "Lauren, if you'd ever said it was what you truly wanted, I would have considered it seriously. You know that. Being a stay-at-home dad makes our choices that much easier. I'm more concerned about your real estate business."

She'd run this scenario in her mind several times before. Brian and Nell could run the place, and she'd open a new location in Florida if they could afford it.

Jeff had always been supportive of her needs and dreams. But a part of her had held back from fully voicing her desire to live in Florida, afraid that it would seem selfish or impractical.

"We can make it work. I've wanted to expand before, but with the fire and Daniel's birth, life felt too complicated to plan anything new. Most of all, whatever I do, I don't want to fail."

"There's no failure in recognizing what makes you happy," Jeff countered. "And your connection to your family isn't something to be ashamed of."

Lauren sighed, feeling the truth of his words. "When did you get so wise?"

"I've always been wise," he replied with a teasing smile. "It's why you married me."

She laughed softly, the tension easing. "So, what now? Do we consider this? Moving to Florida?"

"I think we have to," Jeff said, his expression turning serious again. "For Olivia's sake, at minimum. But also..." He hesitated, then continued, "I've been watching you these past few months, Lauren. You light up when you're on the phone with your mom. How much happier you were after visiting Captiva at Christmas. How torn you've been since Eloise's birth, wanting to be here for Becca and Chris but feeling pulled south."

Lauren felt tears welling, surprised by his perceptiveness. "I didn't realize it was so obvious."

"Only to someone who loves you," he assured her, squeezing her hand. "And who wants you to be happy? And there's something else. You know how much I love being with the children but have talked about finding something I could do while they were in school."

"Yes, I remember. Does moving to Florida change that?"

He shook his head. "I wouldn't go that far, but I think it's important that we stay flexible. We don't know how to navigate Olivia's tennis training or how you're expanding your real estate business. And the adjustment Lily will have to make may be significant."

"What are you saying?"

I'd rather we put my career—or lack thereof —on hold until we're truly settled. I want to be there for Daniel, Lily, *and* Olivia. I'm not dropping my daughter off at a tennis camp and letting others raise my child."

"Oh, Jeff, I think you might be overreacting. The camp has been around forever. It has amazing credentials." She held his hand. "But I understand what you're saying, and I love you for it. You are the best father in the world."

She kissed him on the lips and squeezed his hand. "We both will do what's right for the children. Whatever sacrifices we have to make, we'll do it together."

Jeff took a deep breath. "None of it is insurmountable. We'll be fine if we stay close and keep communicating. I know sometimes you keep things inside, not wanting to upset anything, but that isn't the way. Lauren, you have to talk to me."

"I know. Of course, you're right. Old habits…"

Jeff nodded. "I understand, but it's important if we want to work as a team."

Lauren felt a bubble of hope rising in her chest, tempered by practical concerns. "We'd need to sell the house," she said.

"In this market? It would go in a week," he answered.

"And find a new place down there."

"Your mother would know the best neighborhoods," Jeff pointed out. "And we could stay at the inn temporarily if needed."

"The academy is in Tampa, not Captiva," Lauren remembered suddenly. "That's at least two hours away."

Jeff nodded. "I looked into that, too. They have boarding options for students who live farther away, but that's not my first choice for Olivia at twelve." He hesitated, then added, "There are communities midway between Tampa and Captiva. Places where we could live would put us within a reasonable distance of the academy and your family."

The thoroughness of his research told Lauren how seriously he'd been considering this possibility, even before today's news. "You've thought this through."

"I've been thinking about what would make our family happiest," he corrected gently. "And I'm not convinced it's staying here, especially with your mother and grandmother getting older and Sarah's kids growing up without knowing their cousins."

The mention of her sister's children sent a pang through Lauren. Sophia, Noah, and little Maggie were growing up so fast, their faces changing between FaceTime calls. Their lives proceeded parallel to her children's but rarely intersected except for the occasional holiday visit.

"I want them to know each other," she said softly. "To have what we had growing up—cousins like siblings, family traditions, shared memories. The hard part is that wherever we live I'm separated from family. Living in Florida will mean that we won't see my brother, Michael's kids. Olivia and Lily love Quinn, Cora and Jackson."

"I know it isn't perfect, but it's a perfect solution for us, at least for the foreseeable future," Jeff suggested. "Olivia's opportunity opening the door to what you've been wanting for a long time."

Lauren took a deep breath, feeling the possibilities expanding before her. "We'd need to talk to the kids. Well, to Lily, at least.

Olivia would move to the moon if it meant training with Coach Davis."

"Lily's adaptable," Jeff reminded her. "And she adores your mother, her aunt, and Grandma Sarah. Plus, beaches, dolphins, year-round swimming... I don't think it would be a hard sell."

"And Daniel's too young to care as long as we're there," Lauren added, thinking of their easygoing baby boy.

There was so much to consider. It wasn't just about Olivia's tennis career or Lauren's desire to be closer to her family. It was about changing their lives—Jeff's need to watch over Olivia while still caring for Lily and Daniel when Lauren worked, the children's education and social circles, daily routines, and long-term plans.

"We don't have to decide tonight," Jeff said, sensing she was overwhelmed. "The academy needs an answer by August 1st. That gives us time to research, talk to the kids, and make sure this is right for all of us."

Lauren nodded. "I can't wait to run this by Mom."

Jeff laughed. "No doubt she'll be over the moon."

Lauren felt the tension in her shoulders ease, replaced by a sliver of excitement. "So, we're considering this, aren't we?"

"We are," Jeff confirmed. "And for what it's worth, I think it could be wonderful for all of us, not just Olivia. A new adventure."

Looking into his eyes, Lauren knew they were on the same page. Whatever concerns he might have about his career, about starting over in a new place, he was willing to set them aside for her happiness and Olivia's opportunity.

"I love you," she said simply. "And whatever we decide, I'm grateful we're deciding it together."

"Always," he replied, lifting her hand to kiss her palm. "That's the one constant, no matter where we live."

Later, lying awake in bed while Jeff slept peacefully beside her, Lauren let herself fully imagine it for the first time—Florida, the warm embrace of family, the rhythm of island life, the sun-drenched days and star-filled nights of Captiva. In her mind's eye, she saw Olivia flourishing at the academy, Lily collecting shells with Grandma Sarah, and Daniel taking his first steps on the same beaches where she'd learned to walk.

And beneath these specifics, a deeper truth: the sense of belonging, of continuity, of being part of something larger than her immediate family unit. The Wheeler-Moretti clan, spread across two states but bound by unbreakable ties, now potentially reuniting in a way she hadn't dared to hope for.

There were practicalities to consider, details to iron out, and conversations to have. But in the quiet darkness of her Massachusetts bedroom, Lauren allowed herself to feel the full force of her yearning for her mother.

Sleep came eventually, and with it, dreams of salt air and mangrove trees, of her mother's kitchen and her grandmother's knowing smile, of her children running along the shore while she and Sarah watched from beneath a palm tree, picking up the threads of their sisterhood as if they'd never been stretched by distance.

Tomorrow would bring questions and plans, research, and discussions. But tonight, Lauren rested in the possibility that the pull she'd been feeling for so long might finally draw her to where she truly belonged.

CHAPTER 9

When they arrived in Boston, the first thing Maggie and Paolo Moretti did was to get a taxi to the hospital. Her son, Michael, had offered to pick them up, but Maggie didn't want to take anything away from Becca and Christopher's needs. Michael insisted they weren't the burden Maggie declared, but Maggie got her way.

Once at the hospital, they stayed with Becca and Christopher for several hours before they agreed to let Michael drive them to Maggie's former home, now Christopher and Becca's. For the next couple of days, they visited Becca, but when it was finally time for her to leave the hospital, Maggie stayed back at the house, preparing Lauren's food for her son and daughter-in-law.

"Mom, please stop doing so much. Chris said all we had to do was pop everything in the microwave. You're going overboard making salads and appetizers."

"You're still my child, Christopher Wheeler, and I'll do what I think is right for my family; thank you very much."

Christopher smiled despite himself, recognizing the familiar tone that meant his mother was not to be deterred. He checked his watch—he needed to leave for the hospital in fifteen minutes to pick up Becca.

"I know, Mom. I just don't want you and Paolo exhausting yourselves."

Maggie waved a wooden spoon dismissively. "Nonsense, this is what grandmothers do." She turned back to the stove where a pot of homemade soup simmered.

Christopher leaned against the counter, watching his mother move efficiently around the kitchen that had once been hers. "How is it, being back here? In the old house?"

Maggie paused briefly, a soft smile crossing her face. "It feels right, seeing you and Becca making it your own. Your father would have loved seeing his grandchild come home to this house."

Christopher felt his throat tighten. "I wish he could have met Ellie."

"He knows her," Maggie said with certainty, reaching to squeeze her son's hand. "Now, how's our little one doing today? Any updates from the morning rounds?"

"Dr. Winters says she's gaining weight right on schedule. Twenty grams yesterday." Christopher's face brightened. "And she's taking more formula each feeding."

"That's wonderful," Maggie said, her eyes shining. "She's a fighter, just like her grandmother." She winked.

Christopher laughed, then grew serious. "Mom, I'm... I'm terrified. Bringing Becca home without Ellie—it doesn't feel right. And I don't know if I'm ready to be responsible for this tiny human when they finally let her come home."

Maggie set down her spoon and turned fully to her son. "Christopher Wheeler, I watched you grow from a boy who couldn't remember to feed his goldfish into a man who puts everyone else first. I've seen you with Becca through this whole difficult pregnancy. You are more ready than you know."

"But what if—"

"There will always be 'what ifs.' That's parenthood." She cupped his face like she did when he was small. "You and Becca will figure it out together, and when you can't, that's what Paolo and I are here for. And Michael, Lauren, and Beth. You have a village, sweetheart."

Christopher took a deep breath, nodding. "I need to go. Becca's probably already packed and waiting." He glanced at his watch again and straightened.

"Bring her straight home. Everything will be ready." She hesitated, then added, "And Christopher? It's okay if she cries on the way home without the baby. It's okay if you both do."

Christopher nodded, throat tight again. "I know, Mom." He grabbed his keys from the counter. "I love you."

"I love you too," Maggie said. "Now go get your wife. And tell my granddaughter her grandma will be there to see her tomorrow morning with fresh stories."

As Christopher headed for the door, Maggie called, "And don't forget to use the seat warmer for Becca. She'll be tender still!"

Christopher smiled again as he closed the door behind him. Some things never changed, and his mother's loving, overwhelming attention to detail was one of them. Right now, he couldn't be more grateful.

After nearly a week of family occupation, Becca's hospital room had become homey. Cards and flowers covered every surface, and the family had taped photos of Eloise's daily progress to the walls where Becca could see them easily. Someone—Lauren suspected Beth—had strung fairy lights along the window to soften the institutional fluorescents.

Lauren sat in the visitor's chair, Daniel asleep against her chest, while Becca prepared for her discharge. After six days of intensive monitoring, her blood pressure had stabilized enough for the doctors to release her, though she'd be returning to the hospital daily to be with Eloise.

"Are you nervous?" Lauren asked, watching Becca fold the nightgown Beth had brought her days earlier.

Becca paused, considering the question. "About going home without her? Terrified." She placed the nightgown in the small duffel bag Crawford had bought at the hospital gift shop. "But also relieved, in a way. I need to regain my strength if I'm going to be any use to her, and I can't do that properly here."

Lauren nodded, understanding the complex emotions. "The first night will be the hardest," she said gently. "But it gets easier. And you'll be back first thing in the morning."

"That's what Dr. Patel said. She's arranging for me to have unlimited NICU access." Becca zipped the bag closed, her movements deliberate.

She sat on the edge of the bed, suddenly looking very young and vulnerable despite the maturity she'd shown throughout the crisis. "How do you do it, Lauren? Being a mother. It's so..." She gestured vaguely, searching for words.

"Overwhelming?" Lauren suggested. "Terrifying? Exhausting? The most incredible thing you've ever done?"

"All of that," Becca agreed with a small laugh. "I keep thinking I'm not ready and don't know enough. And then I remember that Eloise didn't ask for my permission before deciding to arrive."

"No baby ever does," Lauren said, smiling down at Daniel's sleeping form. "They come when they come, ready or not. And somehow, we figure it out."

"I hope so."

"I know so," Lauren assured her. "I've watched you this week, Becca. How you talk to Eloise, how you've learned every detail of her care, the questions you ask the doctors. You're already an amazing mother."

Becca's eyes filled with tears. "Thank you for saying that."

"I'm only stating facts," Lauren replied, reaching out to squeeze Becca's hand. "And you're not doing this alone. You have Christopher, your dad, brothers, all of us Wheelers... plus your medical training, which gives you a head start most new mothers don't have."

"That's true," Becca acknowledged, wiping at her eyes. "Though sometimes I think the medical knowledge makes it worse. I know too many things that could go wrong."

"Focus on what's going right," Lauren advised. "Eloise is gaining weight; her oxygen needs are decreasing, and she takes more milk daily. She's a fighter."

"Like her mother," Christopher said from the doorway, startling both women.

"How long have you been standing there?" Becca asked, though her expression softened at the sight of her husband.

"Long enough to hear my wise sister dispensing maternal wisdom," Christopher replied, crossing to kiss Becca's forehead. "The car's ready whenever you are. Dad and the boys are on their way to the house with seafood, of all things. Mom's prepared what she's calling a 'welcome home feast,' which I should warn you appears to involve an alarming amount of appetizers. Now, with your father's seafood, our parents think food is the answer for every situation.

Becca laughed. "Of course they do. Powells consider crab legs the ultimate comfort food."

"Is there anything else you need before we go?" Christopher asked. Are there any last-minute items?"

"Just one more visit with Eloise," Becca replied. "I want to feed her before we leave."

"Dr. Winters is expecting you," Christopher confirmed. "And Lauren, Mom asked if you could swing by the house on your way home. She said something about not getting to talk to you enough while she and Paolo are here."

Lauren nodded, carefully shifting Daniel as she stood. "I'll head over there now. She and Paolo are flying back tomorrow, right?"

"First thing in the morning," Christopher confirmed. "Though I think Mom would stay forever if they didn't have the inn to manage."

"That's Mom," Lauren said fondly. Once she latches onto a grandbaby, wild horses can't drag her away." She hugged Becca. I'll see you at the house, but don't forget to call me if you need anything, promise?"

"I promise," Becca said. "And Lauren? Thank you so much for the meals, the support, everything."

"Of course," Lauren replied, gathering her purse and diaper bag. "See you soon."

As she walked down the hospital corridors to the parking garage, Lauren reflected on family bonds and obligations, on the invisible ties that pulled at her even from hundreds of miles away. Watching Becca and Christopher navigate the crisis of Eloise's premature birth and seeing the Powells and Wheelers unite in support had only strengthened her conviction that family mattered more than geography or convenience.

And now, with Olivia's unexpected opportunity opening a door to the move she'd been secretly craving, Lauren felt a sense of alignment—as if the universe was finally bringing her desires and circumstances into harmony.

She settled Daniel into his car seat, the warm June air wrapping around them as she opened the car doors to let the heat escape. As she waited, her phone chimed with a text from her mother: *Don't forget my grandbabies!*

Lauren smiled, imagining her mother's excitement at having three grandchildren together. It would be chaotic and noisy, exactly the kind of family gathering Maggie thrived on.

We'll be there, she texted back. *And Mom? I have some news to share.*

The response came instantly: *Good news or concerning news?*

Lauren hesitated, then typed: *Life-changing news. But good. Very good.*

As she drove toward her house to pick up Jeff and the girls, Lauren felt a curious lightness in her chest, as if a weight she'd been carrying had begun to lift. Whatever happened with their potential move—whether they ended up in Tampa, Captiva, or somewhere in between—she was finally allowing herself to acknowledge what she truly wanted, to voice the longing that had been growing for the last five years—to feel settled once and for all.

CHAPTER 10

$\mathcal{T}$he Wheeler family home buzzed with energy. After a week of medical anxieties and worries, Becca was finally home, though little Eloise remained in the NICU. The house had been transformed in anticipation of Becca's return. Fresh flowers were arranged in the entryway, the refrigerator was stocked with prepared meals, and a "Welcome Home Eloise" sign was hung in the living room.

"Sorry about the sign, but our little Ellie will be home before you know it," Lauren said.

Becca shook her head. "No, that's fine. The doctors said she shouldn't have to stay in the hospital for more than a few days. She's doing well and will manage on her own soon. I'm hopeful."

"Beth and Gabriel couldn't make it but wanted us to let you know they're so happy you're home and they'll visit soon. Michael's on call, so he couldn't make it either."

Becca nodded. "Thanks, Lauren. You and Jeff have been great."

Maggie Wheeler Moretti moved efficiently through the kitchen, directing Paolo's placement of serving dishes with the precision of someone who had orchestrated countless family gatherings.

"The seafood platter needs to be on the sideboard, not the table," she instructed, rearranging the cluster of appetizers. "And we'll need the larger serving spoons for the pasta salad."

Paolo smiled indulgently at his wife's management style. "As you wish, cara mia. Though I doubt anyone will be looking at the food with Becca finally home."

"It's precisely because of what she's been through that everything needs to be perfect," Maggie insisted. "Becca and Chris are exhausted. The least we can do is make sure everything else runs smoothly. Besides, did you see her brothers? They've been hovering around the kitchen island since they arrived."

"They're growing boys," Paolo answered.

From the living room came the boisterous laughter of Becca's brothers—Finn, Luke, and Joshua Powell had arrived early to help, and their father's anxious-looking face relaxed the minute his daughter stepped into the house.

"Dad, I'm pretty sure Becca can manage to walk from the sofa to the armchair without assistance," Luke teased as Crawford adjusted the placement of a footstool for the fifth time.

Crawford straightened his weathered face, a mixture of defensiveness and concern. "You try having a C-section and visiting your preemie in the hospital every day, then tell me about what she can manage."

"He's got you there," Finn remarked, elbowing his younger brother.

Lauren caught her mother's eye over the children's heads, an unspoken question passing between them. Maggie nodded subtly —yes, there would be time for their private conversation later. For now, the focus remained on preparing for Becca's homecoming.

Jeff found his way to the kitchen, baby Daniel babbling contentedly in his arms. "Lauren told me to deliver this little guy to whoever needs baby snuggles," he announced. "Any takers?"

"I think that would be me," Maggie volunteered instantly, her hands reaching for her grandson.

"I'm so glad you're home, even if our little fighter has to stay behind a few more days," Crawford said, his arm steady around Becca's shoulders. "She'll be home before you know it, Bec."

The family moved to the living room, arranging themselves around Becca as she settled carefully on the sofa. Christopher sat beside her, his arm protectively encircling her shoulders.

"How are you feeling?" Lauren asked, perching on the coffee table across from Becca.

"Sore. Tired. Heartbroken about leaving Eloise. Relieved to be home," Becca replied honestly. "Sometimes, all within the same minute."

"Sounds about right," Lauren nodded sympathetically. "The separation must be so hard."

"The doctors say it won't be long," Christopher assured everyone, though his eyes held the same hope and worry as Becca's. "Her breathing has improved dramatically, and she's gaining weight on schedule."

"That's wonderful news," Maggie said, reaching out to squeeze Becca's hand. "In the meantime, you can rest and regain your strength."

Crawford cleared his throat, emotion making his voice gruff. "Your mother would be so proud of how you've handled this, Bec. She had that same strength—that ability to face whatever comes with grace."

A brief, tender silence fell over the room at the mention of Julia Powell. Becca's eyes met her father's, a lifetime of shared loss and love passing between them.

"Did you bring new pictures?" Lily asked, breaking the emotional moment with a child's perfect timing. "Mom said Eloise is getting bigger every day."

Christopher smiled, pulling out his phone. "We have a whole new album from this morning."

The family gathered around as Christopher displayed the latest photos of Eloise in the NICU. Though still small, the improvement from her earliest days was remarkable—her face fuller, her color healthier, and the medical equipment surrounding her noticeably reduced.

"She has your chin, Chris," Joshua observed, peering at a close-up.

"And Becca's eyes, thank goodness," Luke added with a teasing grin.

"Powell nose, though," Finn declared. "Perfect for detecting which way the wind is blowing when she's old enough to sail."

Paolo disappeared into the kitchen, returning with trays of appetizers that he distributed with quiet efficiency.

"You must eat," he insisted, placing a plate directly in Becca's line of sight. "New mothers need proper nutrition, especially after such an ordeal."

Becca accepted the plate gratefully. "Thank you, Paolo. It looks amazing."

As the family ate, the conversation centered on Eloise—her progress, the nurses' reports, and the preparations for her homecoming. Christopher had finished setting up the nursery with Beth's help. The pediatrician had been selected, follow-up appointments had been scheduled, and a specialized monitor had been purchased for when Eloise finally came home.

"We're taking shifts at the NICU," Christopher explained. "I'll return this evening, and Becca will visit tomorrow morning. The nurses suggested we both try to rest to prepare for the sleepless nights ahead."

"Smart advice," Jeff nodded. "Sleep deprivation is the hardest part of those early weeks, even without the NICU experience beforehand."

"So, NICU life for just a few more days," Luke said, settling onto the ottoman near her feet. "How are you holding up, Bec?"

"It's harder than I expected," Becca admitted. "Walking out of the hospital without her felt impossible."

Finn squeezed her hand. "She's where she needs to be right now, getting the care that will make her stronger when she comes home."

"I know." Becca nodded. "The nurses are wonderful, and she's making such good progress. It's just the separation that's killing me. I'm her mother—I should be with her."

"You are with her," Joshua insisted. "Every day, every moment you can be. And when you can't physically be there, you're recovering and preparing so you can be the mother she needs when she comes home."

"That's why we're staying through the weekend," Finn added. "Extra hands while you get your strength back."

Becca smiled gratefully at her brothers. Despite their teasing and occasional overprotectiveness, they had always been her steadfast supporters. "Thanks. I'm sure Dad has already drawn up a 24-hour schedule for the next month."

"Dad's in his element." Luke laughed. "He's been researching premature infant care like it's his new doctoral thesis. Pretty sure he could write a medical textbook by now."

Becca felt a lump form in her throat. "He's been amazing through all of this. I don't know what we would have done without him."

"That's what family's for," Finn said. "We're heading back to Captiva on Monday, but Dad's staying another week. And we're just a phone call away if you need reinforcements."

"Or a seafood delivery," Luke added. "I've already packed the cooler with stone crabs for tomorrow."

In the kitchen, Maggie cornered Lauren near the pantry, their voices low but animated.

Lauren explained everything about the move to Florida as Maggie pressed a hand to her heart, tears springing to her eyes. "Oh, Lauren. I can hardly believe it's happening."

"Me neither," Lauren admitted. "It seems impossible that it's coming together."

"And the children? They're excited?"

"We haven't told them everything, but Olivia expects it. She's thrilled about the tennis academy."

"And Jeff?" Maggie asked.

"Surprisingly enthusiastic," Lauren said. "We're already planning to put the house on the market as soon as possible."

Maggie enfolded her daughter in a tight embrace. "I can't tell you what this means to me, having you all close by. I wish all of my children lived in Florida."

Lauren returned the hug, allowing herself to feel the complete rightness of her decision. "You might get your wish. Don't quote me on this, but I think Becca and Chris will move to Captiva eventually."

"Really? Why do you say that?"

"Because I heard them talking about looking into having her residency in Florida. It's a hunch, and it's probably another year away. You should get more info from Chris about it."

They were interrupted by Paolo calling everyone to the dining room for lunch. The meal was a masterpiece of casual elegance—Crawford's requested seafood platter supplemented by Paolo's Italian pasta creations and various sides that accommodated everyone's preferences.

Throughout lunch, Christopher kept his phone next to his plate, occasionally darting his eyes to check for updates from the NICU. Becca tried to focus on the conversation around her, but her thoughts kept straying to Eloise.

"I'm going with you in the morning, Becca. I want to spend some time with my granddaughter," Crawford said.

"Mom, Paolo, and I will come in around noon and take you back home," Christopher added.

"And we'll come by before heading to the airport on Monday," Finn added, speaking for himself and his brothers.

"We'll want to say goodbye to our niece and remind her that her uncles expect her to visit Captiva as soon as she's cleared for travel."

"Paolo's already planning what Italian lullabies to sing to her," Maggie added.

"You don't all have to—" Becca began.

"Yes, we do," Luke interrupted firmly.

"Just remember that you all can't go into the NICU simultaneously. They're very strict about that. You might have to go in one at a time."

"We'll do whatever they tell us to, honey. Don't worry," Crawford said.

By early evening family members began to depart. Lauren and Jeff gathered their sleepy children, and Lily extracted a promise that she could visit baby Eloise in the hospital before she came home.

"Of course," Becca assured her niece. "She needs to meet all her cousins. It will make her stronger."

Soon, only Maggie, Paolo, and Crawford remained, helping with the final cleanup while Christopher prepared for his evening hospital visit. Finn, Joshua, and Luke get an Uber to their hotel.

"I'll stay here tonight," Crawford whispered to Christopher. "Keep an eye on Becca while you're with Eloise."

"That would be great." Christopher nodded gratefully. "I won't be gone too long." Looking at Becca, Christopher added, "She keeps saying she's fine, but—"

"She's still recovering from major surgery and emotional trauma," Crawford finished. "I know my daughter. She'll push herself too hard if someone's not watching."

When the house was quiet and Maggie and Paolo had gone to bed, Christopher found Becca in the nursery, slowly rocking in a chair.

"Ready for me to go?" he asked softly.

Becca nodded, though her eyes remained on the waiting crib. "Tell her I love her. That I'll see her first thing tomorrow."

"I will," Christopher promised, leaning down to kiss her. "Try to get some real sleep, okay? Doctor's orders, and mine."

"I'll try," Becca agreed. "It feels so strange—being home but not having her here. Like I've left part of myself behind."

"Just for a few more days," Christopher reassured her. "The doctors are amazed at her progress. Before you know it, she'll be home, and sleeping in your arms."

He kissed her on the cheek as she held his arm. "I love you."

"I love you too," she said, squeezing him.

After he left, Becca remained in the nursery, unable to tear herself away from the room prepared with such love for a baby still fighting to be strong enough to come home.

Crawford momentarily stood in the doorway before making his presence known.

"Want company?" he asked gently.

Becca glanced up, summoning a tired smile for her father. "Sure."

Crawford entered, his weathered hands looking oversized and awkward among the delicate baby things. He picked up a tiny pink cardigan from the changing table, marveling at its smallness.

"Your mother knitted something like this for each of you," he recalled. "Stayed up nights working on them, wanting everything to be perfect for when you arrived." His voice softened with memory. "She was always so prepared."

"I tried to be," Becca said, gesturing to the carefully organized nursery. "But nothing prepared me for Eloise coming so early or for how hard it would be to come home without her."

Crawford set the cardigan down and moved to kneel beside the rocking chair, his focus entirely on his daughter. "Listen to me, Becca. You are doing everything right. Eloise is getting the best possible care, and in a few days, she'll be home where she belongs. In the meantime, you need to heal, rest, and prepare for the marathon of new parenthood ahead."

Tears filled Becca's eyes. "I know you're right. It's just—"

"The hardest thing in the world," Crawford finished. "Believe me, I understand. When you kids were small and your mother got sick the first time, having to leave her in the hospital while I cared for you at home nearly broke me. But we do what we have to for the ones we love. Sometimes that means being apart for a little while to be together much longer."

Becca leaned forward, resting her forehead against her father's shoulder as she had since childhood. "Thank you for being here, Dad."

"Where else would I be?" Crawford replied simply. "This is what fathers are for."

Later, after Becca settled in bed with pain medication and a cup of tea, Crawford made his bed in the guest room, positioning the phone carefully beside him in case Christopher called with any updates from the hospital. The house felt strangely suspended—not quite in crisis anymore, but not yet fully embracing joy—a home waiting for its missing piece to complete it.

According to the doctors, Eloise would fill that emptiness in three or four days. Until then, the Wheeler and Powell families would do what they'd always done—support each other through whatever came, one day, one hour, one breath at a time.

CHAPTER 11

"*H*ow's my little brother?" Sarah Hutchins asked Christopher on an early morning phone call. "Mom's been filling me in but I wanted to hear it from you."

Christopher rubbed his eyes, "Everything is going well."

Sarah laughed. "You sound exhausted. I imagine everyone is. How's Becca?"

"Emotional," he answered.

"I can imagine."

"She'll be fine as soon as they release Ellie. How are you doing?"

Sarah sighed. "I'm fine. It's always hard when Trevor travels. Having the kids to myself has been fun though. Working part-time instead of full-time helps."

Christopher yawned. "So, when are you coming up to see Ellie? I'd like my little girl to meet her Aunt Sarah."

"I know. We all want to meet her, too. It's just that Trevor's work makes it so hard for me to get away, and it's not easy traveling with three children. I'll figure it out, and as soon as possible I'll get up there. In the meantime, take care of your family and send me pictures and videos."

"You bet. Love you, sis."

"Love you, too. Give Becca and Ellie kisses from us. Talk soon."

They ended the call, and Christopher looked at the clock and fell back into his bed and pulled the blanket over his body. He'd get to the hospital in a few hours, but for now he needed sleep, and then a strong cup of coffee.

The weekend passed in a blur of hospital visits, family meals, and quiet conversations. Each day brought small victories—Eloise taking an extra ounce of formula, maintaining her temperature without assistance, or showing improved oxygen levels that had the nurses smiling and the doctors nodding with cautious approval.

Becca grew stronger physically, though the emotional strain of traveling back and forth to see Eloise took its toll. Christopher maintained his vigilant presence at the NICU, learning every detail of Eloise's care from the nurses who had grown so fond of the determined little girl and her devoted parents.

Crawford stayed steady and supportive, coordinating the family's efforts with quiet efficiency. He slept on a cot in the hospital's parent room one night when Eloise had a brief respiratory setback, his solid presence a comfort to both Becca and Christopher during those tense hours. By morning, their little fighter had stabilized, and the episode became just another entry in the journal Becca kept of Eloise's journey.

Becca's brothers visited Eloise one last time before reluctantly returning to Captiva, extracting promises of daily photo updates and video calls. Each Powell man had his own moment with his tiny niece, whispering hopes and promises that brought tears to the nurses' eyes.

Finn, typically the most reserved of the brothers, spent a full hour just watching Eloise, his hands looking enormous as he gently stroked her arm through the incubator port. "She's got the Powell tenacity," he observed to the night nurse. "You can see it in the way she holds onto your finger. That grip's going to serve her well on a fishing boat someday."

Joshua, always the most talkative, read Eloise a children's book about sea creatures, complete with exaggerated voices for each animal and improvised additions to the story that had the NICU staff stifling laughter. "Never too early to start her marine biology education," he insisted when Christopher teased him about the performance.

Lauren and her family maintained their supportive presence, bringing meals and offering welcome distractions when the worry became too heavy. Olivia proved surprisingly adept with baby Daniel, giving Lauren time to help Becca with practical matters like organizing medication schedules and arranging the nursery for optimal efficiency. Lily insisted on drawing a new picture for Eloise each day, creating a colorful gallery on the refrigerator at home since she wasn't allowed to bring them to the NICU.

Beth came by Sunday morning, bringing fresh produce and the practical help that was her particular gift. She arrived one afternoon with baskets of early summer fruits and the latest news on her and Gabriel's apple orchard journey.

By Monday afternoon, with goodbyes said and promises to return made, Maggie and Paolo also prepared to head back to Captiva. The Key Lime Garden Inn couldn't run itself forever, even with the capable staff they'd left in charge. Before leaving, they had one last hospital visit with tiny Eloise, whose improved breathing and steady weight gain had all the doctors optimistic about a homecoming by midweek.

"I'm going to want a video call when that happens," Maggie instructed Becca, embracing her gently in the hospital corridor.

"Of course." Becca smiled, the exhaustion in her eyes

tempered by growing confidence. "And we can't wait for that day."

"You have no idea how proud I am of both of you," Maggie said, including Christopher in her gaze. "The way you've handled this crisis with such grace and strength—it's remarkable."

"We have good examples," Christopher replied, hugging his mother. "Wheeler resilience, right?"

Maggie smiled through tears. "That, and something uniquely your own. You're going to be wonderful parents. You already are."

Paolo had his own moment with Eloise, singing a traditional Italian lullaby in a gentle baritone that had the baby turning toward his voice, her tiny face relaxed in what almost looked like a smile. "That's my secret weapon," he told Christopher. "The grandparent advantage—we know all the old songs that soothe babies. I'll teach you when you come to Captiva."

As Paolo and Maggie boarded their flight back to Florida, a sense of cautious optimism had replaced the crisis atmosphere of the previous last few days. The Wheeler-Powell extended family had weathered another storm together, emerging battered but intact, their bonds strengthened by shared struggle and mutual support.

Maggie and Paolo pulled into the driveway of the Key Lime Garden Inn after the drive from the airport, the familiar sight of weathered clapboard siding and wide verandas bringing a wave of relief. As much as she had needed to be with Christopher and Becca during the crisis, Captiva Island was home now, the inn her particular domain.

"Home sweet home." Paolo sighed, cutting the engine. "Though I won't feel fully settled until I see what Oliver has on the menu for dinner. I can't believe what the airline thinks is food. My stomach wasn't meant to live on chips and soda."

Maggie laughed. "You're spoiled, you know that?"

"I do, and I wish for it to continue," he answered.

The front porch of the inn was decorated with fresh-cut flowers in blue ceramic pots—Iris's work, Maggie recognized immediately. The plants looked well-tended, the walkways swept, and the wooden rocking chairs arranged in the conversational groupings Maggie preferred. Whatever had happened in their absence, the inn's appearance hadn't suffered.

"Ah, look who's back!" Grandma Sarah called from her customary position on the porch swing, a pitcher of sweet tea and a well-worn paperback on the table beside her. "Just in time, too. This place can't thrive without you two. Even the garden looks like it's giving up."

Maggie laughed, hurrying up the steps to embrace her mother. "That's hard to imagine considering we were only gone for ten days. How are you, Mother? Everything running smoothly?"

"As smoothly as can be expected with you and Paolo gallivanting off to Massachusetts," Grandma Sarah replied without heat. Her silver hair was pulled back in its usual neat bun, her linen clothing crisp despite the humidity. At eighty-one, she remained the elegant matriarch of the Wheeler family, her posture as straight as her opinions. "Enough about all this. How's my great-granddaughter?"

Maggie smiled. "Oh, Mom. You should see her. She's so beautiful and getting stronger by the day. I think this coming week they'll send her home."

Grandma Sarah nodded. "Well, of course she's beautiful and strong. She's a Wheeler isn't she? Although the truth is she's more a Garrison than a Wheeler, but I'll give the Wheeler name some credit."

Maggie rolled her eyes. "Tell me everything about what's been going on here."

Grandma Sarah put her eyeglasses down on the table and

looked at Maggie. "We've managed, though Millie threatened to quit twice and Oliver nearly came to blows with that new seafood supplier."

Paolo raised his eyebrows as he joined them, carrying their overnight bags. "The Sanderson boy? What happened?"

"Tried to deliver second-rate grouper and call it prime." Grandma Sarah sniffed. "Oliver sent him packing with a few choice words."

"That boy has always tried to pass off inferior fish," Paolo shook his head. "His father would never have attempted such a thing. Standards have slipped since Edward retired."

"Well, Oliver made it very clear that the Key Lime Garden Inn has not lowered its standards, regardless of who's manning the kitchen," Grandma Sarah reported with evident satisfaction. "I thought the boy might cry when Oliver inspected each fish and rejected more than half the delivery."

The screen door opened, and Millie emerged out onto the porch, her practical cotton dress and sensible shoes a constant outfit. Her face lit up at the sight of Maggie and Paolo.

"Oh thank goodness you're back," she exclaimed. "Mrs. Henderson in Room 4 has been asking about that special pillow you promised her, and the Wilsons want to extend their stay but Iris couldn't find the reservation book, most likely because Gretchen put it somewhere and couldn't remember. The Simpson wedding party called to increase their booking from two rooms to four for October, and—"

"Take a breath, Millie," Maggie interrupted gently. "One thing at a time. The hypoallergenic pillow is in the linen closet, top shelf, labeled with her name. And we switched to the digital system last month, remember? The reservation changes are all on the tablet in the office."

Millie looked embarrassed. "I never did figure out that tablet nonsense. Iris tried to show me but then got busy with lunch preparations. And then that Gretchen woman made things worse when she tried to help." She pressed a hand to her mouth. "Oh, I shouldn't have mentioned that. Iris said not to ambush you with problems the moment you arrived."

Maggie raised an eyebrow. "Gretchen? Chelsea's sister was here helping out?"

"'Helping' is a generous description," Grandma Sarah remarked dryly. "But we'll get to that. First, sit down and have some tea. You look exhausted, both of you."

Paolo set down their bags with a sigh of relief. "Tea sounds wonderful, but I should check on the dinner menu first."

"Oh, Oliver's been very careful to follow your instructions to the letter," a new voice assured him. Iris appeared in the doorway, wiping her hands on her ever-present apron. Despite the Florida heat and the demands of running the inn's kitchen, she looked as put-together as always.

"Welcome back. How's the baby? And Becca?"

"Both improving daily," Maggie reported, accepting Iris's quick embrace. "Eloise should be home by midweek if all continues as planned. She's gained almost a pound since birth and her breathing is much stronger."

"Christopher's been sending updates and photos." Iris nodded. "That child has more determination in her tiny finger than most adults have in their entire bodies. The guests have been asking—word travels fast on a small island, and several regulars were concerned when they heard you'd left so suddenly."

"I'll make the rounds at dinner," Maggie promised, settling into a wicker chair and accepting the glass of sweet tea her mother poured. "Thank everyone for their good thoughts. The support from near and far has meant everything to Becca and Christopher."

"And you'll need to speak with the Lovells," Millie added, hovering nearby with her ever-present notebook. "They're interested in booking the entire property for their fiftieth anniversary next spring. I told them you'd discuss the details when you returned."

Maggie nodded, mentally shifting from grandmother-mode back to innkeeper. "I'll catch up on all the business matters tomorrow. For now, catch me up on what's happened here while we were gone. Start with the minor things, then we'll get to whatever situation occurred with Gretchen."

Millie and Iris exchanged glances, a silent communication that immediately put Maggie on alert.

"What?" she asked. "What happened that you're not telling me?"

"Nothing serious," Millie assured her quickly. "The inn has been running fine. Full occupancy, good reviews, minimal complaints." She consulted her notebook. "The new gardener has worked out well—the flower beds have never looked better. The coffee supplier sent the wrong beans last week, but we managed until the correct order arrived. Oh, and the Martinsons in the cottage requested an extra night, which we were able to accommodate since it was vacant for the following day."

"All routine matters," Maggie nodded, sipping her tea. "So why do you all look like you're hiding something?"

Iris sighed, trading glances with Grandma Sarah. "It's just... there was a bit of a situation with Gretchen."

"Chelsea's sister," Maggie clarified. "What sort of situation?"

"She showed up last Wednesday offering to help," Oliver explained, joining them from the kitchen. His tall frame filled the doorway, flour dusting his apron. "Said she knew you were away and thought we could use an extra pair of hands."

"That was... unexpectedly thoughtful of her," Maggie said carefully. Gretchen had many qualities, but spontaneous helpfulness rarely featured among them.

"Yes, well, her helping lasted exactly four hours," Grandma Sarah reported dryly. "She reorganized the brochure display in the lobby—quite nicely, I'll admit—then started taking photographs of guests without permission for what she called her 'island hospitality portfolio.'"

"When the Carmichaels complained, she told them they should be flattered to be included in her artistic vision," Millie added. "Then she spilled coffee on the new reservation tablet while trying to show me her photography website."

Maggie closed her eyes briefly. "And then what happened?"

"Then she received a phone call, said something had come up, and left without another word," Iris finished. "Haven't seen her since, though Chelsea stopped by yesterday looking for her."

"Did she find her?" Paolo asked, concern evident in his voice. For all Gretchen's flighty ways, she was still family of sorts through Chelsea's connection to the inn.

"Apparently not," Oliver replied. "Chelsea seemed quite aggravated—said something about Gretchen missing an important appointment about a real estate showing at the Barlowes.'"

"The Barlowe cottage?" Maggie clarified. "I thought that sale was proceeding smoothly. Isabelle mentioned it was nearly finalized before we left."

Grandma Sarah settled back in her chair, clearly enjoying being the most informed as usual. "Well, according to what Chelsea told me when she stopped for tea yesterday, the people couldn't get financing and then Gretchen wanted to see it. However, I don't think a P&S was created, even though Gretchen was certain it was the place she wanted to settle. Then she disappeared the night before another walkthrough. Chelsea finally tracked her down at some photographer's studio in Naples, where she was, and I quote, 'building her portfolio instead of her future.'"

"Oh dear." Maggie sighed. "That sounds like classic Gretchen —enthusiasm followed by distraction when the real work begins."

"Much like her sisters Tess and Leah if memory serves. The good news," Grandma Sarah continued, "is that I think she's finally moving forward with the purchase, although don't quote me on that. Chelsea practically dragged her sister to the bank to sign papers but then Gretchen pulled out at the last minute. It's been a roller-coaster ride." She adjusted her reading glasses.

"I suspect Chelsea may have threatened bodily harm if Gretchen jeopardized the sale. She had that particular look in her eye—you know the one she gets."

Maggie laughed. "Chelsea's patience has limits, especially where her sister is concerned. Did Gretchen say why she suddenly felt compelled to help at the inn? It seems out of character, especially with her looking for a place to live."

Iris and Millie exchanged another glance.

"Well," Iris began carefully, "she might have mentioned something about getting out of Chelsea and Steven's hair, and also that she wanted to prove to Chelsea that she's responsible and serious about getting work."

"Ah." Maggie nodded, understanding dawning. "That makes sense. Chelsea's been hospitable, but she'll lose her mind if Gretchen thinks she's going to live with them for months. For the life of me I can't understand why Gretchen didn't stay in the rental she found when she first got here. I think she's afraid to commit to anything because she can't decide where to live permanently. She's got one foot out the door at all times."

"Well, if you're right, the attempt backfired rather spectacularly," Grandma Sarah observed. "Hard to prove you're dependable when you abandon the task after less than half a day."

Oliver leaned against the doorframe, arms crossed. "She did reorganize the brochure display quite artistically before she left. And she took some lovely photos of the garden that she emailed to Iris. So it wasn't a complete waste."

"Always the optimist, Oliver," Grandma Sarah said with a fond smile. "You'd find the silver lining in a hurricane."

"Speaking of weather," Paolo interjected, "how did the neighbors weather the storm? It didn't look too bad when we left. Thankfully, it wasn't a hurricane."

This question launched a detailed account of the storm's passage—minor compared to what they'd initially feared, but still requiring cleanup of fallen branches and debris. Millie had photos on her phone of the aftermath, which she shared while describing how the staff had worked together to restore the gardens to their usual pristine condition.

"Byron Jameson's place had extensive damage, but I think everything's cleaned up now," Iris added.

As they talked, Maggie felt herself easing back into the rhythm of inn life, the familiar concerns and small crises a stark contrast to the life-and-death intensity of the NICU. She hadn't realized how much tension she'd been carrying until she felt it begin to release, her shoulders loosening as she sipped her tea and listened to the staff's animated recounting of the week's events.

Paolo, ever attuned to his wife's moods, placed a hand on her shoulder. "Perhaps we should unpack and rest a bit before dinner," he suggested. "It's been a long day of travel."

"Good idea," Maggie agreed, rising from her chair. "I'll check in with the Hendersons about their pillow situation, then take a proper look at the reservation changes." She glanced around at her staff—her friends, really, after all these years—and felt a surge of gratitude for their steadfast management in her absence. "Thank you all for keeping things running smoothly. I know it wasn't easy with both of us away."

"It's what family does," Iris said simply, echoing words that had been repeated often by Maggie.

"Besides," Grandma Sarah added, "it gave Millie a chance to exercise her authority as assistant manager. She's quite good at it when she stops worrying about making mistakes."

Millie blushed at the unexpected praise. "I just did what needed doing. Though I'll be glad to hand the tablet back to you, Maggie. That thing and I do not get along."

Maggie laughed, feeling another knot of tension ease. "We'll schedule some refresher training. I forget that not everyone adapts well to new technology."

As they headed to the carriage house to unpack, Maggie paused at the door. "One more thing—now that we're back, we don't need Gretchen's help anyway, but I wonder what's going on between Chelsea and her sister. I should give her a call, see if everything's all right."

Paolo laughed. "I have no doubt that your best friend has a million things to talk about, but for now, it's time to rest. If I were a betting man, I'd say Chelsea will be here first thing in the morning."

"You're right about that. I'm not complaining but that woman can smell my croissants from two streets away," Iris added.

CHAPTER 12

"*S*ebastian, mon coeur, you must eat something," Isabelle Barlowe urged, setting the breakfast tray on the table beside her husband's wheelchair. The morning sun streamed through the floor-to-ceiling windows of their Captiva mansion, turning the Gulf waters beyond into a dazzling expanse of diamonds.

Sebastian Barlowe barely glanced at the carefully arranged plate—fresh fruit, poached eggs, whole grain toast with the crusts trimmed off, just as he preferred. "Not hungry," he muttered, his gaze fixed on the water.

Isabelle bit back a sigh, studying her husband's profile. At sixty-four, Sebastian remained handsome despite the ravages of time and illness—silver hair still thick, aristocratic features that spoke of his French heritage, the dignified bearing he maintained even after so many years in a wheelchair. But the past few months had etched new lines into his face, and the tremors in his hands had worsened noticeably.

"The medication works better with food," she reminded him gently. "Just a few bites, perhaps?"

Sebastian turned to her, irritation flashing in his gray eyes. "I said I'm not hungry, Isabelle. Must you always hover?"

The words stung, but Isabelle maintained her bright smile. "Of course not. I will leave you to enjoy the morning view." She bent to kiss his cheek, inhaling the familiar scent of his after-shave. "I am going to yoga with Chelsea, remember? Maggie is back from Massachusetts and joining us."

"Another one of your ridiculous activities," Sebastian grumbled. "Grown women contorting themselves on mats. Undignified."

Two years ago, Sebastian would have delivered such a comment with a playful twinkle in his eye, teasing her about her "bohemian pursuits" while secretly admiring her vivacity. Now, there was only acid in his tone, the barb meant to wound.

"Perhaps," Isabelle conceded, refusing to be provoked. "But it makes my body happy, and a happy body makes for a happy wife, non?"

"Do as you please," Sebastian said, turning back to the window. "You always do."

Isabelle straightened, adjusting the colorful silk scarf around her neck—a habitual gesture when she was trying to maintain her composure. "Natalia will be here at nine to help with your physical therapy. I've left lunch in the refrigerator, clearly labeled. I should be home by one."

Sebastian didn't respond, his silence a dismissal as effective as any words. Isabelle lingered a moment longer, searching for a glimpse of the man she'd fallen in love with—the brilliant, cultured man who had found his way back to her after many years apart. The man who had laughed at her outrageous stories, who had matched her zest for life despite the constraints of his wheelchair, who had proposed to her in a moonlit café in Paris, promising adventures despite his physical limitations.

That man was disappearing by increments, replaced by a bitter stranger who seemed to resent her very presence.

"Je t'aime," she said softly before turning to leave. Sebastian didn't reply, but his shoulders tensed slightly.

In the expansive marble foyer, Isabelle gathered her yoga mat and water bottle, checking her reflection in the ornate mirror that dominated the wall. At fifty-three, she remained strikingly beautiful, her dark hair cut in a stylish bob that emphasized her strong cheekbones and expressive brown eyes. Living in Florida had added golden highlights to her hair, and regular yoga kept her figure as lithe as it had been in her dancing days.

Sebastian's children, all in their forties now, frequently remarked—not kindly—that she could be mistaken for a woman fifteen years younger. They saw it as evidence of her unsuitability as their father's wife, as if her vitality were an affront to his disability. They had never accepted her, this vibrant French-woman who had captured their widowed father's heart.

"Gold-digger," they whispered behind her back, conveniently forgetting that she had come into the marriage with her own modest fortune, earned through years as a successful interior designer in Paris.

"Trophy wife," they sneered, dismissing the genuine love that had bloomed between two unlikely souls—he, the proper investment banker; she, the free-spirited artist who didn't seem to care what people believed.

Pushing these thoughts aside, Isabelle stepped out into the morning sunshine, instantly feeling lighter once free of the mansion's oppressive atmosphere. She loved the house's spectacular setting on one of Captiva's most pristine stretches of beach, but the structure itself—a Mediterranean-style behemoth built to Sebastian's first wife's specifications—had never felt like home.

Too grand, too formal, and not what she would select for herself. She had tried to warm the space with color and art, but Sebastian had resisted most of her changes, preferring to keep the house as his first wife had designed it. Another ghost she could never quite exorcize.

Chelsea's car was already waiting in the circular driveway, top down to catch the morning breeze. Isabelle waved, pasting on the bright smile that had become her public mask.

"Bonjour, ma belle!" she called, sliding into the passenger seat. "You are looking particularly radiant this morning. Married life agrees with you, yes?"

Chelsea laughed, her no-nonsense demeanor softening as it always did in Isabelle's presence. "I'd be more radiant if I'd had a full night's sleep. Steven snores when he's been drinking, and we had wine with dinner."

"The price of love," Isabelle teased, securing her scarf against the wind. "Though there are excellent nasal strips he could try. Sebastian used them when his allergies were bad."

At the mention of Sebastian, Chelsea's expression grew more serious. "How is he today?"

Isabelle shrugged, the gesture deliberately casual. "The same. Difficult. Refusing breakfast. The usual charming morning routine."

Chelsea reached over to squeeze her friend's hand briefly before putting the car in gear and heading toward the Key Lime Garden Inn. "I'm sorry, Isabelle. Is he any more receptive to the idea of the mainland move?"

"He has agreed it is necessary, which is progress," Isabelle replied. "The reality of his declining health is becoming impossible to ignore. I try to explain that we need to downsize, but...I don't know." She kept her voice steady with effort. "The cottage sale is proceeding, at least. Diane called yesterday to say the buyer has been approved for financing."

"About that," Chelsea began, navigating the winding drive that led from the Barlowe estate to the main road. "I should probably tell you—"

"Wait," Isabelle interrupted, a genuine smile breaking through her composed façade. "Is that Maggie?"

Sure enough, Maggie Wheeler Moretti stood waiting at the

end of the drive, yoga mat under one arm, her blonde hair pulled back in a casual ponytail that somehow only emphasized her elegance. She waved enthusiastically as the car approached.

The car had barely stopped before Isabelle was out of her seat, engulfing Maggie in a characteristically exuberant embrace. "Ma chérie! You are back! How is the tiny baby? How is the mother? You must tell us everything!"

Maggie returned the hug with equal warmth. "The tiny baby is getting less tiny by the day, thank goodness. And Becca's recovering well. But let me look at you, Isabelle! It's only been a few weeks since I last saw you, but I swear you've gotten more gorgeous."

"Flattery." Isabelle laughed, linking arms with Maggie as they walked to the car. "But please, continue. A woman my age thrives on such delicious lies."

"Nothing about you is old," Maggie countered affectionately. Her expression grew more serious as they walked. "Chelsea mentioned Sebastian's been having a rough time. I'm sorry to hear it."

Isabelle's smile dimmed slightly. "It has been... challenging. But today is not for sad stories. Today is for friends and yoga and perhaps a mimosa or two afterward, yes? I want to hear about the baby and your handsome son and his brave wife."

Maggie recognized the deflection but didn't push. "Well, Miss Eloise Julia Wheeler is absolutely the most perfect baby ever created in the completely objective assessment from her grandmother," she began, her face lighting up as she launched into stories about her granddaughter.

Isabelle listened with genuine interest, asking questions and exclaiming appropriately, but a part of her mind remained with Sebastian, alone in that cavernous house with only his dark thoughts for company. His increasing moodiness worried her not just for its effect on their relationship, but as a potential symptom of his deteriorating health.

The neurologist in Fort Myers had warned her to watch for personality changes—increased irritability, mood swings, depression. All potential indicators that the Parkinson's was progressing more rapidly than expected.

"Isabelle? Earth to Isabelle?" Chelsea's voice broke through her thoughts. They had reached the yoga studio, and both her friends were looking at her with concern.

"Pardonnez-moi," she said quickly. "My mind wandered. What were you saying?"

"I was asking if you'd heard from Sebastian's children about the move," Chelsea repeated. "Are they on board with the plan?"

Isabelle's expression tightened momentarily before she controlled it. "Samantha is coming next week to 'assess the situation,' as she puts it. His son Peter is too busy with his banking career to be bothered, and Jordan..." She shrugged expressively. "Jordan has never warmed to me at all."

What she didn't say was that Sebastian's eldest daughter had made it clear she was coming to evaluate her father's mental competence, convinced that Isabelle was manipulating him into selling his beloved Captiva properties for her own financial gain. The fact that they were moving to be closer to specialized medical care—at Sebastian's doctor's strong recommendation—apparently counted for nothing in Samantha's assessment.

"Vultures circling," Chelsea muttered, holding the studio door for her friends. "I've never understood why Sebastian's children are so hostile toward you., but then again, when we were dating they were like that with me as well. You've been nothing but good for him."

"They loved their mother," Isabelle said simply. "And to them, I will always be the woman who took her place." She smiled to soften the words. "It is natural, perhaps. And they are right to be concerned for their father's well-being."

"There's concerned, and then there's just being unkind," Maggie pointed out as they found places for their mats in the sunlit studio. "But enough about that. Let's focus on the present moment, as our lovely yoga instructor would say."

Chelsea pulled onto the main road and headed to the yoga studio on the Sanibel town line. They made it just in time as the class was about to begin.

As if on cue, the instructor—a serene woman in her thirties—entered the room, bringing a wave of calm energy that seemed to reset the emotional atmosphere. "Good morning, ladies," she greeted them. "Let's begin by setting our intentions for today's practice."

Isabelle closed her eyes, attempting to center herself as she'd been taught. But instead of peaceful emptiness, her mind filled with images of Sebastian—as he had been when they met, vibrant despite his wheelchair, his gray eyes sparkling with intelligence and humor; as he was now, diminished and angry, slipping away from her by increments.

Her intention formed with crystal clarity: strength. Strength to face whatever came next, to weather the storm that she sensed was gathering on the horizon.

CHAPTER 13

$\mathcal{T}$he house was unnaturally quiet when Isabelle returned home shortly after one o'clock. Normally, Sebastian would be in his study at this hour, classical music playing softly in the background as he managed his investments or corresponded with former colleagues.

"Sebastian?" she called, setting her yoga mat and the bag of fresh pastries she'd picked up on the way home on the marble-topped entry table. "I've brought those almond croissants you like from Captiva Bakery."

No response.

"Natalia?" she tried instead, wondering if the physical therapist was still with him. Again, silence.

A frisson of unease shivered down Isabelle's spine. She moved quickly through the house, checking the kitchen, the living room with its panoramic Gulf views, and finally Sebastian's study.

Empty.

The French doors leading to the deck stood open, gauzy curtains billowing in the warm breeze. Isabelle stepped outside, scanning the expansive space with its infinity pool and carefully landscaped gardens that gave way to pristine beach.

And there, at the far end of the deck where the ramp provided wheelchair access to the beach path, she spotted him. Sebastian sat motionless in his chair, facing the water, his silver head bowed slightly.

Relief flooded through her, followed immediately by irritation. "Sebastian!" she called, walking briskly toward him. "You gave me a fright, not answering."

He didn't turn or acknowledge her approach, which only stoked her annoyance. "I know you heard me calling. Is this another of your sulking episodes? Because truly, mon coeur, I am not in the mood today. I've brought your favorite pastries, and Chelsea and Maggie send their love."

Still no response.

Isabelle reached his side, her irritation evaporating as she registered the unusual stillness of his posture. Sebastian was never completely still—the Parkinson's tremors saw to that, especially when his medication wore off.

"Sebastian?" she said again, softer now, reaching to touch his shoulder.

His skin was warm beneath the fine cotton of his shirt, but there was a limpness to his body that sent alarm bells clanging in her mind. She moved around to face him, dropping to her knees on the sun-warmed decking.

His eyes were open but unfocused, gazing somewhere beyond her. The left side of his face had a strange slackness to it, and a thin line of saliva traced from the corner of his mouth down his chin.

"Oh God," Isabelle breathed, recognition and terror flooding through her simultaneously. "Sebastian, can you hear me?"

She grasped his hand, noting the complete laxity of his fingers. No answering pressure, no acknowledgment of her touch. With shaking hands, she reached for the pulse point at his neck, finding it weak and erratic.

Stroke. The word flashed in her mind with terrifying clarity.

"I'm calling an ambulance," she told him, pulling her phone from her pocket. "Stay with me, my love. Stay with me."

The 911 operator answered almost immediately, her calm voice a lifeline as Isabelle reported the situation, following instructions to check Sebastian's breathing (labored but present) and to position his wheelchair to prevent him from slumping over.

"The ambulance is on its way," the operator assured her. "They should be there in less than ten minutes. Is there someone who can wait at the entrance to direct them to your location?"

Isabelle realized with a jolt that they were alone in the house. Natalia must have left after the physical therapy session, and their housekeeper wasn't due until tomorrow.

"No, there's only me," she said, fighting to keep her voice steady. "But the front gates are open, and the house is visible from the drive."

"Stay on the line with me until they arrive," the operator instructed. "Keep talking to your husband, even if he doesn't respond. Sometimes stroke patients can hear and understand, even if they can't communicate."

Isabelle nodded, then realized the gesture was meaningless over the phone. "Yes, I'll stay with him. Thank you."

She set the phone on speaker and placed it on the arm of Sebastian's wheelchair, then took both his hands in hers. The left one was completely limp, but she thought she detected a faint pressure from the right.

"Sebastian," she began, forcing steadiness into her voice. "The ambulance is coming. You are having a stroke, but help is on the way. You must fight, my love. You must stay with me."

His eyes flickered slightly, focusing on her face for just a moment before drifting away again. But it was something—a sign that he was still present, still fighting.

"That's it," she encouraged, squeezing his right hand. "Stay with me. Think of all we still have to do together. Our trip to

Provence that we've been planning. And Samantha is coming next week—you know how much you love it when your children visit."

She kept talking, a stream of consciousness that ranged from mundane household matters to their shared memories, from practical concerns about his medical care to whispered endearments in French that had been part of their private language since the beginning. All the while, she monitored his breathing and fought her own rising panic.

By the time the paramedics arrived, sirens cutting through the peaceful afternoon, Isabelle had moved past fear into a kind of crystalline clarity. She answered their questions precisely, providing Sebastian's medical history, medication list, and the timeline of events as they transferred him onto a stretcher.

"Probable right-hemisphere stroke," one paramedic said to the other as they secured Sebastian for transport. "BP 190 over 110. Patient is on multiple medications for Parkinson's disease, which complicates the treatment options."

"Are you coming in the ambulance, ma'am?" the younger paramedic asked Isabelle.

"Of course," she replied, already gathering her purse and phone. "He is my husband. I will not leave his side."

The ride to the mainland hospital was a blur of sirens and urgency, Sebastian's condition deteriorating visibly despite the paramedics' interventions. By the time they reached the emergency department, he was unconscious, his breathing increasingly labored.

Isabelle found herself pushed aside as a medical team swarmed around Sebastian, their rapid-fire medical terminology washing over her in waves of incomprehensible English. Words like "thrombolysis" and "hemorrhagic versus ischemic" floated past as they wheeled him away for immediate imaging.

A kind-faced nurse guided Isabelle to a small waiting area, pressing a cup of tepid coffee into her hands. "The doctor will come speak with you as soon as they've completed the CT scan," she assured her. "Is there someone I can call for you? Family or friends who could be here with you?"

Isabelle shook her head, then reconsidered. "Yes, actually. Could you hand me my phone? It's in my purse."

She called Chelsea first, the words tumbling out in a mixture of English and French as she explained the situation. Chelsea promised to come immediately, stopping first to pick up Maggie, who would know what to do—Maggie always knew what to do in a crisis.

Next, with greater reluctance, Isabelle called Samantha, Sebastian's eldest daughter. The call went to voicemail, which was perhaps a blessing. Isabelle left a message, her voice formal and controlled, providing the essential information without emotional overlay. Samantha would come, she knew. Whatever their differences, the woman loved her father.

Jordan and Peter were more problematic. Sebastian's other daughter and son lived in London and Sydney respectively, half a world away. Should she call them immediately, or wait until she had more definitive information about their father's condition?

Before she could decide, a doctor appeared in the waiting room doorway—a woman about Isabelle's age, with tired eyes and a grave expression.

"Mrs. Barlowe? I'm Dr. Reynolds, the neurologist on call. We've completed your husband's initial assessment."

Isabelle stood, suddenly aware that her legs were trembling. "How bad is it?"

Dr. Reynolds gestured to the chairs. "Let's sit down. I'm afraid the news isn't good."

And as the doctor explained the devastating extent of Sebastian's stroke—a massive cerebral hemorrhage affecting critical areas of his brain—Isabelle felt the future she had carefully constructed with Sebastian crumbling around her. The doctor's words blurred into a litany of worst-case scenarios: severe brain damage, minimal chances of recovery, difficult decisions to be made.

"He's currently stable but critical," Dr. Reynolds concluded. "We've transferred him to the ICU, where our team will continue to monitor him closely. But Mrs. Barlowe, I need to be clear—given the extent of the bleeding and your husband's pre-existing Parkinson's, you should prepare yourself for the possibility that he may not regain consciousness."

Isabelle absorbed this, her face composed even as her heart shattered. "May I see him?"

"Of course. I'll have someone take you to the ICU." Dr. Reynolds hesitated, then added with genuine compassion, "Is there family we should contact? These next hours and days will be difficult to face alone."

"His children are being notified," Isabelle replied, her voice remote, as if coming from somewhere outside herself. "And my friends are on their way."

The ICU was a landscape of beeping monitors and hushed voices, the antiseptic smell burning Isabelle's nostrils as a nurse led her to Sebastian's bedside. She barely recognized her husband amid the tangle of tubes and wires—his proud face slack and gray, his silver hair flattened against the institutional pillow, his strong hands limp atop the thin blanket.

A ventilator breathed for him now, the rhythmic whooshing sound a mechanical parody of life. His chest rose and fell in artificial cadence, but the essential Sebastian—the keen intelligence, the dry wit, the passionate engagement with life despite his physical limitations—was nowhere visible in this still form.

Isabelle sank into the chair beside his bed, taking his right hand carefully in hers, mindful of the IV line. "Je suis là, mon amour," she whispered. "I am here."

Outside the window, the Florida afternoon continued in brilliant sunshine, oblivious to the tragedy unfolding within these sterile walls. Isabelle gazed at Sebastian's face, tracing with her eyes the features she had loved for many years, before, when they were only friends and had not begun dating—the strong nose, the well-shaped mouth, the slight cleft in his chin that his son had inherited.

"We have had a good life together, non?" she said softly, stroking his hand. "Not long enough, perhaps. Never long enough. But good. Very good."

Memories washed over her—Sebastian proposing at the café, the moonlight silvering his hair; their wedding, intimate and joyful despite his children's barely disguised disapproval; countless evenings watching the sunset from their deck, his hand warm in hers as they shared wine and conversation.

"I will not say goodbye," she told him fiercely. "Not yet. You are still here, and I am still here, and while there is breath, there is hope."

There was no response, only the steady beep of the monitors and the mechanical whoosh of the ventilator. Isabelle continued talking anyway, switching between English and French, sharing memories and plans, anecdotes and endearments, as if the sheer force of her will could keep Sebastian tethered to life.

She was still talking when Chelsea and Maggie arrived, their faces grave with concern. They entered the ICU room quietly, Maggie immediately moving to embrace Isabelle while Chelsea stood at the foot of the bed, visibly shocked by Sebastian's appearance.

"Oh, Isabelle," Maggie murmured, her arms tight around Isabelle's shoulders. "I'm so sorry."

Isabelle accepted the embrace briefly before straightening, her composure firmly back in place. "The doctors say it is very serious," she reported, her voice steady. "A massive cerebral hemorrhage. They are not... they are not optimistic about recovery."

Chelsea moved closer, taking Sebastian's other hand with uncharacteristic gentleness. "He's so still," she said softly. "I've never seen him so still."

"The machines are keeping him alive," Isabelle explained, the clinical terminology a shield against the emotional reality. "The bleeding in his brain has damaged the areas that control breathing, among other functions."

"Have you reached his children?" Maggie asked, ever practical even in crisis.

"I left a message for Samantha. She was already planning to visit next week, so she may be able to come sooner. The other two..." Isabelle shrugged, a gesture that conveyed volumes about the complicated relationships within the Barlowe family. "I will try again later, when there is more news."

"You shouldn't be alone right now," Chelsea said firmly. "We'll stay with you."

Isabelle started to protest, then stopped, recognizing the truth in her friend's words. The ICU room felt suddenly cavernous and cold, the gravity of Sebastian's condition pressing down like a physical weight.

"Thank you," she said simply. "I would be grateful for the company. I'm not sure they'll let all three of us in here at the same time. Did anyone stop you?"

Chelsea shook her head. "No. We'll stay as long as we can and if they kick us out, we'll be in the lounge area."

As evening descended over the hospital, Isabelle remained at Sebastian's bedside, Chelsea and Maggie forming a protective circle around her. They took turns fetching coffee and bland cafeteria sandwiches, fielding phone calls, and speaking with the rotating medical staff who didn't seem to mind the three women by Sebastian's side.

Samantha called shortly after seven, her voice breaking with uncharacteristic emotion as she confirmed she would be on the first available flight from London. For once, there was no hint of the usual antagonism toward Isabelle—just shared concern for the man they both loved, albeit in different ways.

"How bad is it, really?" Samantha asked after the practicalities had been discussed. "The doctors, I mean. What are they actually saying?"

Isabelle hesitated, weighing honesty against kindness. "They believe the damage is... extensive," she said finally. "They are preparing us for the worst, while doing everything possible to save him."

There was a long pause. "I see," Samantha said, her voice tight with controlled emotion. "Please... please tell him I'm coming. Even if he can't hear you. Tell him I'll be there soon."

"I will," Isabelle promised, surprised and touched by this moment of connection with her stepdaughter. "And Samantha? Travel safely. Your father would not want you taking risks, even for him."

Another pause, then: "Thank you, Isabelle."

The call ended, Since her marriage to Sebastian, it was possibly the first time Samantha had addressed her by name rather than the coolly formal "Mrs. Barlowe" or simply avoiding direct address altogether.

"Progress?" Maggie asked, having overheard Isabelle's side of the conversation.

"Of a sort," Isabelle replied with a wan smile. "It only took a medical catastrophe to thaw the ice queen slightly."

"Crises have a way of clarifying what matters," Maggie said, her gaze drifting to Sebastian's still form. "And what doesn't."

Isabelle nodded, turning back to her husband. "Samantha asked me to tell you she's coming," she said, addressing Sebastian directly as she had been all afternoon. "Your daughter is on her way, mon coeur. She sends her love."

The ventilator continued its mechanical rhythm, the monitors their steady electronic vigilance. But something in the atmosphere of the room had shifted—a softening, perhaps, or simply the acceptance that this vigil might be a long one, requiring reserves of strength that Isabelle wasn't certain she possessed.

"You should rest," Chelsea said, concern evident in her voice. "There's a small waiting room down the hall with a couch. Maggie and I can take turns sitting with Sebastian so he's never alone."

Isabelle shook her head firmly. "I will stay. He would do the same for me."

"At least eat something more substantial," Maggie urged, pushing the remains of the cafeteria sandwich toward her. "You'll need your strength."

Before Isabelle could respond, the ICU doors opened to admit Dr. Reynolds, accompanied by another physician in surgical scrubs. Their expressions sent a chill through Isabelle's body before they'd spoken a word.

"Mrs. Barlowe," Dr. Reynolds began, her voice gentle but direct, "there's been a change in your husband's condition."

Isabelle stood, her legs surprisingly steady beneath her. "What has happened?"

"The intracranial pressure has continued to increase despite our interventions," the surgeon explained. "We've detected signs of brainstem involvement, which is extremely serious."

"What does that mean?" Chelsea asked sharply, moving to stand beside Isabelle.

Dr. Reynolds met Isabelle's gaze directly. "It means we need to discuss whether surgical intervention is appropriate at this point, given your husband's overall condition and prognosis."

"You're suggesting we should not operate?" Isabelle clarified, her French accent becoming more pronounced in her distress. "That we should simply... let him go?"

"I'm suggesting that we need to have a realistic conversation about Sebastian's quality of life, even in a best-case scenario following surgery," Dr. Reynolds replied gently. "Given the extensive brain damage he's already suffered, combined with his advanced Parkinson's..."

"He has an advance directive," Isabelle interrupted, her voice steadier than she felt. "Sebastian was very clear about his wishes. He would not want extraordinary measures if there was no reasonable chance of meaningful recovery."

The doctors exchanged glances. "We'll need to see that document," the surgeon said. "And ideally, we'd want his next of kin to be involved in this decision."

"I am his wife," Isabelle said, drawing herself up with quiet dignity. "I am his designated healthcare proxy. His daughter is on her way from London, but she will not arrive for many hours. This decision cannot wait that long, can it?"

Dr. Reynolds shook her head. "No, it can't. If we're going to operate, it needs to be within the next hour. And Mrs. Barlowe, I need to be completely honest with you—even with surgery, the chances of meaningful recovery are extremely low. We'd be looking at severe neurological deficits, likely permanent ventilator dependency, and the possibility that he might never regain consciousness."

Isabelle closed her eyes briefly, thinking of Sebastian as he had been that morning—difficult and irritable, yes, but still himself, still the proud, intelligent man she had married. He had made her promise that she would never allow him to linger in a vegetative state, never permit his dignity to be sacrificed for the mere extension of biological function.

"No surgery," she said firmly, opening her eyes to meet the doctor's gaze. "That would not be what Sebastian wants."

"You understand what this means?" the surgeon asked, his expression grave.

Isabelle nodded, grief a physical ache in her chest. "I understand that my husband is leaving me," she said simply. "But I will honor his wishes, even as it breaks my heart."

The next hours passed in a blur of paperwork and decisions,

of hushed consultations and tearful phone calls. The ventilator settings were adjusted, medications reconfigured—not to hasten the end, the doctors assured her, but to ensure Sebastian's comfort as nature took its course.

Samantha was somewhere over the Atlantic, unreachable. Peter had finally been contacted in London, his shock and grief palpable even across thousands of miles. Jordan remained elusive, her phone going straight to voicemail despite multiple attempts.

Through it all, Isabelle remained at Sebastian's side, holding his hand, speaking to him in a mixture of English and French, ensuring that love was the last thing he would know in this life. Chelsea and Maggie created a protective barrier around her, fielding questions from medical staff, bringing tissues and water, their steady presence a lifeline in the storm.

Just after midnight, Sebastian's condition began to deteriorate rapidly. His blood pressure dropped, his oxygen levels fell despite the ventilator's efforts, and the monitors registered increasingly erratic cardiac activity.

"It won't be long now," the night nurse said gently, adjusting his medication.

In the end, it was surprisingly peaceful. Sebastian's breathing slowed, the spaces between heartbeats lengthened, and then, with no drama or fanfare, the monitors flatlined into the steady tone that signaled the end.

"Time of death, 12:47 AM," the nurse noted quietly, reaching over to silence the alarms. "I'm so sorry for your loss."

Isabelle sat motionless, still holding Sebastian's hand as it grew cool in hers. The essential him had already been gone for hours, but the finality of this moment—the absolute certainty that she would never again see his smile, hear his voice, feel his touch—crashed over her in a wave of raw grief.

"Oh, Sebastian," she whispered, bending to press her lips to his forehead. "Bon voyage, mon amour. Until we meet again."

Chelsea and Maggie moved closer, their hands warm on her shoulders as she said her final goodbye. Outside the hospital windows, the Florida night continued, stars gleaming indifferently over the Gulf, the world spinning on despite the hole that had just been torn in Isabelle's heart.

Life would go on, she knew. There would be funeral arrangements and legal matters, Sebastian's children to face, a house to sell, a future to reimagine without the man who had been its centerpiece. But for now, in this sterile room with its silenced monitors and the shell of the man she had loved, Isabelle allowed herself to simply feel the enormity of her loss.

"Adieu, mon coeur," she whispered, pressing a final kiss to Sebastian's lips. "Thank you for loving me."

And somewhere in the vastness beyond life, Isabelle had to believe that Sebastian heard her, and understood, and was at peace.

CHAPTER 14

The kitchen of the Key Lime Garden Inn was a sanctuary of sorts, especially after guests settled in the parlor or outside on the back porch in the early evening.

Maggie stood at the counter, methodically kneading dough for the next morning's scones, the rhythmic motion soothing after days of hospital stress and grief.

Chelsea sat across from her at the island, nursing a glass of white wine.

"I still can't believe he's gone," Chelsea said finally, breaking the quiet. "Sebastian always seemed so... permanent, somehow. Even with the wheelchair, even with the Parkinson's. He had such force of personality."

Maggie looked up, studying her friend's face. "You two had quite a history."

Chelsea's laugh held no humor. "That's one way to put it. Ancient history, really."

"Still," Maggie said gently, "you were close once. This can't be easy for you."

Chelsea traced the rim of her wineglass with one finger, her gaze distant. "It was over three years ago, Maggie. So much has changed for all of us since then."

"Some feelings don't disappear entirely, no matter how much time passes," Maggie observed, her hands never pausing in their work. "It's okay to grieve for what was, not just what is."

Chelsea sighed, taking a sip of her wine. "I'm not sure what I'm feeling, to be honest. Sad, of course. Sebastian was a good man, despite his... complexities. But mostly I'm worried about Isabelle. Those children of his are going to make her life hell, especially Jordan. I don't even know why I'm calling them children, they're grown up people."

"They're already circling," Maggie confirmed grimly. "According to Isabelle, Peter arrived this morning, barely stopped to drop his bags at the mansion before he was on the phone with their family attorney. Jordan will be here tomorrow."

"Poor Isabelle." Chelsea shook her head. "She was devoted through the Parkinson's diagnosis, the decline, the increasing difficulty. And her reward is going to be a legal battle over every teacup and throw pillow."

"Let's hope it doesn't come to that," Maggie said, though her tone suggested she shared Chelsea's pessimism. "Sebastian was meticulous about his affairs. Surely he made provisions for Isabelle."

"Men like Sebastian often believe they'll live forever, despite evidence to the contrary," drawled a voice from the doorway. Grandma Sarah stood there, one hand on the frame for support, the other clutching a well-worn paperback. Despite being just shy of her eighty-first birthday, she stood tall, her silver hair arranged in a neat bob, her eyes sharp behind stylish glasses.

"Mom," Maggie greeted her with a smile. "I thought you were resting."

"At my age, resting too much is just practice for the grave," Grandma Sarah retorted, making her way to a stool at the island. "Besides, I thought you might need me to supervise your baking."

"Since when? I've been making scones for years and no one's complained yet."

"Well, they're certainly good, but I've been making them since before you were born. I think I know a thing or two about baking."

Maggie looked at Chelsea who was smiling. "Mom, why are you here exactly? I thought you were heading back to your place. Didn't you tell me you had an interview with a nomad or someone like that?"

"A nomad?" Chelsea asked.

"Yes, Mom has suddenly become interested in women of a certain age who live in their SUVs."

"You mean like camping?"

"Something like that. She's interviewing a woman who has turned her SUV into a fantastic camper. They take the seats out and everything," Maggie explained.

"Maggie, dear, I'm staying one more night so I can be at Sebastian's funeral. I don't want to go home only to drive back here in all that island traffic. I postponed the interview for next Saturday. I'm not surprised that Sebastian died. He looked gray around the gills, as my late husband would have said."

"Mother!" Maggie admonished. "He was seriously ill."

"And now he's seriously dead," Grandma Sarah replied matter-of-factly. "Which leaves his French wife in a pickle with those vultures he called children." She fixed Chelsea with a keen gaze. "You dodged a bullet as far as I can see."

Chelsea choked slightly on her wine. "I didn't think you knew Sebastian that well."

"Please." Grandma Sarah waved a dismissive hand. "This island has no secrets, just varying degrees of polite amnesia. Besides, I remember hearing all about the two of you from Maggie."

Chelsea shot Maggie a look. "Some friend you are."

Maggie put her head down and focused on the scones.

"Well, anyway, he's gone now, and you're married to a real looker. Steven isn't hard on the eyes that's for sure."

"Mother, really," Maggie interjected.

"What matters now is supporting Isabelle," Chelsea added.

"Well, of course," Grandma Sarah agreed, undeterred. "Though I suspect our French friend is tougher than she appears. Behind all that Parisian silk and perfume is a woman with a spine of steel."

"She'll need it," Chelsea muttered. "Jordan Barlowe would make Cruella de Vil look like a humanitarian."

The kitchen door swung open, and Iris and Millie carried in grocery bags, apparently returning from a supply run.

"Are we discussing Isabelle Barlowe? Because if so, I have thoughts."

"Doesn't everyone?" Chelsea asked.

"We're discussing the Barlowe situation generally," Maggie clarified, dividing her dough into precise portions. "Sebastian's funeral is the day after tomorrow, and Isabelle is apparently facing an uphill battle with his children."

"Poor Isabelle," Iris said with genuine sympathy. "She truly loved that man. Anyone with eyes could see it wasn't about his money."

"Try telling that to Jordan," Chelsea replied. "I ran into Diane Mueller at the post office this morning. Apparently, Peter's already making noise about contesting the sale of the cottage to Gretchen, claiming Sebastian wasn't of sound mind when he agreed to it."

"That's ridiculous," Maggie exclaimed, looking up from her scones. "Sebastian was sharp as a tack right up until the stroke. And that sale was his idea in the first place!"

Chelsea rubbed her temples. "The truth is that I'm not sure Gretchen will go through with the purchase."

Maggie stared at her. "What? After all they've been through? The back and forth on this sale has been a mess from the start."

Looking at Chelsea, Iris said, "Well, I'm guessing if they don't want to sell and your sister doesn't want to buy it, then that's the end of that."

A thoughtful silence fell over the kitchen as each woman contemplated the situation. Iris returned to unpacking groceries, Millie wiped down counters that were already spotless, and Maggie continued her methodical scone preparation. Grandma Sarah, however, fixed her keen gaze on Chelsea.

"You never answered my question, dear," she said abruptly. "How are you feeling about Sebastian's passing? And don't give me that 'ancient history' nonsense again. The man was important to you."

Chelsea's head snapped up, her eyes wide with surprise. "Grandma Sarah!"

"Oh, stop acting so shocked. I'm old, not blind or stupid. I remember how you felt about him. No shame in acknowledging that."

The room had gone very still, all eyes on Chelsea, who looked like she wanted to disappear through the floor. After a moment, she squared her shoulders, meeting Grandma Sarah's gaze directly.

"Fine. Yes, Sebastian was... important to me once. And yes, it hurt when he chose Isabelle. But I'm happy that he had a few years with her. More to the point, I'm very much in love with my husband. We haven't been married a year and I still feel like I'm on my honeymoon. As happy as I am, I don't think this is the time to flaunt my good fortune. Can we please focus on Isabelle and help her through this?"

"Of course. And, I'm truly happy for you, Chelsea. I'm surprised you were able to trust again, after Sebastian."

Mother," Maggie interjected firmly. "That's enough."

Chelsea held up a hand. "It's all right, Maggie." She turned back to Grandma Sarah, a wry smile tugging at her lips. "Some people never get even one chance at love. I've been very blessed to have had three men in my life. My first husband, Carl, Sebastian Barlowe, and Steven Ellis Thompson. I consider myself one of the luckiest women in the world."

Grandma Sarah nodded. "I'm happy for you, Chelsea. Maybe before I kick the bucket, I'll get another chance at falling in love."

She pushed herself to her feet with the help of her cane. "Now, I'm going to lie down before dinner. Being wise and insightful is exhausting at my age."

Chelsea laughed, the tension in her shoulders easing. "Thank you, Grandma Sarah. For the wisdom, insightful or otherwise."

"You're welcome, dear. Come see me anytime when you need advice."

Maggie shook her head. "I'm so sorry about her," she whispered.

Chelsea laughed. "I think everyone should have a Grandma Sarah in their life. She does keep us on our toes."

"That's putting it mildly," Maggie responded.

"Well, I think I'll head home. Steven is flying in tomorrow morning. I want to get to bed early. I need my beauty sleep."

"You'll be back in the morning to enjoy my scones?" Maggie asked.

"Bright and early. . .Nite all."

"Goodnight, Chelsea," Iris and Millie responded.

Chelsea decided to walk through the garden path to the beach. Several people were still on the beach catching the last of the sunset. Several couples held each other close making Chelsea long to see her husband.

She thought about Grandma Sarah and her constant teasing about Sebastian. The sadness at his passing hit her again, and to honor his memory, she thought back to happier times when they dated. Chelsea knew she would forever think of him as a lovely person who opened her heart to love again after her husband died from cancer years before. If not for Sebastian, she would never have met her husband, Steven, and for that she would be forever grateful.

Some paths, once closed, could never be reopened. And perhaps that was as it should be. After all, the path she'd ultimately chosen had led her to Steven, to a life she valued, to deep friendships and meaningful work on the island she loved.

Sebastian had been a chapter in her story, not the whole book. An important chapter, perhaps even a formative one, but still just a part of the larger narrative of her life.

And at the funeral, she would help Isabelle write the final lines of his.

CHAPTER 15

*T*he Barlowe mansion was eerily quiet when Isabelle returned from her meeting with the lawyers. Samantha had remained behind, ostensibly to discuss "family matters" with the attorney—matters from which Sebastian's widow was apparently excluded.

Isabelle moved through the cavernous entryway, her footsteps echoing on the marble floor. She had never loved this house, with its formal elegance and emotional chill, but now it felt actively hostile—a monument to his first wife's taste and his children's expectations, with very little of Sebastian himself evident in its carefully curated spaces.

The only room that had truly been his was the study, with its wall of books, the antique desk where he'd spent countless hours, and the collection of nautical instruments that reflected his love of sailing. Even after the accident that confined him to a wheelchair, he'd maintained his connection to the sea through meticulous models of famous ships, charts of distant harbors, and books on maritime history.

It was funny how Sebastian's life changed over the years. As a young boy his grandparents ran a dairy farm in Pennsylvania, but there was little evidence of it in family photos. Instead, his mother's ancestral home in France where he grew up until returning to America as a teenager, was displayed in photos throughout the house.

Isabelle headed to the study, seeking some sense of connection to her husband in the silence left by his absence. As she approached the heavy oak door, however, she was surprised to hear movement within—drawers opening and closing, papers rustling.

She paused, then pushed the door open. Peter Barlowe stood behind Sebastian's desk, methodically going through the contents of the drawers, occasionally setting documents aside in a leather portfolio.

Isabelle turned quickly when she heard movement near Sebastian's desk.

"What are you doing?" Isabelle asked sharply, her accent thickening with emotion.

Peter started, looking up with the guilty expression of a child caught raiding the cookie jar. At forty-six, he was the spitting image of a younger Sebastian—tall and lean, with the same aristocratic features and silver beginning to touch his dark hair. Unlike his father, however, his face lacked the warmth and humor that had made Sebastian so charismatic.

"Isabelle," he said, composing himself quickly. "I didn't hear you come in."

"Evidently not," she replied, crossing the room with deliberate steps. "I asked what you are doing in your father's private study, going through his papers without permission."

Peter drew himself up, his expression cooling. "I'm looking for some family documents that belonged to my mother. Samantha thought they might be here."

"And it could not wait until after your father's memorial

service? Two days was too long to allow him to rest in peace before ransacking his belongings?"

A flush crept up Peter's neck. "That's hardly fair. These are family papers, documents that rightfully belong to my mother's estate—"

"Which was settled many years ago," Isabelle interjected. "If these papers were so important, why wait until now to search for them?"

Peter had no immediate answer for that, his gaze dropping to the documents he'd been sorting. Isabelle moved closer, noting with growing anger that he'd been focused on Sebastian's personal correspondence.

"Those are private letters," she said, her voice dangerously quiet. "Between your father and me."

"They were in his desk," Peter said defensively. "A desk that belonged to our grandmother, which will now return to the family."

Isabelle took a deep breath, forcing herself to remain calm. "Peter, I understand you are grieving. We all are. But this behavior—sneaking into your father's study while I am out, going through his personal papers without permission—it is disrespectful to his memory and hurtful to me."

Peter had the grace to look somewhat abashed. "I apologize if it seemed underhanded," he said stiffly. "That wasn't my intention."

"What was your intention then?" Isabelle asked, genuinely curious. "What are you really looking for?"

A flash of something—uncertainty? fear?—crossed Peter's face before his expression settled back into polite neutrality. "As I said, family documents. Nothing more."

Isabelle studied him, sensing the lie but too emotionally exhausted to press further. "I would appreciate it if you would leave your father's study untouched until after the memorial service," she said finally. "There will be time enough for sorting through possessions later."

Peter hesitated, clearly reluctant to abandon his search. "Samantah wanted—"

"I don't care what Samantah wants," Isabelle interrupted, her patience finally snapping. "This is still my home, and Sebastian has been gone less than seventy-two hours. Show some respect, if not for me, then for your father's memory."

They stared at each other for a long moment, the tension palpable. Finally, Peter nodded curtly, closing the leather portfolio and tucking it under his arm.

"I'll continue this another time," he said, moving toward the door.

"Leave the portfolio," Isabelle said, holding out her hand. "I don't know what you've already taken, but nothing more leaves this room until I've had a chance to review it."

Peter's jaw tightened, but after a moment's hesitation, he handed over the portfolio. "Samantha won't be pleased, not to mention Jordan."

"Good night, Peter," Isabelle replied dryly.

After he left, Isabelle sank into Sebastian's chair. The portfolio sat on the desk before her, but she made no move to open it. Whatever Peter had been searching for, whatever Samantha and Jordan had sent him to find, it could wait.

Instead, she ran her hands over the smooth wood of the desk, lingering on the worn patch where Sebastian had rested his right arm when reading. Traces of him were everywhere in this room —the faint scent of his cologne, the dog-eared books on the side table, the half-finished crossword puzzle still open on the ottoman by the window.

For the first time since his death, Isabelle allowed herself to truly feel his absence, the crushing certainty that he was gone forever. Tears came silently at first, then in wracking sobs that bent her double, her grief too enormous to contain.

"Oh, Sebastian," she whispered when the storm had passed, leaving her drained and hollow. "What am I going to do without you?"

There was no answer, of course. Only the ticking of the antique clock on the mantel, the distant sound of waves against the shore, and the growing awareness that she was now alone in a house that had never really been her home, facing a future she had never planned for.

Soon, she would meet with Maggie and Chelsea to talk about the memorial service. Tomorrow, she would stand up to Samantha's demands and Peter's machinations. Tomorrow, she would begin the long process of rebuilding her life without Sebastian at its center.

But tonight, in the quiet sanctuary of his study, surrounded by the evidence of the life they had shared, Isabelle allowed herself one night of pure, unrestricted grief for the man she had loved, and lost, and would never stop missing for the rest of her days.

A soft breeze carried the scent of salt and jasmine across the stretch of beach behind the Barlowe mansion, where nearly a hundred people had gathered to say goodbye to Sebastian.

Isabelle stood at the water's edge, barefoot in the sand despite the formality of her black dress. Her dark hair lifted gently in the breeze, her face composed into a mask of dignified grief. To her right stood Samantha, Peter, and Jordan Barlowe, a unified front of mourning—Samantha in a severe black suit, Peter in a dark jacket despite the Florida heat, and Jordan, in a black dress and pearls. All three maintaining a careful physical distance from their father's widow.

Behind them, the island's residents and Sebastian's business associates mingled quietly, their murmured conversations creating a gentle backdrop to the lapping of waves. Wooden chairs had been arranged in semicircles facing the water, though many guests chose to stand, holding the slender white candles that had been distributed as they arrived.

Chelsea watched from near the back of the gathering, her fingers laced with Steven's, drawing strength from his solid presence. Samantha nodded to Chelsea, her cold gaze sweeping over her father's former girlfriend with barely disguised disapproval before returning to her rigid surveillance of Isabelle's every move.

"You'd think they were at different funerals," Steven murmured in Chelsea's ear, nodding toward the stark contrast between Isabelle's smiles and concern for her guests and the Barlowe children's formal rigidity.

"They are, in a way," Chelsea replied softly. "Isabelle is saying goodbye to the man she loved. They're guarding the family legacy."

Steven's arm tightened around her waist, a silent gesture of understanding. Steven was a quieter presence than Chelsea—thoughtful where she was outspoken, deliberate where she was impulsive. His salt-and-pepper hair and kind eyes gave him a distinguished appearance, and his steady temperament had proven to be exactly what Chelsea needed after years of resisting commitment.

"I'm glad Sebastian introduced us," he said, his voice pitched for her ears alone. "Whatever else he was or wasn't, he got that right."

Chelsea smiled, leaning into his embrace. "He did, didn't he? Even when playing matchmaker, he was calculating the angles."

Before Steven could respond, a hush fell over the gathering as the string quartet positioned near the flower garden began to play—something classical and elegiac that Sebastian had apparently specified in the detailed instructions he'd left for his memorial. Isabelle turned to face the assembled mourners, the setting sun behind her creating a golden halo around her slender figure.

"Thank you all for coming," she began, her French accent more pronounced than usual, betraying her emotional state despite her outward composure. "Sebastian would be touched—and perhaps a little surprised—to see so many gathered to bid him farewell. He was not always an easy man, but those who knew him well understood that beneath the reserve was a passionate soul, full of curiosity and joy."

Jordan shifted visibly at this characterization of her father, her mouth tightening, but she remained silent.

"Sebastian loved this beach," Isabelle continued. "Every evening that his health permitted, he would have his chair brought to this spot to watch the sunset. He said there was no better reminder of life's beauty and brevity than watching day transform into night over the Gulf waters."

She gestured to the small table that had been set up at the water's edge, where a simple wooden box rested alongside a framed photograph of Sebastian—not the formal portrait the family might have chosen, but a candid shot of him laughing on the deck of a sailboat, his face alight with pleasure.

"In accordance with Sebastian's wishes, there will be no traditional service, no eulogies or readings. Instead, he asked that we simply gather as the sun sets, remember him as he was in life, and then celebrate with good food, fine wine, and perhaps a few stories of happier times."

From her position at the back, Chelsea could see Samantha practically vibrating with disapproval. The woman's hands were clasped so tightly in front of her that her knuckles showed white, and she kept throwing sidelong glances at Isabelle as if expecting her to suddenly break into inappropriate song or dance.

Isabelle, either oblivious to or deliberately ignoring her stepdaughter's discomfort, continued with quiet dignity. "Sebastian specified that his ashes should rest in two places he loved—half to be scattered here, on his beloved Captiva, and half to be returned to France, to his family's country estate where he spent his childhood summers."

This concession to his French heritage seemed to slightly soften Samantha's rigid posture, though her expression remained guarded.

"For those who wish to participate, I invite you now to join me at the water's edge as we return Sebastian to the sea he loved, with the sunset he cherished."

As Isabelle lifted the wooden box, Chelsea was surprised to see Samantha step forward, her hand extended in what appeared to be a silent request. After the briefest hesitation, Isabelle nodded, allowing her stepdaughter to take the box. Jordan and Peter moved to their sister's side, and after an awkward moment, Isabelle joined them, the four forming an uneasy circle at the water's edge.

The quartet played softly as the family opened the box, each releasing the ashes. Jordan, her composure finally cracking, spoke a few words too quiet for the gathered mourners to hear, then released the ashes into the gentle waves. Samantha and Peter followed suit, their composure crumbling slightly.

Finally, Isabelle took her turn, kneeling at the water's edge to let the ashes slip from her fingers into the Gulf. Her lips moved in a private farewell, and for just a moment, she allowed her hand to linger in the water, as if reluctant to break this final physical connection to her husband.

Chelsea felt tears prick her eyes at the raw grief evident in Isabelle's posture. Whatever calculation might be happening among the family regarding the inheritance, Isabelle's loss was real and profound.

Maggie appeared silently at Chelsea's side, slipping an arm around her friend's waist. "She's holding up well," she murmured.

"Barely," Chelsea replied, watching as Isabelle finally rose, accepting a hand from Peter.

"Almost over," Maggie reassured her. "The reception will be easier—more people around to buffer the family tension."

As the last notes of music faded, Isabelle turned back to the gathered mourners. "Thank you all for sharing in this farewell. Sebastian would not want us to linger in sadness. The house is open for those who wish to join us for refreshments and, perhaps, a toast or two to a life well-lived."

The formalities concluded, the crowd began to disperse, some heading toward the path that led back to the Barlowe mansion, others lingering to offer personal condolences to the family. Chelsea hesitated, uncertain of her place in this delicate choreography of grief and obligation.

"We should pay our respects," Steven said gently, reading her reluctance. "Then we can escape to the reception if it gets uncomfortable."

Chelsea nodded, allowing him to guide her toward Isabelle, who stood slightly apart from her stepchildren, accepting condolences with gracious exhaustion.

"Isabelle," Chelsea said, embracing her friend carefully. "That was beautiful. Sebastian would have approved."

"Thank you both for helping me to decided how best to handle everything. You're wonderful friends, but if you don't mind, I'm going to think of you as my sisters. I don't know what I'd do without your support."

"Captiva Sisters," Chelsea said.

Isabelle smiled. "Sebastian would have complained about the music selection and criticized the wine choices," Isabelle replied with a sudden, genuine smile that transformed her face. "But yes, in his heart, he would have approved."

"Is there anything you need? Anything we can do?" Steven asked, clasping Isabelle's hand warmly.

Isabelle's gaze drifted to Samantha, who was deep in conversation with several of Sebastian's business associates, her expression intent. "Just stay close," she said quietly. "I suspect the real battle begins now that the public ceremony is over."

"We're not going anywhere," Chelsea assured her. "Maggie, Grandma Sarah, and I are organizing a rotating guard duty. You won't face them alone."

Gratitude flashed across Isabelle's features. "Merci, my friends. I—"

"Isabelle," Samantha's cool voice cut through their conversation like a blade. "The Harringtons are asking for you. Mother's cousins," she added, as if Isabelle might have forgotten her predecessor's family connections.

"Of course," Isabelle replied smoothly. "I'll be right there." She squeezed Chelsea's hand once more. "Duty calls. Save me some champagne for later—I suspect I'll need it."

As Isabelle allowed herself to be led away, Chelsea fought the urge to say something cutting to Samantha, whose dismissive glance spoke volumes about her opinion of Isabelle's friends. In Chelsea's opinion, the fact that they'd had history gave her permission.

"Easy," Steven murmured in her ear, sensing her tension. "Not the time or place."

"I know." Chelsea sighed. "But that woman makes it so tempting."

They made their way up the path to the house, where the reception was already in full swing. The Barlowe mansion had been transformed for the occasion, with flowers in Sebastian's favorite colors—deep blues and whites—adorning every surface. Catering staff circulated with trays of champagne and hors d'oeuvres, while a jazz trio played softly in the corner of the grand living room.

Chelsea accepted a glass of champagne, scanning the room for familiar faces. Maggie and Paolo stood near the fireplace with Grandma Sarah, who appeared to be regaling several guests with a story that involved expansive hand gestures.

"Chelsea, Steven—a word?" Peter Barlowe appeared at their side, his expression carefully neutral. Up close, his resemblance to Sebastian was even more striking, though he lacked his father's natural charisma.

"Peter," Chelsea greeted him with practiced politeness. "I'm sorry for your loss."

"Thank you," he replied automatically. "I've been meaning to speak with you about the cottage sale. Samantha mentioned you're quite close to the buyer—your sister, I believe?"

Chelsea felt Steven tense beside her and placed a warning hand on his arm. "Gretchen is indeed my sister, but any questions about the property transaction should be directed to Diane Mueller or to Sebastian's attorney. I'm not involved in the sale."

"But you are aware of it," Peter pressed. "You must have known my father had been... unwell for some time. His judgment was not always sound in these last months."

"On the contrary," Chelsea replied, maintaining her pleasant tone with effort. "Sebastian was sharp as a tack right up until the end. The cottage sale was entirely his idea, part of his and Isabelle's planned relocation to be closer to his medical care."

Peter's expression hardened slightly. "Yes, the relocation. Another decision that seems to have been made rather hastily, without proper family consultation."

"Peter," Steven interjected, his voice calm but firm. "This is hardly the time or place to discuss business matters. Your father's memorial service deserves more respect than that."

For a moment, Peter looked as though he might argue, but then his gaze traveled past them to Isabelle, who was watching their interaction with barely concealed concern.

"Of course," he said stiffly. "My apologies. We can discuss this another time."

As he moved away, Chelsea released a breath she hadn't realized she was holding. "Well, that confirms what we suspected. They're going after the cottage sale."

"And probably everything else Sebastian left Isabelle," Steven agreed grimly. "This is just the opening salvo."

Before they could discuss it further, a sharp sound of silverware against crystal cut through the murmur of conversation. Samantha stood at the center of the room, champagne flute raised.

"Ladies and gentlemen, if I could have your attention," she said. "While my father's wishes specified no formal eulogies, I hope you'll indulge me in a brief toast to the man we all loved."

Isabelle, standing near the French doors that led to the terrace, made no move to join her stepdaughter, though her gaze was alert and wary.

"Sebastian Barlowe was many things to many people," Samantha continued, her voice carrying a rehearsed quality. "A brilliant financier, a generous philanthropist, a dedicated sailor. But to Peter, Jordan, and myself, he was simply Father—steadfast, principled, and unfailingly devoted to our mother during their twenty-five years of marriage."

The emphasis on Sebastian's first marriage was subtle but unmistakable. Around the room, guests shifted uncomfortably, sensing the undercurrent of tension. Chelsea glanced at Isabelle, whose expression remained composed, though a flush of color had risen to her cheeks.

"After Mother's death, and the accident that so dramatically altered his life, Father found his way to Captiva, where he built a new chapter of his story," Samantha continued. "And while the last decade brought... changes we could not have anticipated, his connection to his true home in France remained unbroken."

The implication that Sebastian's life on Captiva—including his marriage to Isabelle—had been somehow less authentic than his French existence hung in the air, pointed enough to raise eyebrows but just vague enough to maintain plausible deniability.

"So please, raise your glasses to Sebastian Barlowe," Samantha concluded. "May he finally rest in peace, reunited with our beloved mother in whatever lies beyond this life."

A ripple of discomfort passed through the gathering as glasses were raised. The toast, with its deliberate exclusion of Isabelle and subtle undermining of her place in Sebastian's life, was a masterclass in polite aggression.

Chelsea glanced around the room, noting the various reactions—Peter and Jordan looking smugly satisfied, Isabelle's friends rallying protectively closer to her, the island residents exchanging uncomfortable glances.

Isabelle herself remained still for a long moment, her gaze fixed on Samantha. Then, with deliberate grace, she moved to the center of the room, stopping alongside her stepdaughter.

"Thank you, Samantha, for those heartfelt words," she said, her voice carrying a warmth that belied the tension evident to anyone paying attention. "Sebastian would be touched by your remembrance."

She turned to address the gathering, champagne flute raised. "If I might add a brief toast of my own? To Sebastian—who taught me that love can arrive unexpectedly at any age, that courage means facing each day's challenges with humor and grace, and that a true partnership is built on honoring each other's independence as well as connection."

Samantha's expression froze, but she could hardly object without appearing petty.

"Sebastian loved his children deeply," Isabelle continued, nodding toward Samantha, Peter, and Jordan. "He spoke often of his pride in each of you. And he cherished the legacy of his first marriage, the family it created, and the memories it held."

This acknowledgment seemed to momentarily catch Samantha off guard, her defensive posture easing slightly.

"But Sebastian also embraced the fullness of his second chapter here on Captiva—a place that brought him peace after tremendous loss, and joy in unexpected forms." Isabelle's gaze swept the room, including each person present. "To Sebastian—who taught us all that life can begin anew at any age, if we have the courage to open our hearts to possibility."

"To Sebastian," the room echoed, the atmosphere warming perceptibly as Isabelle's genuine affection for her late husband cut through Samantha's calculated performance.

As the toast concluded, Chelsea caught Isabelle's eye across the room and gave her a subtle nod of approval. Round one to Isabelle, she thought. But the evening—and the battle for Sebastian's legacy—was far from over.

CHAPTER 16

*T*wo days after Sebastian's memorial service, Isabelle stood in the middle of his study, surrounded by cardboard boxes and colored stickers. Green for items to be shipped to the house in Paris, yellow for things to be stored until she decided their fate, red for objects the Barlowe children had requested or that she had decided to give them.

The task of dismantling a life shared was overwhelming in its emotional weight and logistical complexity. Every item held memories, associations, decisions to be made. Sebastian's leather-bound collection of maritime history—green sticker, for he had read from them to her on lazy Sunday afternoons. The ancestral portrait of some stern-faced Barlowe patriarch—red sticker, for Samantha had claimed it as family heritage before Sebastian was even cold in his grave. The antique compass Sebastian had given Isabelle on their fifth anniversary—no sticker yet, for she couldn't bear to pack it away but didn't know where it belonged in her uncertain future.

"You don't have to do this alone, you know," Chelsea said from the doorway, causing Isabelle to startle slightly. She hadn't heard her friend arrive.

"I gave the staff the day off," Isabelle explained, setting down the compass. "I wanted some peace to sort through Sebastian's things without an audience."

Maggie appeared beside Chelsea and entered the study, carrying a wicker basket. "Hence why we brought reinforcements," she said, lifting the cloth to reveal a bottle of wine, three glasses, and an assortment of cheeses and fresh bread. "Sorting through memories requires sustenance."

Isabelle's face softened with gratitude. "You two are the best," Isabelle said.

"We're nosy friends who wanted to make sure you weren't drowning in grief alone in this mausoleum," Chelsea said, setting her basket on a relatively clear corner of the desk. "How are you really doing?"

Isabelle sighed, gesturing at the half-packed boxes surrounding them. "I feel like I'm dismantling Sebastian piece by piece. Each book, each memento I pack away, another part of him disappears."

"Not disappears," Chelsea countered gently, uncorking the wine. "Transforms. Changes shape. Like grief itself."

"Is that what happened for you? When Carl died?" Isabelle asked, accepting the glass Chelsea offered.

Chelsea nodded, leaning against the edge of the desk. "Eventually. At first, it felt like I was betraying his memory every time I put something away or gave something of his to Goodwill. As if I were erasing him from existence. But later, I realized that the objects weren't Carl—just shadows he'd left behind. The real essence was inside me, in my memories, in how his love had shaped who I am."

"Even though Daniel and I were going to divorce, I still felt the same way when he died. We had so many years together. It's impossible to disconnect from all that overnight," Maggie added.

"I hope I can reach that perspective," Isabelle said, her gaze wandering to the wall of photographs behind Sebastian's desk—

images spanning his life from childhood in France to their last trip to Paris the previous year. "Right now, it still feels like I'm losing him all over again with each item I pack away."

Chelsea followed her gaze to the photos. "Tell me about this one," she said, pointing to an image of Sebastian and Isabelle on what appeared to be a sailboat, both laughing into the camera, the wind tousling their hair.

A smile touched Isabelle's lips. "Our honeymoon. Sebastian insisted on taking me sailing, even though he couldn't physically manage the boat himself anymore. He hired a captain but planned the entire itinerary—a tour of the Greek islands. I had never sailed before and was terribly seasick the first two days."

"Yet you're laughing in the photo," Chelsea observed.

"Because by the third day, I had found my sea legs, and it was as if a whole new world opened up to me. Sebastian was so proud, so delighted to share his love of the water with me." Isabelle touched the frame gently. "He said that was the moment he knew our marriage would work—when I embraced something so important to him, despite my initial discomfort."

"That's Sebastian," Chelsea agreed fondly. "Always testing boundaries."

Isabelle selected another photo—Sebastian in his wheelchair on the deck of their home, silhouetted against a spectacular sunset. "This was just last year. His Parkinson's was already quite advanced, but he still insisted on watching every sunset possible. He said each one was unique, never to be repeated. 'Pay attention, Isabelle,' he would say. 'Life gives us only so many sunsets. Don't miss a single one.'"

Chelsea and Maggie sipped their wine, listening as Isabelle moved from photo to photo, sharing memories, laughing and occasionally wiping away tears. The exercise seemed to lift some of the weight from her shoulders, transforming the task of packing from a solitary burden to a shared celebration of Sebastian's life.

After a while, Isabelle paused, her gaze falling on the compass she'd set aside earlier. "Sebastian gave me this on our last anniversary," she explained, lifting it carefully. "He said that even though his body was confined to the wheelchair, his spirit still navigated wild seas with me. That I had given him back the horizon when he thought it lost forever."

"That sounds like him," Chelsea said softly. "Poetic and a bit dramatic."

Isabelle laughed, the sound brightening the somber room. "He was that. Especially when he wanted something."

She ran her fingers over the compass's brass casing, her expression growing more thoughtful. "I've been thinking a great deal about horizons since Sebastian died. About what comes next for me."

"And?" Maggie prompted when Isabelle fell silent.

"And...I'm not sure." Isabelle set the compass down carefully. "I'm not certain Captiva is where I belong."

Isabelle looked at her friends, her dark eyes full of uncertainty. "Where does a middle-aged widow with no children, no career, and no real homeland fit in this world?"

"First of all, you might be 'middle-aged' but that doesn't mean your life is over. Besides, I'm surprised to hear you talk like this. You're not sounding like our wild and carefree Isabelle Barlowe." Chelsea replied. "And second, you have a successful design business in Paris that you put on hold for Sebastian. You're hardly without options."

"True," Isabelle acknowledged. "I've had several calls from old clients since the news of Sebastian's death spread. Apparently, they've been waiting for Isabelle Barlowe, the designer, to return."

"And will she?" Chelsea asked.

Isabelle shrugged, a very French gesture that conveyed volumes of complex emotion. "I don't know. Paris feels like another lifetime now. And yet Captiva..."

"Holds too many memories of Sebastian?" Chelsea guessed.

"Yes. And no." Isabelle gestured to the mansion around them. "This house was never truly mine. Always Shelly's design, his children's inheritance, Sebastian's past. I lived here, but I never belonged here."

"So maybe neither Paris nor Captiva is the answer," Chelsea suggested. "Maybe it's time for an entirely new horizon."

Isabelle's gaze turned contemplative. "Perhaps. Though I'm not sure I have the courage to start over completely, not at my age."

"Says the woman who moved from Paris to a tiny island in Florida for love," Chelsea pointed out with a smile. "I'd say courage isn't something you lack."

This drew a reluctant laugh from Isabelle. "Fair point."

She moved to the window, gazing out at the Gulf stretching to the horizon. "I do love it here," she admitted. "Not this house, perhaps, but the island itself. The light, the water, the sense of being at the edge of the world."

"Then stay," Chelsea said simply. "Not here, not in this mausoleum of memories, but somewhere on Captiva that could be truly yours. Somewhere new."

Isabelle turned, a spark of interest lighting her eyes. "Like the cottage, you mean? Something simple, on the water?"

"Exactly," Chelsea agreed, warming to the idea. "Something sized for one person but with room for guests. Something you design completely to your own taste, without compromise."

"Samantha would be apoplectic," Isabelle observed, a mischievous smile playing at her lips. "She's convinced I'll retreat to Paris now that Sebastian is gone, leaving the Captiva property empire intact for the Barlowe heirs."

"All the more reason to stay," Chelsea replied, refilling their wine glasses. "Besides, we need you here. Who else is going to scandalize the Yacht Club with inappropriate cocktail attire and French opinions on American prudishness?"

Isabelle laughed, the sound freer than Chelsea had heard since before Sebastian's death. "It would be worth staying just for that."

"Not only that, but I've also come to appreciate wine since you moved here. Remember our late nights on the beach with a few bottles of France's best Bordeaux?" Maggie asked.

"And the night we climbed the lifeguard chair in the middle of a glorious full moon?" Chelsea added. "I want to do that again."

Isabelle's expression grew more serious as she sipped her wine. "The legal battles aren't over, you know. Samantha is still contesting portions of the will, especially Sebastian's decision to leave me the house in Paris, with no entailment to the Barlowe estate."

"Let her contest," Chelsea said firmly. "Sebastian's attorney assured you the will is ironclad, and Steven says the same. Samantha's just making noise because she can't bear the thought of you walking away with anything of 'real value.'"

"As if Sebastian's money was what mattered to me," Isabelle said, a flash of genuine anger coloring her tone. "I had my own career, my own savings. I didn't need his fortune."

"We know that," Chelsea assured her. "Anyone who saw you together knew that."

Isabelle's anger ebbed as quickly as it had risen, replaced by a weary sadness. "I just want to honor his wishes, to respect the provisions he made. Is that so much to ask?"

"Not at all," Chelsea replied, moving to stand beside her friend at the window. "And you will. Samantha can bluster and threaten, but in the end, Sebastian's will is a legal document, and his intentions were clear. You'll get through this, Isabelle. One day at a time."

They stood together, watching as the afternoon light shifted across the water, painting the Gulf in shades of turquoise and blue.

"I do believe I'll stay on Captiva," Isabelle said finally, a new resolve in her voice. "Not because of Sebastian or in spite of Samantha, but because it feels right for me. It's who I am now."

"And who is that?" Chelsea asked gently.

Isabelle considered the question, her gaze still on the horizon. "I'm not entirely sure yet," she admitted. "But I think I'd like to find out." She turned to her friends, a smile lightening her features. "And I believe I'd like to do that here, surrounded by friends who knew me as Sebastian's wife but are willing to know me as simply Isabelle."

"Count us first among them," Chelsea replied, raising her glass in a small toast, and Maggie did the same.

"To new horizons, new beginnings, and finding out who Isabelle is when she's standing on her own," Chelsea said.

"To new horizons," Isabelle echoed, clinking her glass against Chelsea's and then Maggie's. "And to old friends who help us find them."

"Captiva Sisters now and forever!" they said in unison.

Outside, the sun began its descent toward the Gulf, the first hints of pink and gold touching the edges of the sky. Sebastian's voice seemed to echo in the room, a memory so vivid Isabelle could almost hear it: *Pay attention, Isabelle. Life gives us only so many sunsets. Don't miss a single one.*

"Come on," she said suddenly, setting down her glass. "Bring the wine. We're going to watch the sunset from the beach, the way Sebastian always insisted we should."

Chelsea followed without question as Isabelle led the way through the house and down to the shore, where they kicked off their shoes and walked to the water's edge. The sky was transforming now, the subtle pastels deepening into vibrant oranges and reds as the sun neared the horizon.

"Sebastian always said the best sunsets happen after storms," Isabelle remarked, settling onto the sand. "When the air is cleared of dust and pollution, the colors are more vivid."

"Sounds like a metaphor," Chelsea observed, joining her.

"He was full of those," Isabelle agreed with a fond smile. "Some profound, others ridiculous. But this one, I think, has merit."

As they watched the sun sink into the Gulf, its final rays painting the sky in a spectacle of color, Isabelle felt a sense of peace settle over her. The future remained uncertain, the legal battles with Sebastian's children unresolved, the tasks of packing and moving still before her. But for this moment, watching another sunset from the shore Sebastian had loved, she was exactly where she needed to be.

And perhaps that was enough for now—not to know the entire path forward, but simply to take the next step, and the next, trusting that each sunset would lead to a new dawn, each ending to some new beginning.

Sebastian would have appreciated the poetry in that, she thought. And for the first time since his death, the thought brought a smile rather than tears.

CHAPTER 17

*B*ecca Wheeler stared at the small collection of baby clothes spread across her bed, uncertainty clouding her face. After three long weeks in the NICU, Eloise was finally coming home tomorrow. The moment Becca had both dreamed of and dreaded in equal measure was upon them.

"What if none of these fit her?" she asked, holding up a mint-green sleeper that looked impossibly tiny despite Eloise's prematurity. "She's still so small."

Christopher looked up from the bassinet he was assembling, a screwdriver in one hand and an expression of infinite patience on his face. "Then we'll buy new ones," he said simply. "Or my sisters will. Lauren's been threatening to do some baby girl shopping."

Becca smiled weakly, folding the sleeper with nervous precision. "I should be more prepared than this. Why do I feel so completely out of my depth?"

Setting down the screwdriver, Christopher came to sit beside her on the bed, his hand covering hers. "Because this is different," he said gently. "This isn't a patient or a medical textbook on babies. This is our daughter. Our tiny miracle who's been through more in her first three weeks of life than most people face in years."

"What if I do something wrong?" Becca whispered, voicing the fear that had been growing since Dr. Patel had announced Eloise was ready for discharge. "In the NICU, there were monitors and nurses and doctors. Here, it's just us."

"And my mom. And Beth. And your dad and brothers. And the entire medical staff on speed dial," Christopher reminded her. "We're not alone in this, Bec."

Becca nodded, drawing strength from his steady presence. Over the past three weeks, Christopher had been her rock—shuttling between hospital and home, learning every aspect of Eloise's care, asking questions, taking notes, treating their daughter's NICU stay as both a medical crisis and a masterclass in infant care.

"I know," she said, leaning against his shoulder. "I just want everything to be perfect for her."

"It won't be," Christopher replied with unexpected frankness. "We'll make mistakes. We'll forget things. We'll probably cry from exhaustion at some point. But we'll figure it out, together."

Before Becca could respond, her phone chimed with a text message. She checked the screen and smiled. "Dad says he wants us to video as much as possible."

"I'm not surprised," Christopher said, returning to the bassinet. "This baby is very much loved."

Her father had stayed an extra week after her brothers went back to Florida. When he finally left, Becca was happy to have time alone with Christopher. As much as she loved the company, playing hostess to company wasn't something she needed. What she needed most was to have her daughter out of the NICU and sleeping in her mother's arms.

Becca returned her attention to the baby clothes, selecting a few outfits to pack in the hospital bag. The rest she organized neatly in the freshly painted nursery dresser, each tiny garment a testament to hope and perseverance.

The nursery itself was a labor of love—walls painted a soft sea glass-teal at Becca's insistence ("She's a Powell, she needs to be surrounded by ocean colors"), furniture in natural wood tones, and shelves filled with books and mementos from both sides of the family. A mobile of sailing ships hung above the crib, hand-crafted by Gabriel. On the wall, a quilt made by Grandma Sarah featured fabrics from significant family garments—a square from Maggie's wedding dress, another from Christopher's childhood blanket, a piece of the sundress Becca had worn the day she and Christopher met.

It was a room designed to hold a child securely in the embrace of family history while leaving plenty of space for her to write her own story. Much like the parenting approach Becca hoped to embody, if she could just get past this paralyzing fear of inadequacy.

"Done," Christopher announced, giving the bassinet a final check. "Sturdy enough to withstand a hurricane, which, given that she's half Powell, might be necessary."

Becca smiled, crossing to run her hand along the bassinet's smooth edge. "It's perfect. Thank you."

"I can't believe she'll be sleeping here tomorrow night," Christopher said, wonder evident in his voice. "After all these weeks of monitors and incubators."

"If she sleeps at all," Becca reminded him. "Dr. Patel warned us that NICU babies often have trouble adjusting to a quiet home environment after the constant noise and light of the hospital."

"Then we'll take shifts walking her, singing to her, whatever she needs," Christopher said with the confidence of the not-yet-sleep-deprived. "We've got this, Bec."

Becca wanted to believe him. After the trauma of Eloise's premature birth and the roller coaster of the NICU experience, bringing their daughter home should feel like a triumph. Instead, it felt like stepping off a cliff without knowing if her parachute would open.

"I want to double-check that we have all the medications and supplies on Dr. Patel's list," she said turning back toward the bedroom.

Christopher caught her hand, gently pulling her back. "Hey," he said softly. "Look at me."

Becca met his gaze reluctantly, aware of the anxiety she couldn't quite hide.

"Remember what Dr. Winters told you last week? About the most common complication after bringing a NICU baby home?"

Becca nodded. "Parental anxiety leading to unnecessary emergency room visits."

"Exactly. We're prepared, Becca. We've had more training than most first-time parents get in a lifetime. We know Eloise's patterns, her needs, her signals."

"But what if—"

"What if she stops breathing? We have the monitor. What if she won't eat? We have the breast pump and formula backup. What if she spikes a fever? We have the pediatrician on call." Christopher's voice was gentle but firm. "We can't prepare for every possible scenario, but we can trust ourselves to handle whatever comes."

Becca took a deep breath, letting his words sink in. "I'm choosing to trust your judgment here."

Christopher laughed. "I'm no expert, but I'm thrilled you think so."

That startled a laugh from Becca. "I know you're scared too."

"Are you kidding? I've been petrified," Christopher admitted. "Every time an alarm went off, every time a new doctor came to examine her, every time her weight dropped even slightly. But I didn't want to add to your stress, so I saved my panic attacks for the drive between hospital and home."

The honesty in his confession was oddly reassuring. Becca

wasn't alone in her fear—Christopher had simply been channeling his anxiety differently, protecting her while processing his own emotions privately.

"We make a good team," she said, wrapping her arms around his waist and resting her head against his chest.

"The best," he agreed, holding her close. "And tomorrow, we bring our daughter home."

Home. The word echoed in Becca's mind, carrying weight and meaning beyond its simple syllable. Home to the house Christopher had grown up in, and now the place where little Ellie would grow up too. Home, at last, as a family of three.

The NICU was quieter than usual the following morning, the normal bustle of shift change subdued as if in recognition of the momentous day. Becca and Christopher arrived early, carrying the carefully selected going-home outfit and the infant car seat that had been inspected and approved by the hospital's safety team.

Nurse Elena, who had been caring for Eloise since her first day, met them with a warm smile. "Today's the big day," she said, leading them to their daughter. "Someone's all ready for her grand exit."

Eloise lay in the open bassinet, no longer needing the temperature regulation of the incubator. At four pounds, eight ounces, she was still tiny compared to full-term newborns, her birth weight had increased through sheer Powell-Wheeler determination. Her dark hair had grown into soft curls that framed her face, and her eyes—now definitively dark blue like Becca's—tracked movement with alert interest.

"Good morning, sweetheart," Becca said, reaching in to stroke her daughter's cheek. "Today's your homecoming."

Eloise turned toward her mother's voice, her tiny mouth

making sucking motions in anticipation of her morning feeding. The sight made Becca's heart clench with love so powerful it bordered on pain.

"Breakfast first," Elena said, noting the baby's hunger cues. "Then we'll do the final discharge exam and paperwork."

Becca settled into the familiar rocking chair for Eloise's feeding, a routine they had perfected over several days. After struggling initially with traditional breastfeeding due to Eloise's prematurity, they had established a system of pumping and bottle feeding that ensured the baby received breast milk while building her strength and coordination. Now, Eloise was beginning to nurse directly for short periods, a development that Dr. Patel had encouraged as part of her transition to home.

As Eloise nursed, Christopher sat on the edge of the chair, his arm around Becca's shoulders, the three of them cocooned in a moment of quiet intimacy amid the medical environment. This was what they'd fought for, what they'd endured the emergency delivery and long NICU stay to reach—these ordinary, extraordinary moments of family connection.

Dr. Patel arrived as Eloise was finishing her feeding, her warm smile reflecting the attachment she'd formed with this particular NICU family.

"Ready for the big adventure?" she asked, taking Eloise for her final examination.

"As ready as we'll ever be," Christopher replied, his hand finding Becca's for a reassuring squeeze.

Dr. Patel's examination was thorough but swift, practiced hands checking reflexes, listening to heart and lungs, assessing tone and alertness. "She looks excellent," the doctor pronounced. "All the markers we want to see for discharge are right where they should be."

Becca, the medical professional momentarily overriding the anxious mother, asked, "And her lungs? The last X-ray showed some residual signs of the respiratory distress."

"Which is expected and will continue to improve," Dr. Patel assured her. "The follow-up with the pediatric pulmonologist is scheduled for next week, but I'm very pleased with her progress. Her oxygen saturation has been consistently at 98-100% on room air for over a week."

The clinical confirmation helped settle Becca's nerves. Numbers, data, medical evidence—these were the foundations of her training, the concrete reassurances her mind needed.

"Now," Dr. Patel continued, handing Eloise back to Becca, "time for the fashion show. I believe Nurse Elena has been looking forward to this all week."

Elena laughed, retrieving the going-home outfit from the bag Christopher held. "It's the best part of discharge day. Though I should warn you, even the smallest newborn clothes are going to swallow our little miss."

The outfit in question—a soft yellow sleeper with tiny sail-boats embroidered along the collar—had been a gift from Craw-ford, who claimed it was the exact replica of what Becca had worn home from the hospital thirty years ago. Elena was right; it was comically large on Eloise's tiny frame, the sleeves needing to be rolled multiple times and the legs bunching around her minia-ture feet.

"She'll grow into it," Christopher said, snapping photos to send to the eagerly waiting family members who couldn't be present.

"Faster than you can imagine," Dr. Patel agreed. "Now, let's go over the discharge instructions one more time, and then this little sailor can set course for home."

The next hour passed in a blur of paperwork, instructions, prescriptions, and final checks. Becca, despite having memorized every detail of Eloise's care plan, listened with intense concentra-tion, asking questions and taking notes as if this were the most crucial medical exam of her career. In many ways, it was—her first solo act as both doctor and mother, with her own child's well-being at stake.

Finally, it was time. Elena helped secure Eloise in the car seat, tucking specially designed positioning rolls around her tiny body to ensure proper support. The NICU team gathered to say good-bye, many of them misty-eyed at the departure of a baby they'd cared for since her first breath.

"You've got our numbers," Elena reminded them, bending to kiss Eloise's forehead. "Call anytime, day or night, with questions. No concern is too small."

"And remember," Dr. Patel added, her hand on Becca's shoulder, "she's ready for this. You both are. Trust yourselves and enjoy your baby."

As Christopher lifted the car seat, Becca felt a surge of emotion—gratitude for the medical team that had saved their daughter's life, amazement at the resilience of the tiny person they'd created, and yes, still fear, but now tempered with confidence in their ability to face whatever came next.

"Say goodbye to the NICU, Eloise," Christopher said softly. "We hope you never see it again, but we'll always be grateful for the care you received here."

They walked out together, a family complete at last, stepping from the artificial light of the hospital into the natural sunshine of a New England summer day.

CHAPTER 18

*T*he arrivals area at Logan Airport buzzed with the usual chaos of an early summer afternoon. Gabriel Walker weaved through the crowd, checking the flight information board one more time to confirm his father's flight was on time. Gate C22, arriving from Los Angeles. Just ten minutes late —practically early by airline standards.

Gabriel found an empty spot against the wall and leaned back, stretching his tall frame. The drive from the Boxford had taken longer than expected, traffic clogging the highways as Bostonians escaped to summer destinations. His body ached from the morning's work—he'd been up since dawn, clearing brush from the eastern section of the property, an area that had gone untended for years.

His phone vibrated in his pocket. Beth.

"Hey," he answered, smiling at the sound of her voice.

"Are you there yet? Did his flight land?" The questions tumbled out in quick succession.

"Just got here. The flight's landing now." Gabriel lowered his voice, moving away from a family reuniting nearby. "How are things at home?"

"I've changed the sheets on the guest room bed twice," Beth admitted. "And added some flowers on the night stand. Charlie's been following me around like I've lost my mind."

Gabriel chuckled. "Dad's not going to care about having an organized bedroom, Beth. He's coming to help with the orchard, not inspect our housekeeping."

"I know, I know." He could hear her moving around the farmhouse as she talked. "It's just... it's the first time he's staying with us since we got married. I want him to feel welcome."

"He will." Gabriel's tone softened. "He's excited to see the place, to see what we're building together."

There was a brief silence on the line. "Do you think he'll be surprised at how little progress we've made on the orchard?"

"Beth," Gabriel interrupted gently. "Dad knows what it takes to run the place. Who better than him to understand?"

The announcement overhead indicated that Flight 372 from Los Angeles had landed. Gabriel straightened, scanning the area where passengers would emerge. "His flight's here. I should go."

"Drive carefully coming home," Beth said. "And Gabriel? I love you."

"Love you too. See you soon."

Pocketing his phone, Gabriel moved closer to the security exit, watching as travelers streamed out, reunion scenes playing out all around him—families embracing, lovers reuniting, business travelers striding purposefully toward ground transportation.

And then there he was. At sixty-eight, Thomas still cut an imposing figure—tall like his son, with a full head of silver hair tied back in a short ponytail, weathered skin from decades working outdoors, and the same observant gray eyes Gabriel saw in the mirror each morning.

He wore faded jeans, a chambray shirt with the sleeves rolled up, and carried only a worn leather backpack and his guitar. No matter where he traveled, Thomas always brought his guitar—a cherished Martin that was older than Gabriel.

"Dad!" Gabriel called, raising a hand.

Thomas's face broke into a wide smile as he spotted his son. "Gabriel," he said, setting down his bags to embrace him properly. "Good to see you, son. Am I wrong or have you been working in the field?"

Gabriel laughed, returning the hug with equal enthusiasm. "Nothing gets by you. I've got dirt under my fingernails that won't come out, and Beth says I track more soil into the house than Charlie does."

"Charlie?" Thomas asked, picking up his bags again.

"Our dog. Lab mix. You'll love him—he has the run of the orchard and thinks he's in charge of all of us."

They made their way through the terminal toward the parking garage, Thomas took in his surroundings with the alert curiosity that had always characterized him. Before he retired, he was an environmental consultant who specialized in sustainable agriculture, he'd traveled extensively throughout Gabriel's childhood, sometimes taking his son along, other times leaving him with his mother in their Massachusetts home. When they finally retired, they moved out to California.

"How was the flight?" Gabriel asked as they reached his truck, a practical Ford F-150 that had seen better days but served the orchard's needs.

"Long," Thomas admitted, stowing his guitar case carefully in the backseat. "But worth it to finally see my family. I've missed you guys."

Once they were on the highway heading north, Thomas rolled down his window, breathing deeply. "East Coast air," he remarked. "Heavier than California. Richer somehow, and definitely cleaner."

Gabriel nodded, navigating through the remnants of rush

hour traffic. "I love it. The seasons are so distinct here—you can smell autumn coming weeks before it arrives."

"And how are you and Beth handling the orchard? Your emails have been... optimistic, but not particularly detailed."

There it was—his father's gentle way of asking for the truth behind the carefully edited updates Gabriel had been sending. He should have known Thomas would sense the challenges they'd been facing.

"It's been harder than we expected," Gabriel admitted, keeping his eyes on the road. "The trees need major pruning, the irrigation system is a disaster, and we're finding evidence of disease in some of the older sections."

Thomas made a sympathetic noise. "Heritage varieties?"

"Some. About twenty acres of modern commercial varieties—Honeycrisp, Gala, Fuji—and then five acres of older types: Northern Spy, Baldwin, Roxbury Russet. Those are the ones we're most worried about."

"The old New England apples." Thomas nodded. "Worth saving, if you can. They've adapted to the local conditions over generations. More disease-resistant in the long run, if you can nurse them through this rough patch."

Gabriel felt a weight lift slightly at his father's understanding. "That's what I've been telling Beth. She wants to focus our limited resources on the commercial varieties that will bring quicker returns, but I think the heritage section could be our niche."

"And that's become a point of tension?" Thomas asked perceptively.

Gabriel sighed. "One of several. We're both learning as we go, and we're both stubborn. Beth approaches the orchard like a legal case—researching, analyzing data, making rational decisions. I'm more intuitive, willing to take risks based on feeling."

"Sounds familiar," Thomas said with a small smile. "Your mother and I had similar conflicts in our approach to... well, everything."

The comparison made Gabriel uneasy. Hi mother's passing the year before still hurt him deeply. "Beth and I are not you and Mom," he said more sharply than intended, "but I know what you mean."

Thomas was quiet for a moment. "No, you're not," he finally agreed. "But all partnerships face challenges when dreams meet reality. The question is how you navigate them together."

They didn't talk much as the city gave way to suburbs, then to the more rural landscape of central Massachusetts.

"Beth has struggled with the work because I don't think she was prepared for how much work it is and how long it will take for the orchard to be fully operational. She knows what the orchard meant to you and Mom and she worries you'll think she's playing at farming. That you won't take what we're trying to do seriously."

Thomas shook his head slowly. "Gabriel, I've spent my life working with farmers all over the world. The ones who succeed aren't necessarily those with the most experience or knowledge when they start. They're the ones who care deeply enough to persevere through the inevitable hardships."

He paused, looking out at the passing landscape. "Does Beth care about the orchard itself, or just about you?"

Gabriel considered this. "Both, I think. At first, it was more about supporting my dream, finding a way for us to be together. I think she felt lost after leaving her job, but now... you should see her with the trees, Dad. She talks to them when she thinks no one's listening. She keeps detailed journals about each section of the orchard. She's the one who persuaded the historical society to help us research the heritage varieties' provenance."

Thomas smiled. "Then she's a true orchardist, whether she knows it yet or not."

As they turned off the main road onto the long, gravel drive that led to the farmhouse, Gabriel felt a surge of pride despite the property's obvious challenges. The ancient farmhouse sat nestled against a backdrop of gently rolling hills, its weathered clapboard siding glowing warmly in the evening light. Beyond it stretched the orchard—twenty-five acres of apple trees in various states of growth and repair, the nearest sections pruned and tended, the farther ones still wild and overgrown. It had been his parents' place for years, and now, Gabriel and Beth's.

"When it comes to the orchard, it's not much to look at yet," Gabriel said, suddenly seeing the place through his father's experienced eyes. "But I think it will come along, especially with your help."

As the truck rumbled up the drive, the front door of the farmhouse opened. Beth stepped out onto the porch, Charlie at her heels. She'd changed from her work clothes into jeans and a soft blue sweater, her hair pulled back in a loose ponytail. She raised a hand in greeting, her smile a mixture of welcome and nervousness.

"Welcome to Walker Orchard," Gabriel said, parking the truck. "Ready to get your hands dirty?"

Thomas's eyes crinkled at the corners, his gaze moving from the weathered farmhouse to the sprawling orchard beyond, then finally to Beth waiting on the porch. "Absolutely," he said. "I thought you'd never ask."

As they got out of the truck, Gabriel noticed how Beth straightened, as if preparing to meet an important client rather than her father-in-law. He caught her eye, giving her a reassuring smile.

"Beth," he called, "it's so good to see you. You're as beautiful as ever."

She came down the porch steps, Charlie bounding ahead to investigate the newcomer. Thomas set down his bags and pulled Beth into a big hug.

"Welcome home, Thomas," she said. "We're so glad you're here."

Thomas's face softened as he returned the embrace. "The pleasure is mine, Beth. I'm so glad to be back."

Gabriel watched them, feeling something settle inside him. His father was here, bringing decades of experience and wisdom. Beth was trying, pushing past her natural reserve. And the orchard, for all its challenges, was theirs—a dream they were fighting to make real, together.

As they walked toward the house, Thomas carrying his guitar case and backpack, Beth slipped her hand into Gabriel's and squeezed. The simple gesture conveyed volumes: solidarity, partnership, a shared purpose despite their differences.

"I hope you're hungry," Beth said to Thomas. "I've made my grandmother's pot roast recipe. Gabriel says it's the only thing I cook that's consistently edible."

Thomas laughed. "After airline food, anything home-cooked will taste like a feast." He turned to Gabriel. "What about your brother and his family? Will they come around soon?"

Gabriel nodded. "James will come by in the morning with Willow. They can't wait to see you."

Charlie raced ahead of them, circling back occasionally as if to hurry them along. The evening air was cool and sweet, carrying the scent of newly cut grass and the first summer flowers. In the orchard beyond the house, the apple trees stood in neat, if somewhat neglected, rows—waiting, Gabriel thought, for the attention and care that would bring them back to their full potential.

"Tomorrow I'll show you the heritage section," Gabriel told his father. "The trees there are over a hundred years old. They need the most help, but they're also the most special."

"You don't have to tell me about them. One day at a time," Thomas advised, looking around appreciatively. "Orchards aren't built—or restored—overnight."

"We've got all summer," Beth said, and Gabriel heard the determination beneath her welcoming tone. They had decisions to make, challenges to overcome, a business to build from nearly nothing. But for tonight, at least, they could enjoy this moment of new beginnings.

As they reached the porch, Gabriel paused to look back at the orchard, the trees silhouetted against the darkening sky. His father was right—they couldn't fix everything at once. But with Thomas's help, perhaps they could find their way through the tangle of problems that had been straining his and Beth's relationship these past weeks.

"Come on inside," Beth said, holding the door open. "Let's get you settled."

The farmhouse embraced them with its simple comfort—nothing fancy or pretentious, just honest wood and stone warmed by two centuries of life within its walls. As Gabriel followed Beth and his father inside, he felt a cautious optimism take root. The summer stretched ahead, full of hard work and uncertainty, but also possibility.

Tomorrow would bring its challenges. Tonight was for welcome, for family, for sharing the dream that had brought them all together on this patch of New England soil.

CHAPTER 19

"*A*re you sure about this?" Chelsea asked, arranging a bouquet of fresh-cut hibiscus in the center of her patio table. The evening breeze carried the scent of salt and jasmine across her back deck, which offered a perfect view of the sunset over Captiva's shoreline.

Maggie, busy uncorking a bottle of chilled Sancerre, glanced up at her friend. "About what? The wine? It's one of Isabelle's favorites."

"About inviting Isabelle and Gretchen to the same dinner." Chelsea adjusted a place setting. "Isabelle's still grieving, and Gretchen is... well, Gretchen."

"That's precisely why it's perfect timing," Maggie replied confidently. "Isabelle needs distraction from those vultures Sebastian called children, and your sister needs purpose."

Chelsea made a noncommittal sound as she filled water glasses. In the month since returning to Captiva from Key West, Gretchen had cycled through three potential business ideas, photographed half the historic buildings on the island "for her portfolio," and rearranged Chelsea's spare bedroom wall hangings no fewer than four times.

"Besides," Maggie continued, "Sarah's excited to see Isabelle. They've always gotten along so well, and she needs to get out more. Ever since Trevor started working with Steven, Sarah's been on her own with the children."

"Who's gotten along well?" came a voice from the doorway. Sarah Wheeler Hutchins stepped onto the deck, carrying a platter of appetizers. At thirty-two, she was Maggie's youngest daughter, with the same blonde hair and warm smile as her mother, though with more freckles on her nose than she had when she was a child.

"You and Isabelle," Maggie replied, giving her daughter a quick one-armed hug. "I was just telling Chelsea that tonight's dinner is a perfect combination."

"If you're playing matchmaker again, Mom..." Sarah warned with good-natured exasperation.

"Not romantically," Maggie clarified. "But perhaps... professionally? Creatively? Isabelle needs a project, and Gretchen needs stability. I get the same vibe from both of them these days—two women trying to find their way in the world."

"And you think throwing them together will somehow make both those things happen?" Chelsea asked skeptically.

"I think two intelligent, creative women with complementary skills might benefit from knowing each other better," Maggie replied diplomatically. "What happens after that is up to them."

Chelsea whispered, "What your mother won't say is that I'm going to kill my sister if she continues to spend all her time with me."

The sound of a car door closing in the driveway signaled the arrival of their guest. Chelsea smoothed her sundress and headed inside to greet Isabelle.

"Just promise me you'll be subtle, Mom," Sarah murmured.

Maggie's innocent expression fooled no one. "I'm always subtle."

Moments later, Chelsea returned with Isabelle. Isabelle

looked elegant as always in white linen pants and a cerulean, blue silk top that emphasized her eyes.

Gretchen called out from upstairs, "I'll be right down, don't start without me."

"I've got your favorite wine, let me get you a glass," Chelsea said.

"Thank you so much, Chelsea."

Gretchen ran down the stairs and joined them in the kitchen. She wore a flowing bohemian dress with an assortment of silver bangles jingling on her wrist.

"Isabelle, you remember my sister Gretchen," Chelsea said, making the reintroduction.

Recognition flickered in Isabelle's eyes. "Yes, of course. You were here with your sisters a few years ago, looking for investment in a Key West business."

"That's right," Gretchen said, offering her hand. "The famous Lawrence sisters and our misguided CoiffeeShop. Not our finest moment."

"What happened with that?" Isabelle asked, accepting a glass of wine from Maggie.

Gretchen shrugged good-naturedly. "Reality intervened. The property was more dilapidated than advertised, renovation costs tripled, and we discovered none of us actually knew anything about running a business. Tess and Leah are currently bartending, and my daughter has moved to Key West as well. I'll go down here and there in the coming months to visit, but Captiva Island is more my style."

"Gretchen's been doing architectural photography," Chelsea explained as they settled around the table. "Specializing in historic buildings and renovation projects."

"Really?" Isabelle's interest seemed genuinely piqued. "Here on Captiva?"

"Mostly Naples and Fort Myers," Gretchen replied, accepting the platter of grilled shrimp Sarah passed her. "There aren't many truly historic structures left on the islands after the hurricanes over the years. Though a few gems remain."

"Speaking of historic properties," Maggie interjected, her tone deliberately casual, "Isabelle's been looking at that old storefront near the post office."

"Just exploring options, nothing decided," Isabelle explained.

"What kind of business are you considering?" Gretchen asked.

"I haven't settled on anything specific," Isabelle admitted. "After running my design atelier in Paris, I miss creative work. But Captiva's market has different needs than Paris."

"That's an understatement," Gretchen said with feeling. "This island desperately needs some authenticity in its commercial offerings. Everything's so tourist-focused, so... manufactured."

"Gretchen has complained about Captiva's businesses since she arrived," Chelsea explained, rolling her eyes. "Apparently, we're doing everything wrong."

"Not everything," Gretchen clarified. "Just most things food and beverage related."

"Like what?" Sarah asked, genuinely curious.

"Like the fact that there's nowhere to get a proper espresso on this entire island," Gretchen said with surprising passion. "The coffee situation here is criminal."

Isabelle's eyes widened in agreement. "The brown water they serve at the Sandbar? It is an offense to coffee everywhere."

"Exactly!" Gretchen leaned forward eagerly. "You're from Paris—you understand. Coffee should be an experience, not just caffeine delivery."

"In Paris, my apartment was above a small café," Isabelle recalled, her expression softening with the memory. "The owner, Marcel, roasted his own beans. The aroma would drift up through my windows every morning, better than any alarm clock."

"That's what's missing here," Gretchen insisted. "A café with soul—not another beach-themed tourist trap serving mediocre drinks with cutesy names."

"You two sound like coffee snobs," Chelsea observed.

"Connoisseurs," Isabelle and Gretchen corrected in unison, then exchanged surprised smiles.

"Gretchen worked as a barista on Cape Cod for a while," Chelsea added.

"That was years ago, but it was a great experience. I trained under an Italian champion," Gretchen added, without false modesty. "I can pull a perfect ristretto and identify single-origin beans in a blind taste test."

"And yet you've never once made coffee when staying here," Chelsea noted dryly.

"Because your equipment is inadequate," Gretchen retorted. "That pod machine is an abomination."

As dinner progressed, the conversation flowed easily between island gossip, updates on Maggie's other children, and Sarah's work with the Outreach Center. But Maggie noticed that Isabelle and Gretchen kept returning to their shared appreciation for authentic experiences—whether in coffee, design, or photography.

"So what's your vision for the storefront?" Gretchen asked Isabelle over dessert. "If you could create anything there, what would it be?"

Isabelle twirled her wine glass thoughtfully. "Something that brings a bit of Paris to Captiva, perhaps. Not in a themed, artificial way, but in essence. A space with character and history, where people feel the pleasure of being exactly where they are."

"Like a proper café," Gretchen suggested. "Not just a place to grab coffee, but somewhere to linger. To connect. You could have tables and chairs outside, just like they do in Paris."

"Yes, exactly." Isabelle's eyes brightened with genuine interest. "With good coffee, comfortable seating, perhaps a selection of international newspapers and magazines..."

"Fresh pastries," Gretchen added. "Real ones, not those sugar bombs they sell at the bakery."

"You two should see the space together," Maggie suggested, unable to contain herself any longer. "It sounds like you have complementary visions."

Chelsea gave her a look that clearly said *So much for subtle.*

"I'd be happy to offer my perspective," Gretchen said to Isabelle. "Architecturally speaking. That's kind of my professional wheelhouse now."

Isabelle hesitated, then nodded. "I would appreciate another set of eyes. The real estate agent's assessment was... less than thorough."

"They never are," Gretchen agreed. "I've photographed dozens of renovation projects. You learn to spot potential problems— and opportunities—that others miss."

"Would tomorrow morning work?" Isabelle asked. "Say, ten o'clock?"

"Perfect," Gretchen agreed readily. "I'll bring my camera, if that's all right."

As they exchanged phone numbers, Maggie caught Sarah's eye across the table and gave a small, satisfied nod. Her daughter shook her head in amused resignation at her mother's transparent matchmaking Even Chelsea seemed impressed.

Later, as they gathered on the lanai, Isabelle found herself beside Chelsea at the railing.

"Thank you for this little get-together," Isabelle murmured. "I needed to get out of that house and talk to friends."

"Of course," Chelsea replied. "You are welcome here anytime."

"It was perhaps not a coincidence that your sister was here?" Isabelle asked looking at Chelsea and Maggie both.

Maggie laughed softly. "I merely create opportunities. What you do with them is entirely up to you."

"She's interesting, your sister," Isabelle conceded, watching

Gretchen animatedly discuss something with Sarah across the deck. "Passionate about her subjects. That quality is rare."

"Rather like you," Chelsea observed.

Isabelle was quiet for a moment. "Sebastian always said I threw myself completely into whatever captured my interest. It was one of the things he loved about me." Her voice held more fond remembrance than grief, a subtle but significant shift that Chelsea noted with approval.

"He wouldn't want you to lose that part of yourself," Maggie said gently.

"No," Isabelle agreed. "He wouldn't." She straightened, a new resolve in her posture. "Well, it seems I have a property viewing tomorrow morning. With an architectural photography expert, no less."

"How fortunate," Maggie said blandly, knowing full well that Gretchen wasn't an expert on anything.

Isabelle laughed—a genuine sound that had been too rare since Sebastian's passing. "You are incorrigible, Maggie Wheeler Moretti."

"So I've been told." Maggie clinked her glass against Isabelle's. "Here's to new possibilities."

"To new possibilities," Isabelle echoed, her gaze drifting toward Gretchen, who was now showing something on her camera to Chelsea. "And unexpected connections."

The small storefront in the center of town had stood empty for nearly two years. Dusty windows obscured the view inside, and a faded "For Lease" sign hung crookedly in the corner of the door. Isabelle stood on the sidewalk, keys in hand, waiting for Gretchen to arrive.

After last night's dinner at Chelsea's home, she'd found herself unexpectedly energized by the possibility of creating something new. The conversation with Gretchen about Parisian cafés had awakened memories of places Isabelle had loved—spaces where the atmosphere was as carefully curated as the coffee itself.

A bright yellow Jeep pulled up, and Gretchen hopped out, her camera bag slung over one shoulder.

"Right on time," Isabelle greeted her.

"For coffee and renovation potential? Always." Gretchen's smile was bright as she surveyed the building's exterior. "This has great bones. Those original transom windows above the door are architectural gems."

Isabelle unlocked the door, which protested with a creak. "The real estate agent said it was originally a bookshop in the 1970s, then a series of tourist stores. It's been vacant since the previous tenant left during COVID."

They stepped inside, and Gretchen immediately began taking photos, capturing the sunlight streaming through the dusty windows, the worn wooden floors, the pressed tin ceiling partially hidden by a dropped panel system.

"Look at that," she said, pointing upward. "Those acoustic panels are hiding original tin ceiling tiles. That's a treasure if they're intact."

Isabelle moved further into the space. Despite its neglected state, she could feel the potential—the high ceilings, the natural light, the inherent character of an older building.

"So," Gretchen said, lowering her camera. "A café? Like we talked about last night?"

"I'm considering it," Isabelle admitted. "Though I know nothing about running such a business."

"But you know design, and you know what makes a space special." Gretchen ran her hand along a built-in wooden shelf. "That's half the battle with a café. Anyone can serve coffee; creating an experience is the hard part."

"And you know coffee," Isabelle observed.

"I do." Gretchen's expression turned more serious. "Look, I

know we've only reconnected, but I've been thinking about our conversation last night. We both need a new direction. Maybe..."

"Are you suggesting a partnership?" Isabelle asked directly.

"I'm suggesting we explore the possibility." Gretchen gestured around the space. "This place has incredible potential. Together, we could create something unique on the island—something with authenticity and soul."

Isabelle studied her thoughtfully. "Why would you want to partner with me? You barely know me."

"I know enough," Gretchen countered. "You have exquisite taste, you understand what makes spaces special, and you're not afraid to start over. Plus, Chelsea tells me you ran a successful design business in Paris for years before marrying Sebastian. That kind of experience is invaluable."

"And what would you bring to this hypothetical partnership?"

"Besides my love of coffee? Contacts with specialty suppliers, knowledge of the local market from my time in Naples, and..." she patted her camera, "the ability to document the transformation in a way that builds anticipation and a customer base before we even open."

Isabelle wondered if Gretchen was exaggerating her past experience with anything. Walking to the large front windows, wiping away some of the dust to look out at the street she wondered if enthusiasm was enough to trust this adventure. The location was ideal—just off the main tourist path but still accessible, with the potential to attract both visitors and locals seeking something beyond the typical island offerings.

"It would be a significant investment," she said. "Both financially and emotionally."

"I can't match your resources financially," Gretchen acknowledged frankly. "But I can contribute sweat equity, practical knowledge, and complete commitment. This wouldn't be another of my passing interests. Coffee is my passion, and the truth is, I need a job."

Isabelle nodded, understanding completely.

Gretchen gestured to the empty space around them. "Maybe this is where we both find what we're looking for."

They spent the next hour examining the property in detail—testing floors for soundness, looking behind panels to assess the condition of the original features, discussing where plumbing and electrical would need updating, and without a stove and kitchen area, they couldn't make it work.

"The square-footage is here, but it would need significant construction to make it just right," Isabelle said. "Perhaps we can talk to Steven about it? With his and Trevor's knowledge, they could tell us if this place works."

Gretchen nodded. "That's a great idea. The built-ins along that wall could display local art or specialty goods," she suggested. "Things that complement the café experience without turning it into a gift shop."

"Exactly! And the lighting needs to be completely redone. Cafés are all about atmosphere—too bright and it feels sterile, too dark and people can't read or work."

As they collaborated, Isabelle found herself genuinely excited for the first time since Sebastian's death. Here was something constructive, creative—a project that would demand her full attention and design expertise while creating something lasting for the community.

"We would need to be clear about expectations," she said as they finally took a break, sitting on the front steps of the shop. "Roles, responsibilities, financial arrangements. My attorney would have to draw up a business plan and partnership documents."

"Absolutely," Gretchen agreed. "I'm not naive about business partnerships, despite my track record of abandoned ventures. This would need proper structure."

"And a name," Isabelle mused. "Something that captures the essence of what we're creating."

"Something that bridges Paris and Captiva," Gretchen suggested. "The sophistication of a European café with the relaxed island attitude."

They fell into speculative silence, watching people pass on the sidewalk—tourists headed to the beach, locals running errands, all potential customers if they could create something special enough to draw them in.

"Café de la Mer," Isabelle said suddenly. "The Sea Café. Simple, evocative, bilingual."

"I love it." Gretchen's face lit up. "But as much as I love the name, I think the coffee and pastries will speak for themselves. The name should probably be something as simple as Captiva Café."

Isabelle felt a flutter of genuine excitement. "Yes, you're right. Captiva Café, it's perfect. This is happening rather quickly."

"Sometimes the best decisions do," Gretchen replied. "Chelsea says I'm impulsive to a fault, but occasionally my impulses lead to something worthwhile."

"I propose we take two weeks," she said decisively. "I'll have an architect and contractor assess the space professionally. You research equipment, suppliers, and the permit process. We both develop a business plan from our respective areas of expertise, and I'll talk to my attorney. Then we reconvene to make a final decision."

"Two weeks," Gretchen agreed. "Practical, measured, responsible. Very un-Gretchen-like, but I can adapt."

Isabelle laughed. "And very unlike my usual approach as well. But we both have much at stake here—you, a chance to build something lasting; me, a new chapter after significant loss."

They shook hands, the gesture formal yet charged with possibilities.

"To Captiva Café," Gretchen said. "May it be everything we hope for."

"And perhaps," Isabelle added softly, "exactly what we both need."

As they locked up the storefront and parted ways, Isabelle felt lighter than she had in weeks. Sebastian had often said that the universe provided what you needed when you were ready to receive it. Perhaps this unexpected connection with Gretchen—a woman so different from herself yet aligned in important ways— was exactly that provision.

A new beginning. A purpose. A future on Captiva that belonged to Isabelle alone, not defined by her status as Sebastian's widow.

For the first time since his death, she found herself looking forward rather than back. And it felt, if not quite like happiness, then at least like its possibility.

CHAPTER 20

*L*auren tapped her pen nervously against the desk calendar, watching the clock as she waited for her team to arrive. The morning sun streamed through the windows of Phillips Realty, highlighting the awards and certificates that lined the walls—tangible evidence of the business she'd built from nothing over the past decade.

Brian arrived first, as always. Punctuality was his trademark, along with an encyclopedic knowledge of local zoning regulations that had saved countless deals from falling through.

"Morning, boss," he said cheerfully, setting his messenger bag on his desk. "Got your text. Sounds mysterious."

"Not mysterious," Lauren assured him. "Just important."

Nell breezed in five minutes later, juggling her oversized purse, a laptop case, and a tray of coffees. At forty-five, she was the veteran of the team, with twenty years in real estate and connections throughout Massachusetts that routinely brought in high-end listings.

"Sorry," she said, distributing the coffees. "Line at Franklin's was ridiculous. But I figured we'd need caffeine for whatever warranted an early morning meeting."

Lauren accepted her cup gratefully—a vanilla latte with an extra shot, exactly as she preferred. That was Nell—attentive to details, especially when it came to people.

"Thanks for coming in early," Lauren began, gesturing for them to take seats in the comfortable client chairs across from her desk. "I wanted to talk to you both before the day gets busy."

Brian and Nell exchanged quick glances, a flicker of concern passing between them.

"The business isn't in trouble, is it?" Brian asked.

"Not at all," Lauren assured them quickly. "In fact, we're on track for our best year yet. That's part of what I want to discuss."

She took a deep breath, organizing her thoughts. She'd rehearsed this conversation with Jeff multiple times, but now that the moment had arrived, she found herself unexpectedly emotional.

"Jeff and I have made a decision that will affect the business," she said. "Our daughter Olivia has been accepted into the Tampa Bay Elite Tennis Academy in Florida. It's an incredible opportunity for her, one we can't pass up."

Understanding dawned on their faces.

"You're moving," Nell said quietly.

Lauren nodded. "To Florida, yes. Likely by the end of summer, to get Olivia settled before the program begins in September."

"That's... wow. Big news," Brian said, leaning back in his chair. "What does this mean for Phillips Realty?"

"That's exactly what I want to discuss with you both." Lauren pulled a folder from her desk drawer. "Jeff and I met with our financial planner last week to explore options. I've built this business from the ground up, and I'm not willing to simply walk away from it—or from the two of you."

"We wouldn't want that either," Nell said firmly.

"My proposal is this: I would retain ownership of Phillips Realty, but step back from day-to-day operations. You two would become managing partners, running the Massachusetts office while I establish a Florida branch."

Brian sat forward, interest piqued. "What exactly would that entail for us?"

"More responsibility, more autonomy, and more compensation," Lauren said, sliding documents across the desk. "You'd handle local client relationships, staff management, and operational decisions. I'd remain involved in strategy, branding, and expansion plans, primarily remotely but with regular visits north."

Nell picked up the paperwork, scanning it quickly. Her expression remained carefully neutral, but Lauren could see her mind working through the implications.

"There's something else," Lauren continued. "The business has grown to the point where you two can't handle all the listings alone, especially with me leaving. We need to hire at least two more agents."

"We've been saying that for months," Brian pointed out with a small smile.

"And I should have listened sooner," Lauren acknowledged. "That's on me. But now it's not optional—it's necessary. I'd like you both to be involved in the hiring process, since you'll be working directly with whoever we bring on."

Nell set down the papers and met Lauren's gaze directly. "Can I ask the obvious question? Why keep the Massachusetts business at all? Wouldn't it be simpler to sell and start fresh in Florida?"

It was a fair question, one that she and Jeff had debated extensively.

"Two reasons," Lauren replied. "First, Phillips Realty has a sterling reputation in this market that would take years to rebuild elsewhere. That has real value. Second..." She hesitated, then continued with honesty, "This business represents a decade of my life. It's part of me. I'm not ready to let it go completely."

Brian nodded, understanding. "And the Florida expansion?"

"Initially modest," Lauren explained. "A small office, focusing on residential properties in areas around Tampa. I'd be using our established brand and systems, just in a new market."

"Which means we might need to travel south occasionally to help set things up," Nell surmised, always quick to connect dots.

"Possibly," Lauren confirmed. "If you're willing. All expenses covered, of course."

"Winter trips to Florida? Twist my arm," Brian joked, breaking some of the tension.

Nell was more contemplative. "This is a lot to process, Lauren. You're asking us to essentially take over the daily management of the business you built."

"I'm asking you to help me preserve what we've all built together," Lauren corrected gently. "And to grow with me as the business evolves. I wouldn't consider this if I didn't have complete faith in both of you."

The room fell quiet as Brian and Nell absorbed the information. Lauren sipped her coffee, giving them space to think. She understood the magnitude of what she was proposing. It would fundamentally change their professional roles and relationships.

"The compensation package is generous," Brian noted, reviewing the paperwork.

"It reflects the increased responsibility," Lauren said. "And there would be performance bonuses tied to agency growth."

Nell set down the papers and met Lauren's eyes. "I'm in," she said decisively. "I've been with you since you opened this place. I'm not stopping now just because you're getting a tan year-round."

Relief washed over Lauren. She'd been confident about Nell, but hearing the commitment meant everything.

"Brian?" she asked, turning to her younger agent.

He grinned. "Are you kidding? Managing partner before I'm thirty-five? My mother will finally stop asking when I'm getting a 'real job.'"

Lauren laughed, feeling tension drain from her shoulders. "Thank you both. This means more than I can express."

"We should start the hiring process immediately," Nell said, already shifting into planning mode. "The market is heating up, and training new agents takes time."

"I've drafted job postings," Lauren said, pulling more papers from her folder. "And compiled a list of promising candidates from the last licensing course at the community college."

"Of course you have," Brian said with fond exasperation. "Always ten steps ahead."

"Not always," Lauren admitted. "This move has plenty of unknowns. I'm certain about this part, though—keeping Phillips Realty strong here while building something new there is the right path forward."

The conversation shifted to practical matters—hiring timelines, training plans, office procedures that needed documentation. As they talked, Lauren felt a curious mixture of emotions. Sadness at stepping back from the business she'd nurtured, excitement about new opportunities in Florida, and pride in the capable team she'd built.

"What about Beth?" Nell asked suddenly, during a lull in the conversation. "Have you told her you're moving yet?"

The question hit a tender spot. "Not yet," Lauren admitted. "That's... a difficult conversation I'm still preparing for."

Brian and Nell exchanged looks; they knew how close Lauren was to her sister.

"She'll understand," Nell said gently. "Family comes first."

"I hope so," Lauren replied. "But she's so rooted here now, with the orchard, and Gabriel's furniture-making business. But she's the only sister who won't be in Florida." She sighed. "It feels like I'm abandoning her."

"You're supporting your daughter's future," Brian reminded her. "Beth will see that. I'm sure your brothers, Michael and Christopher will still be close."

Lauren nodded and then looked at Nell. "But it's not the same as having a sister to talk to."

Nell smiled. "Michael's wife and Becca will fill those rolls. Just think how it's been for Sarah living in Sanibel, but your family adjusted and you've remained close. You Wheelers don't let anything get in the way of your connection to one another. I don't think anything could ever get in the way of that."

Lauren agreed though uncertainty lingered. The business aspects of the move were manageable—paperwork, procedures, organizational charts. The emotional landscape was far more complex.

"We should celebrate," Nell declared, changing the subject. "This is a big moment for all of us. Dinner at Franklin's tonight? Partners meeting, official business expense." She winked.

"I'd like that, but let's plan for tomorrow night. I want to talk to Beth in person so I may have to drive to Boxford."

"Sounds good," Brian said.

As they moved on to reviewing current listings and the day's appointments, Lauren felt a weight lift from her shoulders. This part, at least, had gone better than expected. The business would continue to thrive under Nell and Brian's capable management.

Now she just needed to find the right words to tell her sister that after years of building their lives in parallel, their paths were finally diverging.

Beth, who had walked away from a prestigious legal career to put down roots in New England soil, would soon be the only Wheeler sister not basking in Florida sunshine.

That conversation would be far more difficult than this one had been. But as Lauren had learned through years of challenges, the hardest conversations were often the most necessary ones.

The business would adapt and grow. The question was whether her relationship with Beth would do the same.

CHAPTER 21

*B*eth stood in the middle of the heritage apple orchard section, hands on her hips, frustration evident in every line of her body. The morning sun filtered through the gnarled branches of trees that had been producing fruit for over a century, casting dappled shadows across the three figures engaged in what was becoming an increasingly tense conversation.

"All I'm saying is that we should prioritize the commercial varieties this season," Beth insisted, gesturing toward the larger section of the orchard where newer trees grew in orderly rows. "We have limited resources, and those trees will produce marketable fruit sooner."

Gabriel shook his head, not even looking up from the soil sample he was examining. "That's short-term thinking, Beth. These heritage trees are what will set us apart in the market. They need our attention now if they're going to produce at all this season."

"I understand the appeal of heirloom varieties, but we need income," Beth countered. "The mortgage doesn't care about agricultural heritage."

"If we become just another orchard producing the same apples as everyone else, we'll never establish ourselves," Gabriel replied with the same patient tone that had been grating on Beth's nerves all morning—as if he were explaining something simple to someone who couldn't grasp the basics. "The market is saturated with Honeycrisps and Galas."

Thomas Walker knelt nearby, carefully pruning a branch from one of the oldest trees. His weathered hands moved with practiced efficiency, though his attention was clearly divided between the task and the brewing argument between his son and daughter-in-law.

"We need a balance," Beth tried again. "I'm not saying abandon the heritage section, just prioritize where our limited labor and resources go. I've run the numbers, and—"

"That's the problem right there," Gabriel interrupted, standing up and dusting soil from his hands. "You can't reduce an orchard to spreadsheets and projections. These trees don't follow neat timelines or profit margins."

Beth felt her cheeks flush with anger. "So my business experience is worthless here? Is that what you're saying?"

"I'm saying orcharding isn't like practicing law. Sometimes you have to trust intuition and experience over data."

"Your intuition. Your experience," Beth clarified, her voice cooling. "Not mine."

Thomas cleared his throat, finally intervening. "Why don't we take a break? I could use some water." His calm voice cut through the tension, a practiced mediator's technique.

Gabriel seemed to suddenly realize how dismissive he'd sounded. "Beth, I didn't mean—"

"It's fine," she cut him off, pulling off her gardening gloves. "I have to make some calls anyway. Legal expertise may not be relevant to orchard management, but apparently, I still have value as the business administrator."

She turned and walked briskly toward the farmhouse, aware

she was being overly sensitive but unable to temper her reaction. This had been happening more frequently in the weeks since Thomas arrived—Gabriel and his father falling into seamless collaboration while Beth increasingly felt like an outsider in what was supposed to be a shared dream.

Inside the kitchen, she poured herself a glass of water, trying to cool her frustration. She understood Gabriel's passion for the heritage varieties—it was one of the things she loved about him, his dedication to preserving agricultural history. But his dismissal of her practical concerns was becoming a pattern, not an isolated incident.

Her phone rang, providing a welcome distraction. Lauren's name flashed on the screen.

"Perfect timing," Beth answered. "I was about to call and see if you wanted to have lunch this week."

"Great minds," Lauren replied. "I actually needed to talk to you about something. Are you free today?"

Something in her sister's tone caught Beth's attention. "Everything okay?"

"Yes, just... a lot going on. I'd rather discuss it in person."

Beth glanced out the window where Gabriel and Thomas were deep in conversation, heads bent together over a tree branch. Another day of feeling peripheral to orchard decisions stretched before her.

"Actually, why don't I drive down to your place?" Beth suggested. "Thomas and Gabriel are in full orchard mode today, and I could use a change of scenery."

"That would be perfect," Lauren said, relief evident in her voice. "The kids are with Jeff at Olivia's practice, so we'll have the house to ourselves."

"I'll leave in twenty minutes. See you soon."

After a quick change of clothes and an equally quick explanation to Gabriel—who merely nodded distractedly, confirming her sense of redundancy—Beth was in her car, windows down, enjoying the simple freedom of movement away from the farm.

The drive to Lauren's suburban home took just under an hour, time Beth used to clear her head and gain perspective. By the time she pulled into her sister's driveway, her irritation had mellowed to a more manageable simmer.

Lauren greeted her with a hug at the door. "Thank you for coming. I made that spinach dip you like."

"With the sourdough bread? You're a saint." Beth followed her sister into the kitchen, immediately noticing the tension in Lauren's shoulders. "Okay, what's going on? You're doing that thing where you try to look casual but you're actually stressed."

Lauren laughed nervously. "That obvious, huh?"

"To me, yes. Spill it."

Instead of answering immediately, Lauren busied herself with arranging food on a tray. "Let's sit outside. It's too nice to be indoors."

They settled on Lauren's back patio, a comfortably furnished space overlooking a yard where evidence of three active children was everywhere—a soccer ball, a scattered set of sidewalk chalk, a half-constructed fort in the corner.

After they'd each taken a few bites, Lauren set down her plate. "We've made a decision," she said finally. "About Olivia's tennis academy offer."

Beth felt a flutter of unease. "And?"

"We're accepting. Which means we're moving to Florida at the end of the summer."

Though she'd suspected this was coming, the confirmation still hit Beth with unexpected force. "Florida," she repeated. "All of you? Not just Olivia?"

Lauren nodded. "She's twelve, Beth. We can't send her alone, and the boarding option..." She shook her head. "That's not right for her, not yet."

"So you're uprooting your entire family for a tennis program?" The words came out sharper than Beth intended.

"It's more than that," Lauren said carefully. "It's an elite opportunity for Olivia, yes, but it's also..." She hesitated. "It would put us closer to Mom. To Grandma Sarah. To Sarah and her kids."

Understanding dawned on Beth. "I've always known you'd follow Mom to Florida," she said quietly. "You've been lost without her near ever since she left five years ago."

Lauren flinched slightly. "That's not fair."

"Isn't it?" Beth countered. "Every holiday, every family celebration, the conversation always turns to when you're visiting Captiva next. You've had one foot out the door since Mom moved."

"That's not true. We've built a life here. Jeff's been happy with the children, my business has thrived. But things change, Beth. Opportunities arise."

"Convenient opportunities that happen to take you exactly where you've wanted to go all along."

Lauren set down her glass with deliberate care. "I didn't ask you here to be judged."

Beth immediately regretted her tone. "I'm sorry. That was unfair."

"No, it wasn't entirely wrong," Lauren admitted after a moment. "I have missed Mom. And there's something about Captiva—the light, the pace, the sense of connection to something larger than everyday stress. When this opportunity for Olivia came up, it felt like... permission somehow. To make a change we've been considering anyway."

"What about Phillips Realty?" Beth asked, steering toward practical matters. "The business you've spent a decade building?"

Lauren explained her plan with Nell and Brian, the proposed expansion to Florida, the careful financial considerations she and Jeff had worked through.

"You've really thought this through," Beth said when she finished.

"We have. It's not just about Olivia or about Mom. It's about what makes sense for our family at this stage of our lives." Lauren reached across the table to take Beth's hand. "I know what you're thinking—that you'll be the only one left here."

"The thought had occurred to me," Beth admitted dryly.

"We'll come back for visits. The orchard in autumn is spectacular, and the kids love seeing the apple harvest. And you can come to Florida—not just for holidays but anytime. We'll have plenty of room."

Beth nodded, though the prospect of becoming the family member everyone visited occasionally felt hollow compared to the easy proximity they'd enjoyed for years.

"I'm happy for you," she said, meaning it despite the complicated emotions swirling beneath. "If this is what you want, what your family needs, then you should do it."

"But?" Lauren prompted, knowing her sister too well.

"But I'll miss you. Terribly." Beth's voice caught slightly. "And I'm a little envious, if I'm honest."

Lauren looked surprised. "Of moving to Florida?"

"Of your certainty," Beth clarified. "You know what you want, what's right for your family. I thought I did too, but lately..." She trailed off, thinking of the morning's argument.

"Trouble in orchard paradise?" Lauren asked gently.

Beth sighed. "Gabriel and his father are in perfect sync about everything orchard-related, which would be wonderful if it didn't leave me feeling completely superfluous. Every suggestion I make gets overruled or explained away as if I'm a well-meaning amateur who doesn't understand the complexities of apple growing."

"Have you talked to Gabriel about it?"

"I've tried. He says I'm being overly sensitive, that he values my input. But then the next decision comes along, and suddenly it's all about tradition and intuition and things I couldn't possibly understand without having grown up around apple trees."

Lauren considered this. "It sounds like you need to find your own role at the orchard—something that's distinctly yours, not territory where Gabriel and Thomas naturally dominate."

"Like what? Apple-themed legal services?" Beth's attempt at humor fell flat even to her own ears.

"Maybe. Or maybe something completely different. The farm stand? Educational programs? An event space for weddings and parties? I don't know the specifics, but there must be aspects of running an orchard that could benefit from your particular skills."

Beth hadn't considered approaching the problem that way—carving out her own domain rather than trying to be heard in areas where Gabriel and Thomas clearly felt most confident.

"That's... actually helpful," she admitted. "I've been so focused on making them hear me in their territory that I haven't considered establishing my own."

Lauren smiled. "That's my Beth—always trying to win on someone else's playing field when you could be creating your own game."

They sat in companionable silence for a moment, the earlier tension dissipating.

"I really am happy for you," Beth said finally. "And a little jealous that you'll get to see Mom whenever you want."

"She misses you too, you know. She's just better at respecting your decision to stay here than she is at hiding her wish that we were all in Florida."

"I know." Beth sighed. "But this is home now. Despite the challenges, I love our life here. The seasons, the community, the work—even when Gabriel drives me crazy. I can't imagine leaving it."

"Then don't." Lauren squeezed her hand. "This isn't an ultimatum or a competition. We're just following different paths, but we're still sisters. Nothing changes that."

"Sisters," Beth repeated thoughtfully. "Mom told me something her friend, Isabelle, said. 'Sisters, whether born of the same blood or found in the journey of life, are like the different threads in a tapestry. Alone, each is beautiful—but woven together, they create something far more magnificent.'"

"That's beautiful," Lauren said softly. "And true."

"I think she was talking about her friendship with Maggie and Chelsea, but it applies to us too. Even with miles between us, we're still part of the same tapestry."

Lauren's eyes glistened with unexpected tears. "I was so afraid you'd be angry."

"I'm sad," Beth admitted. "But not angry. Never that. You and your family needs to do what's right for you, just as mine does."

As they continued talking through the details of Lauren's move—the timeline, the logistics, the plans for staying connected —Beth felt a curious sense of clarity beginning to form about her own situation. Perhaps the tension with Gabriel wasn't just about apple trees or differing approaches to business. Perhaps it was about finding her own place, her own purpose within the shared dream they'd committed to.

That evening, driving back to the orchard with the windows down and the summer air flowing through the car, Beth felt lighter despite the news of her sister's impending departure. Lauren's move was inevitable in many ways—the pull of family, of sunshine, of new opportunities too strong to resist.

Beth's path lay elsewhere, rooted in New England soil. The challenge now was to find her unique contribution to the orchard's future—something that utilized her strengths rather than highlighting the knowledge gap between her and the Walker men. Something that would make the farm truly theirs, not just Gabriel's family legacy that she happened to share.

As she turned onto the long drive leading to the farmhouse,

she saw Gabriel and Thomas on the porch, deep in conversation over what looked like old maps of the property. Instead of irritation, she felt a new determination. Tomorrow, she would start carving out her own territory—not in competition with their expertise, but complementary to it.

Different threads in the same tapestry. Each beautiful alone, but magnificent together.

CHAPTER 22

*B*eth pulled into the driveway of the Wheeler family home, a sense of familiarity washing over her as it always did. The two-story colonial and cheerful blue shutters had been the backdrop to her entire childhood—from scraped knees and homework struggles to prom photos and graduation celebrations. After their father Daniel's death and their mother Maggie's move to Captiva, Beth had lived here alone for nearly two years before Christopher and Becca moved in, wanting to set down roots for their future family.

Now, with the hanging flower baskets Becca had added and the ramp Christopher had built along the side of the porch after his return from Iraq, it was still unmistakably the Wheeler family home, but with the distinct touches of its new caretakers.

Beth gathered the canvas bag containing the homemade chicken soup and freshly baked bread she'd prepared that morning. Simple offerings, but she knew from experience that practical help meant more to new parents than extravagant gestures.

As she approached the front door, it swung open before she could knock. Christopher stood there, balancing Eloise against his shoulder with practiced ease despite the prosthetic leg that occasionally threw off his center of gravity.

"I heard you pull up," he explained, stepping back to let her in. "Sharp-eared little miss here was just dozing off, but apparently the sound of her favorite aunt's car is worth waking up for."

Beth smiled, setting down her bag to reach for her niece. "Hello, sweet girl," she cooed as Christopher carefully transferred the baby to her arms. "How's our miracle doing today?"

Eloise blinked drowsily, her tiny hand escaping the swaddle to wave in a random pattern that Beth chose to interpret as a greeting. At almost five weeks old she was still impossibly small but had filled out noticeably since coming home from the NICU. The dark curls on her head had grown thicker, and her eyes, now definitively revealed as Becca's deep blue, seemed more alert and focused each time Beth visited.

"She's been cluster feeding all morning," Christopher reported, leading the way into the living room where the evidence of new parenthood was everywhere—burp cloths draped over furniture, a portable bassinet positioned near the couch, a half-empty bottle of water and several granola bar wrappers on the coffee table.

"I hope the baby isn't getting granola bars," Beth teased.

"Funny. No, it's the best I can do to eat while taking care of this little one in shifts. Becca finally fell asleep about twenty minutes ago. I figured I'd let her rest while I handle the princess."

Beth settled into the familiar armchair by the window, adjusting Eloise against her chest. The weight of the baby, slight as she was, centered her somehow, providing a focal point amid the swirling demands of her own life.

"Where do you want this?" she asked, nodding toward the bag of food she'd brought.

"Kitchen's fine," Christopher replied, reaching for the bag. "Soup, I'm guessing? You're an angel. We've been surviving on whatever Lauren drops off and whatever I can manage to microwave one-handed."

As he disappeared into the kitchen, Beth gazed down at Eloise, marveling as she always did at the miracle of this tiny person who had fought so hard to be here. Whatever stress or worry she carried seemed to recede in the presence of her niece, perspective restored by the simple, profound reality of new life.

"You're good for my soul, you know that?" she whispered to the baby, who responded by making a surprisingly loud sucking noise against her fist. "I see you've got your priorities straight. Food first, existential comfort second."

Christopher returned with two mugs of coffee, setting one on the side table near Beth before lowering himself carefully to the couch. Even after four years, Beth still found herself tracking the subtle adjustments he made to accommodate the prosthetic—the slightly wider stance when standing, the careful distribution of weight when sitting. He'd become so adept at managing it that most people who didn't know him wouldn't notice, but Beth had been there through the grueling rehabilitation, the phantom pain, the frustration and dark days of adapting to life with part of his leg gone.

"So," he said, studying her over the rim of his mug. "You going to tell me what's going on, or do I have to drag it out of you?"

Beth blinked, startled by the direct approach. "What makes you think something's going on?"

Christopher gave her a look that clearly communicated he wasn't buying her deflection. "Because I know that face. It's the same one you wore when you realized the truth about Dad. The 'I'm carrying the weight of the world but don't want to bother anyone about it' Beth special."

She sighed, acknowledging the accuracy of his assessment with a slight nod. Sometimes having a brother who knew you better than you knew yourself was a blessing; other times, like now, it was distinctly inconvenient.

"It's nothing I can't handle," she said finally. "And you and Becca have enough on your plate with Eloise. The last thing you need is my problems added to the mix."

"Try again," Christopher replied, unimpressed. "First of all, Becca's asleep, so this is just between us. Second, you've been showing up here often to help with Eloise, bringing food, doing laundry, basically being our lifeline while we figure out this parenting thing. If you think I'm not going to return the favor by listening when something's obviously eating at you, you don't know me very well."

Beth looked down at Eloise, who had drifted back to sleep against her chest, tiny eyelids fluttering with dreams. "Well, I guess we can start with the orchard and Gabriel. And Gabriel's dad moving back from California. Nothing crisis-level."

"Thomas is back?" Christopher's eyebrows rose in surprise. "Since when?"

"Three days ago. Gabriel picked him up from Logan." Beth adjusted Eloise slightly, buying time as she decided how much to share. "He's staying with us, at least for now. He's helping us with the orchard which I can't complain about. It was his at one time after all. Who would know the land better than he does?"

Christopher studied his sister's face, reading the complex emotions she was trying to conceal. "And that's... not good?"

"No, it's great, actually," Beth said quickly—too quickly. "He knows the orchard inside and out. He's already identified issues we've been struggling with for weeks and proposed solutions. It's exactly what we need right now, with harvest coming up and the new plantings requiring so much attention."

"Uh-huh," Christopher nodded slowly. "So if it's so great, why do you look like someone just told you they're canceling Christmas?"

The direct question, delivered with Christopher's characteristic blend of bluntness and affection, broke through Beth's carefully maintained composure. She sighed, the weight of months of accumulated stress pressing down on her.

"It's not Thomas," she admitted. "It's... everything. The orchard is so much more work than we anticipated, and the money's going out faster than it's coming in. Gabriel's furniture commissions are keeping us afloat, but he's stretched so thin trying to balance both businesses. And I've been trying to be here for you and Becca and Eloise, which means less time at the orchard, which means more pressure on Gabriel, which means..."

"Bethy, why didn't you say something? Becca and I can handle things here. You need to take care of things at home. I'd hate to be the reason you and Gabriel can't fix things."

Beth shook her head. "No. It's not this. Honest, I'm just…"

"Trouble in paradise?" Christopher suggested gently when she trailed off.

Beth looked up, meeting her brother's understanding gaze. "We're not communicating like we used to," she said, the admission painful but necessary. "We're like ships passing in the night —he's in the workshop until all hours finishing commissions, I'm up early to handle orchard tasks before coming here, we're both exhausted when we finally do see each other. And now with Thomas there..."

"Complicated." Christopher nodded. "Extra person in the house, shifting dynamics, the whole father-son thing."

"Exactly." Beth was grateful for her brother's quick understanding. "Thomas is going to be a huge help with the orchard, but it changes things between Gabriel and me. We're used to making decisions together, just the two of us. Now there's this third voice—an expert voice, with decades more experience than either of us. It's really five of us with his brother James and his wife. We all decided to run the orchard together. And that's another issue."

"What do you mean?"

"Gabriel and I are doing most of the work. Julia is busy with

Willow so I understand why she sometimes can't help, but James? I don't understand, and Gabriel doesn't seem interested in addressing the problem. He's non-confrontational."

Christopher laughed. "Unlike you who has to look problems in the eye and do battle until it's resolved. Must you climb every mountain put in front of you?"

Beth chuckled. "You know me so well, I'm thinking that's not a good thing."

"What I think is going on is that you're worried about being sidelined," Christopher guessed.

Beth considered this, trying to articulate her concerns precisely. "Not exactly sidelined. More... I'm worried that having Thomas there makes it too easy for Gabriel and me to avoid addressing our actual issues. We can focus on the practical orchard problems, let Thomas take the lead there, and never get around to talking about what's happening between us."

Christopher nodded, understanding in his eyes. "The classic Wheeler avoidance technique. You're the only family member who isn't afflicted, I can't say the same about Gabriel though. He's probably more the type to ask why have a difficult conversation about feelings when there's physical work to be done instead?"

"Exactly," Beth responded.

"So what are you going to do about it?" Christopher asked after a moment, his tone gentler.

Beth sighed, looking down at Eloise who slept peacefully, blissfully unaware of adult complications. "I don't know. There never seems to be the right time for the conversations we need to have. There's always something more urgent—irrigation problems, furniture deadlines, family obligations."

"There's never a perfect time," Christopher observed, shifting slightly to accommodate his prosthetic. "Trust me on this. If Becca and I had waited for the 'right time' to address issues, we'd still be dancing around the big stuff from when I first came home from Iraq."

Beth nodded, remembering those difficult months after Christopher's injury. He'd returned from his third deployment missing part of his left leg below the knee, the result of an IED explosion that had killed two members of his unit. The physical recovery had been grueling, but the psychological adjustment had been even more challenging. His relationship with Becca was a challenge, to say the least. Their relationship had been severely tested by his depression, anger, and initial refusal to accept help.

"You two got through it," Beth said softly. "Even when it seemed impossible."

"We did," Christopher agreed. "But not by waiting for the perfect moment to talk. Becca basically cornered me one night after a particularly bad physical therapy session and said either we start being honest with each other or she was walking away. Said she hadn't signed up for a relationship with a martyr."

Beth smiled slightly, easily imagining Becca—pragmatic, compassionate, but utterly unwilling to accept bullshit—delivering that ultimatum. "Sounds like Becca."

"It was exactly what I needed," Christopher admitted. "Someone who cared enough to call me on things but loved me enough to stick around while I figured it out. It certainly didn't hurt that a certain sister of mine helped her confront me." He studied his sister over his coffee mug.

Beth laughed. "Well, I might have had something to do with it."

Christopher smiled. "Gabriel's a good man, Beth. But even good men need a kick in the pants sometimes."

Beth nodded, acknowledging the truth in her brother's words. Gabriel wasn't deliberately avoiding difficult conversations—he was simply doing what came naturally to him, focusing on the practical problems he could solve rather than the emotional complexities he found more challenging.

"I'll figure it out," she said, kissing Ellie's forehead.

A sound from upstairs indicated Becca was awake and moving around. Christopher glanced toward the ceiling, then back at his sister.

"Look, for what it's worth, I think Thomas moving back might be exactly what you and Gabriel need," he said. "Not just for the practical help with the orchard, but because it creates space for you two to focus on your relationship. Let him take some of the burden, be strategic about using the time that frees up."

"That... actually makes sense," Beth acknowledged, turning the idea over in her mind. "I've been seeing his presence as potentially complicating things, but maybe it's an opportunity instead."

"Exactly. Instead of 'now we have to manage Thomas plus everything else,' think of it as 'Thomas is handling X, which means Gabriel and I can prioritize Y.'" Christopher smiled wryly. "Where Y equals having actual conversations about your marriage and future, not just squeezing in another orchard task."

Beth laughed. "Leave it to you to have a mathematical solution to my problems. Remember how bad I was at math growing up?"

Christopher laughed. "Bad? I don't think the word bad covers it. It amazes me that you graduated high school and college, let alone law school."

"Very funny. I just assumed I'd never need any of that stuff in real life, but here I am, sitting in your living room having a conversation about Xs and Ys."

"Let's just hope the fate of your marriage doesn't depend on your math skills. If it does, then you're doomed."

CHAPTER 23

*T*he sound of footsteps on the stairs announced Becca's approach. She appeared in the doorway, hair tousled from sleep, wearing what looked like one of Christopher's t-shirts over yoga pants. Despite the casual attire and evident fatigue, there was a glow about her—the particular radiance of new motherhood that transcended physical exhaustion.

"Beth," she said warmly, crossing to kiss her sister-in-law's cheek. "I thought I heard your voice. Sorry I was asleep when you arrived."

"Don't apologize," Beth insisted. "Sleep when the baby sleeps—isn't that the first rule of newborn survival?"

"So they tell me," Becca agreed with a tired smile. "Though Eloise seems to have her own interpretation of that rule." She peered at her daughter, still sleeping peacefully against Beth's chest. "Of course she's angelic for her aunt. For her parents, it's all cluster feeding and diaper explosions."

"Just proving she's got good taste already," Beth replied, carefully transferring the baby back to Becca, who settled into the spot beside Christopher on the couch. The three of them there—Christopher, Becca, tiny Eloise—formed such a perfect tableau of family that Beth felt her chest tighten with an emotion she couldn't quite name. Pride in her brother who had overcome so much to reach this point of contentment? Joy for Becca who had navigated the terrors of premature birth with such grace? Or perhaps a tinge of envy for the evident partnership between them, the seamless way they worked together, even in the chaos of new parenthood?

"Beth brought soup," Christopher reported, his arm settling naturally around Becca's shoulders. "And that applesauce Eloise will be eating in about five months."

"You're an angel," Becca said fervently. "Between you and Lauren, we might actually avoid scurvy. My cooking skills have completely abandoned me since we brought Eloise home."

"It's the least I can do," Beth replied. "You two have enough on your plate right now."

Becca studied her face, much as Christopher had earlier. "And how are things at the orchard? Christopher mentioned you've had some irrigation issues."

Beth hesitated, not wanting to burden Becca with her concerns when the new mother clearly had her hands full. But Christopher caught her eye over Becca's head, giving a slight nod of encouragement.

"Actually, we've had some developments," Beth said, making the decision to be more open. "Gabriel's father has moved back from California. He's staying with us for now, helping with the orchard management."

"Thomas is back?" Becca's eyebrows rose in surprise. "That's... significant. How's Gabriel handling it?"

"It's an adjustment," Beth replied, choosing her words carefully. "Thomas has decades of experience with the orchard, so his input is invaluable. But it changes the dynamic, having him there."

"I can imagine," Becca said, her medical training evident in her perceptive assessment. "It can't be easy navigating that father-son relationship in a professional context, especially when you're all living under the same roof."

"No, it's not," Beth acknowledged, finding it oddly liberating to admit this aloud. "We're figuring it out as we go. The practical help is a godsend, but the personal aspects are... complicated."

Christopher shot her an approving look, clearly pleased that she was being more forthcoming about her situation. Becca shifted Eloise to her shoulder, patting the baby's back gently as she considered Beth's words.

"When my dad visits, it takes at least three days before we stop walking on eggshells around each other," she offered. "And that's just for a week or two, not a permanent arrangement. I can't imagine how much more complex it must be when business decisions are involved too."

Beth felt a wave of gratitude for Becca's understanding, for the absence of platitudes or easy reassurances. "Exactly. Thomas means well, and we genuinely need his expertise. It's just... it shifts the balance of everything. Gabriel and I were just finding our rhythm with the orchard, making our own decisions, and now there's this third voice with far more experience than either of us."

"Have you talked to Gabriel about how you're feeling?" Becca asked gently.

Beth shook her head, a rueful smile tugging at her lips. "Not really. There's never enough time or energy for those conversations lately. We're both so focused on keeping everything afloat."

"Been there," Christopher interjected. "Right after my medical discharge, when I was trying to figure out what came next. Becca and I were like ships passing in the night—her with her medical school schedule, me with physical therapy and veterans' affairs appointments."

"How did you break the cycle?" Beth asked, genuinely curious.

Christopher and Becca exchanged a look laden with shared history. "We crashed and burned first," Becca admitted. "Had a fight so epic the neighbors probably considered calling the police."

"I still maintain that was a necessary catharsis," Christopher added, a hint of humor in his voice despite the serious topic.

"It was," Becca agreed. "But I wouldn't necessarily recommend that approach. What actually helped was what came after—we started scheduling time specifically for us. Not for errands or practical matters, but just to be together, check in with each other."

"Like a date night?" Beth asked skeptically. "Gabriel and I can barely find time to eat dinner together most nights, let alone go out."

"Doesn't have to be elaborate," Christopher explained. "For us, it was Sunday mornings. No matter what, from eight to ten, we had breakfast together and talked. No phones, no distractions, just... reconnecting."

"The content of the conversation wasn't even always deep," Becca added. "Sometimes it was just catching up on each other's weeks, sharing small victories or frustrations. But the consistency mattered—knowing that space was protected, that we'd have that time no matter what else was happening."

Beth considered this, trying to imagine where such protected time might fit into their current chaotic schedule. "With Thomas there to help with the orchard, maybe we could actually make something like that work," she mused. "Sunday mornings are usually quiet—the irrigation system runs on automatic, and no deliveries or pickups are scheduled."

"There you go," Christopher said encouragingly. "Start small, be consistent. The orchard and the furniture business are important, but so is your marriage. It deserves at least as much intentional attention as you give to your work."

The simple statement, delivered without judgment or lecture, hit home. Beth nodded, acknowledging its truth. She and Gabriel had been pouring their energy into their businesses, into supporting family through various crises, into addressing the endless practical demands of each day. Their relationship had been left to sustain itself on shared history and assumed commitment, without the regular nourishment of focused attention.

"You're right," she said, making the decision. "I'll talk to Gabriel tonight, suggest we set aside that time."

"Good," Christopher approved. "And don't let him wriggle out of it with furniture deadlines or orchard emergencies. Channel your inner Beth Wheeler stubbornness—the same determination that got you through law school while working full-time."

Beth laughed, recognizing her brother's accurate assessment of her character. "I'll do my best drill sergeant impression if necessary."

"That's my girl," Christopher grinned.

"In the meantime, there's something else. Did you know that Lauren and Jeff are moving to Florida?"

"What? Are you sure?"

Beth nodded. "Yup. I talked to her about it yesterday. Olivia's been accepted into a tennis training camp starting in September. They're moving fast and expect to leave by the end of the summer."

Christopher looked at Becca and then back at Beth.

"What?" Beth asked. "Is there something more?"

Becca shook her head. "I'm not surprised about Lauren and Jeff moving, but what Chris is thinking about is our recent conversation about us moving back to Captiva."

"No. You guys can't leave. It's bad enough Lauren is going, most of my family will be gone."

"It wouldn't be for at least another year anyway, Beth," Chris said, trying to calm his sister.

"That's right. I've got another year of medical school to get through. It's just I miss my family and I'd hate to have Ellie grow up not knowing her grandfather and uncles."

"So, you'd be a pediatrician in Florida?" Beth asked.

Becca shrugged, "Eventually. What I'd like to do is request a residency in Florida. I'm looking into it now."

Eloise chose that moment to wake fully, announcing her hunger with a surprisingly loud wail for such a tiny person. Becca carried her to the sofa.

"I should leave you two," Beth said, rising from her chair. "Let me know if you need anything else this week. Gabriel's father being back means I might actually have a bit more flexibility in my schedule."

"See? Silver linings," Christopher observed. "And Beth? Take your own advice, the same you've been giving me about asking for help with Eloise. You don't have to handle everything alone."

"I'll try to remember that," Beth promised, gathering her bag. "It's just not always easy to practice what you preach."

"Tell me about it," Christopher agreed ruefully. "Do as I say, not as I do—the Wheeler family motto."

Beth bent to kiss Eloise's downy head, then hugged both Christopher and Becca goodbye. As she headed toward her car, she couldn't tell if she felt better or worse. Her family was changing again, and it felt as if the world shifted beneath her feet, leaving her unbalanced and lost.

She wanted to cry but took a deep breath instead.

The drive back to the orchard gave her time to think, to strategize how she would approach Gabriel about carving out designated time for their relationship. She was under no illusions that a single conversation would address all the strain that had been building between them, but it could be a start—an acknowledgment that their marriage deserved the same care and attention they gave to their businesses and extended family.

As she turned onto the county road that led to Walker Orchards, Beth felt a renewed sense of purpose. The challenges they faced—financial pressures, the complexities of working with Thomas, the demands of building a family business hadn't changed. But perhaps their approach to navigating them could.

Family had always been the cornerstone of Beth's life, the foundation from which she drew strength. Today, her brother had reminded her of that essential truth, not by solving her problems but by creating space for her to voice them, to recognize her own needs amid the clamor of everyone else's. Each member of the Wheeler family had forged a life on their own terms, and she was no different.

Regardless of the distance between them, her family would continue to be her true north, her rock no matter what she faced in the future.

It was time to do the same with Gabriel—to create protected space where they could reconnect, not just as business partners or orchard managers, but as husband and wife. They were building something meaningful and permanent, a family that began with two, but would one day be more than that.

Thomas's return, which she'd initially seen as a complication, might actually be the opportunity they needed to refocus on their relationship.

With that resolution firm in her mind, Beth drove the final stretch toward home, toward the difficult but necessary conversations that awaited, toward the man who was still—despite the strain and stress of recent months—the center of her chosen family.

CHAPTER 24

"*J*f my sister doesn't move out soon, I'm going to list her on eBay as a slightly used, moderately annoying collectible," Chelsea declared, kicking at the wet sand as she and Maggie made their way down to the beach. Their early morning walks had become a ritual over the years—a chance to solve the world's problems, or at least their own, before the rest of the island stirred.

Maggie laughed, nearly spilling her travel mug of coffee. "What do you think the starting bid would be?"

"Two dollars and a sympathy card for the buyer." Chelsea bent to pick up a perfect lightning whelk shell, examined it, and slipped it into her pocket. "Steven keeps saying I'm overreacting, but that's easy for him to say—he didn't grow up with Hurricane Gretchen."

"He does seem remarkably patient with her," Maggie observed. "Though I noticed him gritting his teeth when she complained that her room was too hot."

Chelsea sighed, pausing to let the gentle waves wash over her bare feet. "That's Steven. He's too kind to say anything, but I can tell it's wearing on him too. We've been married less than a year, and we've never actually lived alone together. Gretchen moved in three weeks after our honeymoon."

"And now she wants Steven's professional opinion on the café renovations," Maggie said, connecting the dots. "Which puts you right in the middle."

"Exactly. She and Isabelle have been meeting with him about the construction plans. Every time he suggests something might be structurally unsound or too expensive, Gretchen looks at me like I'm supposed to override my husband's professional opinion."

As they walked by The Mucky Duck, a pelican dive-bombed into the water several yards offshore, emerging with a fish wriggling in its beak.

"Show-off," Chelsea muttered at the bird.

"What does Steven say about the renovation plans?" Maggie asked, steering the conversation back.

"That the building needs more work than they initially thought. The electrical is ancient, the plumbing's a disaster, and there's evidence of termite damage in the back wall. Isabelle took it in stride acting like she was on an HGTV show."

Maggie adjusted her sun hat against the early morning breeze. "And you're caught in the crossfire."

"It's like being the referee in a match where one player doesn't understand the rules and the other is my husband." Chelsea shook her head. "I love my sister, but I forgot how exhausting her particular brand of chaos can be. I've always known she was the more practical sister compared to Tess and Leah, but now… I'm not so sure."

"Isabelle seems to manage her well," Maggie pointed out. "Maybe that's the real partnership miracle—not the café itself but finding someone who can actually work with her."

Chelsea snorted. "Isabelle has the patience of a saint after dealing with Sebastian's children. Gretchen probably seems refreshingly straightforward by comparison."

They reached their favorite spot—a relatively secluded stretch of beach marked by a distinctive twisted palm tree that had somehow survived decades of hurricanes. They placed their Tommy Bahama beach chairs on the sand and settled down to watch the water.

"So what are you going to do?" Maggie asked, passing Chelsea a napkin-wrapped scone from her bag.

Chelsea accepted the cranberry orange scone with a grateful nod. "About which disaster? My homeless sister, the café construction drama, or the fact that I didn't sign up for an eternal houseguest when I married Steven?"

"All of the above," Maggie replied with a smile. "Though let's start with the homeless sister situation."

"I've tried dropping hints. I've tried being direct. Last week, I even left rental listings on the kitchen counter. I knew buying Sebastian's cottage wasn't going to happen. She either genuinely doesn't understand that she's overstayed her welcome or she's deliberately ignoring me."

"Knowing Gretchen, it could be both," Maggie observed. "She's always had a convenient blind spot when it comes to boundaries."

Chelsea sighed, breaking off a piece of scone and watching a sandpiper dart along the shoreline. "The ironic thing is, now she actually has a purpose here—a real opportunity with the café. But that makes it harder to push her to move out when she's finally showing signs of putting down roots."

"Have you thought about suggesting she live above the café? I know Isabelle mentioned the possibility of renovating that space."

"That would be perfect, but Steven says it's not up to code for residential use yet. It would need significant work." Chelsea paused, then added, "Which is another thing Gretchen seems to think I should magically fix. As if marriage to a contractor means I can sidestep building regulations."

Maggie chuckled. "The Thompson family contractor discount doesn't extend quite that far."

"Don't I know it," Chelsea agreed with a rueful smile. "Though Steven has been incredibly generous with his time and expertise already."

"Sounds like you need to have two conversations," Maggie said thoughtfully. "One with Gretchen about moving out regardless of the café situation, and one with both Gretchen and Isabelle about the renovation reality check."

Chelsea groaned. "I was afraid you'd say that. Can't we just go with my eBay plan instead?"

"I'd bid at least five dollars," Maggie offered solemnly. "For friendship's sake."

"Such generosity," Chelsea replied, flicking a bit of sand at her friend. They both laughed, the tension momentarily broken.

A notification sound from Chelsea's phone interrupted their banter. She pulled it out, squinting at the screen in the morning light. "And the fun begins. Gretchen wants to know if we can meet at the café site at nine. Apparently, there's an 'urgent design crisis' that needs my input."

"Translation: Steven said no to something, and she wants you to overrule him," Maggie interpreted.

"Got it in one." Chelsea stood, brushing sand from her clothes. "Want to come? You're much better at diplomatic phrasing than I am."

"I wouldn't miss it," Maggie replied, gathering her things. "Besides, I need to check on Isabelle anyway. She's been doing remarkably well since Sebastian's death, but diving into business with Gretchen might be her way of avoiding grief rather than processing it."

"Sorry, I thought we'd have more time on the beach this morning," Chelsea said, extending a hand to help Maggie up. "Captiva's very own grief counselor and sister wrangler. Do you ever get tired of taking care of all of us?"

"Never," Maggie answered honestly. "Though I might need a vacation after we get through Gretchen's café launch and Lauren's moving plans."

They began walking back toward town, the island slowly coming to life around them as shops opened and early morning tourists ventured onto the beach.

"Speaking of Lauren's plans," Chelsea said, "have you told Grandma Sarah yet? I would think she'd be pleased."

Maggie's nodded. "I did yesterday. She listened to the whole explanation about Olivia's tennis academy, nodded thoughtfully, and then said, 'It's about time. That girl belongs here, not freezing half the year in Massachusetts.'"

"That sounds like Grandma Sarah," Chelsea laughed. "Always acting like she knew the plan all along."

"She also said, and I quote, 'Now we just need to work on Beth.'"

Chelsea shook her head. "Good luck with that. Beth is more rooted to New England soil than those apple trees she and Gabriel are so obsessed with."

"I know." Maggie sighed. "But a mother can dream. Can you imagine if all my children were within a short drive? I'd be in grandmother heaven."

"And they'd be in therapy," Chelsea teased. "Too much mother love all at once might overwhelm them after all these years of independence."

"You might be right," Maggie conceded with a smile. "But I'd risk it."

They reached the path that would take them off the beach and through the inn's garden. The morning had fully bloomed now, the island humming with activity.

"Nine o'clock at the café site," Chelsea confirmed. "Bring your diplomatic skills and possibly a tranquilizer dart for my sister."

"I'll bring scones instead," Maggie countered. "Food always helps diffuse tension. It's my secret weapon."

"In that case, bring a dozen," Chelsea advised. "We might need all the help we can get."

The storefront that would soon become Captiva Café looked considerably worse than it had the previous week. Steven's team had removed sections of drywall to expose the plumbing and electrical systems, leaving the space looking more like a demolition site than a future business.

Gretchen paced among the debris, gesturing animatedly as Isabelle examined a set of blueprints spread across a makeshift table of sawhorses and plywood. Steven stood to one side, his expression a careful mask of professional patience.

"—absolutely non-negotiable," Gretchen said as Chelsea and Maggie entered. "The espresso bar needs to be the focal point when customers walk in. It sets the tone for the entire experience."

"I understand that," Steven replied, his voice measured. "But moving the plumbing to accommodate that layout would add at least five thousand dollars to your budget, not including the structural beam we'd have to relocate."

Gretchen threw up her hands. "It's just pipes! How complicated can it be to move some water from one side of a room to another?"

Chelsea caught Steven's eye, noting the slight tightening around his mouth that indicated he was restraining himself from delivering a construction lecture that would likely go over Gretchen's head.

"Good morning," Chelsea said brightly, stepping into the fray. "I see you're making progress."

Isabelle looked up with evident relief. "Chelsea, Maggie— thank goodness. Perhaps you can help us reach a compromise."

"I've brought reinforcements," Maggie announced, holding up

a bakery box. "Cranberry orange scones and those chocolate croissants Isabelle likes."

"You're an angel," Isabelle said, setting down the blueprints to accept the box. "We could all use a moment to regroup, I think."

Gretchen didn't appear ready to regroup. "Chelsea, please tell your husband that the espresso bar placement is critical to the café's entire concept. It needs to be against that wall with the original exposed brick, not hidden in the corner like it's some shameful secret."

"I'm not suggesting hiding it," Steven corrected patiently. "I'm suggesting placing it where the existing plumbing can support it without requiring us to tear up the concrete foundation and potentially compromise the structural integrity of a century-old building."

"Ah," Maggie murmured to Chelsea. "I might need another dozen scones."

Chelsea ignored her friend's comment and surveyed the space, trying to see beyond the current chaos to its potential. "What about a compromise? Could we feature the espresso equipment prominently but keep it where the plumbing already exists?"

"That's what I've been suggesting," Steven said, while Gretchen simultaneously declared, "That defeats the entire purpose!"

Isabelle, who had been quietly examining the blueprints while the others argued, suddenly spoke up. "What if we created a false wall?"

Everyone turned to her.

"We keep the espresso bar where Steven suggests for practical reasons, but we create a decorative brick feature wall behind it that mirrors the original brick wall Gretchen loves. It would frame the barista station without requiring extensive plumbing relocation."

Steven considered this, then nodded slowly. "That could

work. We could use reclaimed brick to match the original, create a feature arch perhaps, with some custom lighting to highlight it."

"But it wouldn't be authentic," Gretchen protested, though with less conviction.

"In Paris," Isabelle replied, "the most beloved cafés combine authenticity with theater. This would be the perfect marriage of both—practical functionality with deliberate design."

Chelsea watched her sister's objection waver in the face of Isabelle's diplomatic framing. "It could be even more distinctive than just using the existing wall," she suggested, reinforcing Isabelle's idea. "A custom feature designed specifically for showcasing your coffee artistry."

Gretchen's resistance visibly crumpled. "I suppose if we added some vintage Italian coffee posters and the right pendant lighting..." She turned to Steven. "Could you design something like that?"

"I could draw up some options," he agreed, relief evident in his shoulders as the tension diffused.

Maggie caught Chelsea's eye and mouthed "Crisis averted" while distributing scones and croissants to everyone.

With the immediate conflict resolved, they all moved to gather around the blueprints, discussing other aspects of the renovation. Chelsea pulled Steven aside briefly.

"Thank you for being so patient," she murmured. "I know Gretchen can be... challenging."

He smiled, tucking a strand of hair behind her ear. "Runs in the family, that stubborn streak."

"Hey!" she protested with a laugh.

"It's one of the things I love about you," he assured her. "Though I admit I'm looking forward to eventually having our home back to ourselves."

Chelsea sighed. "You and me both. I need to have that conversation with her sooner rather than later."

"Preferably before I start redesigning our living room to

accommodate her growing collection of photography equipment," Steven agreed.

Across the room, Isabelle and Gretchen were deep in conversation about light fixtures, with Maggie occasionally offering suggestions. The easy way they worked together—Isabelle's calm practicality balancing Gretchen's creative enthusiasm—gave Chelsea hope that the partnership might actually succeed.

"So what's the actual timeline looking like now?" Chelsea asked, returning to business matters. "With all these additional structural issues you've found?"

Steven consulted his tablet. "Realistically? Three months minimum before you're ready for a soft opening. The electrical alone will take weeks to bring up to code, and that's before we address the termite damage."

Chelsea winced. "Gretchen was hoping for six weeks."

"Gretchen was also hoping to run a commercial espresso machine off wiring that probably dates back to when Edison was still arguing with Tesla," Steven pointed out. "Some things can't be rushed if you want them done safely and legally."

"You mean I can't just bat my eyelashes and get a contractor discount?" Chelsea teased, mimicking her sister's expectations.

"Your eyelash batting gets you many things, Mrs. Thompson," Steven replied with a grin, "but it doesn't make building inspectors look the other way."

Their moment was interrupted by Gretchen calling Chelsea's name. "You've got to see these light fixtures Isabelle found! They're exactly what I've been imagining."

Chelsea squeezed Steven's hand before rejoining the group. For the next hour, they discussed design elements, budget constraints, and scheduling, gradually forming a realistic plan that accommodated both Gretchen's vision and practical realities.

As the meeting wound down, Maggie pulled Chelsea aside. "Now might be a good time for that other conversation," she suggested quietly, nodding toward Gretchen who was photographing some of the original architectural details. "Isabelle and I can take Steven to see that salvage yard he's been wanting to check out for reclaimed materials."

Chelsea hesitated, then nodded. "You're right. No time like the present."

After Maggie orchestrated the departure of the others with her usual diplomatic efficiency, Chelsea found herself alone with her sister for the first time in days.

"I think it's really coming together," Gretchen said, reviewing the images on her camera. "Isabelle has an amazing eye for design. Did you see the espresso bar sketch she did? It's going to be stunning."

"It will be," Chelsea agreed, formulating her approach. "You two work well together."

"We do, don't we?" Gretchen looked up, her expression unusually serious. "I know what you're thinking—that this is just another of my temporary obsessions. But it's different this time, Chelsea. I'm committed to making this work."

The sincerity in her sister's voice made Chelsea's planned speech more difficult, but she pressed on. "I believe you, Gretchen. And I'm genuinely happy for you. This café could be exactly what you need."

"But?" Gretchen prompted, clearly sensing the unspoken qualifier.

Chelsea took a deep breath. "But Steven and I need our space back. It's time for you to find your own place to live."

Gretchen's expression fell slightly, though not with the shock Chelsea had anticipated. "Is it really that bad having me there?"

"It's not bad," Chelsea corrected carefully. "But Steven and I have been married for less than a year. We need time to establish our own household routines, our own patterns. We can't do that with a permanent houseguest, even one we love."

Gretchen was quiet for a moment, absently clicking through

photos on her camera. "I guess I have been there longer than I initially planned," she admitted finally.

"Three months longer," Chelsea confirmed, relieved that her sister wasn't immediately defensive.

"It's just..." Gretchen hesitated. "Every time I've tried to stand on my own, I've fallen flat on my face. My time in Key West, the CoiffeeShop with our sisters, even my photography business. I keep thinking the next venture will be different, but my track record isn't great."

The vulnerability in her sister's admission caught Chelsea off guard. "The café could be different," she suggested gently. "You have Isabelle as a partner this time, and she brings business experience and financial stability."

"That's true," Gretchen acknowledged. "And she seems to actually value my coffee expertise, even when I get overly passionate about seemingly small details."

"Like espresso bar placement?" Chelsea suggested with a smile.

Gretchen had the grace to look slightly sheepish. "I may have overreacted a bit. But in my defense, the customer's first impression is critical in the café business."

"So Steven tells me," Chelsea replied dryly. "Often. Usually around midnight when he's still redrawing plans to accommodate your latest inspiration."

Gretchen winced. "I have been demanding, haven't I?"

"Let's say 'particular' instead," Chelsea offered diplomatically. "But back to the housing situation—what are your thoughts about finding your own place?"

Gretchen sighed, setting her camera down on the makeshift table. "Honestly? Terrifying. Rents on Captiva are ridiculous, and I'm pouring most of my savings into the café startup costs."

"What about the space upstairs?" Chelsea suggested, gesturing toward the ceiling. "Steven mentioned it needs work, but it could eventually be converted to an apartment."

"He also said it would take months and thousands of dollars we don't have in the current budget," Gretchen pointed out. "Though it would be perfect eventually."

Chelsea considered this, formulating a compromise. "What if we agree to a timeline? You stay with us while you look for a temporary rental. Once the café is up and running and generating income, you and Isabelle can revisit the upstairs apartment renovation."

Gretchen looked thoughtful. "That's fair," she said finally. "More than fair, actually. I knew I was wearing out my welcome; I just kept avoiding thinking about it because the alternatives seemed so daunting."

"You haven't worn out your welcome," Chelsea corrected. "But it's time for a transition. And I'll help you find something reasonable for the interim."

Gretchen nodded, then surprised Chelsea by pulling her into a hug. "I'm sorry for being so oblivious. Sometimes I get so caught up in what I'm doing that I forget to consider how it affects everyone else."

"A lifelong Lawrence trait," Chelsea observed, returning the hug. "But one we're working on."

"Does this mean you'll still help with the café design decisions?" Gretchen asked as they separated.

"Of course," Chelsea assured her. "Though I draw the line at overruling Steven on structural issues. I like having a roof that doesn't collapse on customers."

"So picky," Gretchen teased, her usual buoyancy returning. "But I suppose safety is somewhat important in a successful business model."

"Somewhat," Chelsea agreed with a smile, relief washing through her at how well the conversation had gone. She had expected resistance, drama, perhaps even tears. This mature acceptance was a pleasant surprise.

"Only until I find a place," Gretchen confirmed. "Then I'm out of your newlywed hair. I owe you big time so you can expect family discounts on all future café purchases."

"Deal," Chelsea laughed, feeling as though a weight had lifted. Perhaps this time really was different. Perhaps Gretchen had finally found her path—both professionally and personally.

As they began gathering their things to leave, Chelsea's phone chimed with a text from Maggie: *Mission accomplished? Or should we stay away longer?*

Chelsea typed back quickly: *Coming home. Crisis averted. She's going to start looking for a place. The countdown begins.*

Miracles happen on Captiva, came Maggie's immediate reply. *Bringing celebratory key lime pie for dinner.*

With a smile, Chelsea tucked her phone away and helped her sister lock up the construction site. The challenges were far from over—three months of renovation, establishing a new business, finding Gretchen suitable housing—but for now, one hurdle had been cleared.

And on Captiva Island, sometimes that was victory enough for one day.

CHAPTER 25

*B*eth stood at the kitchen counter, carefully arranging fresh apple slices on a platter beside the cheese board she'd prepared. Charlie lay sprawled at her feet, occasionally thumping his tail when she glanced down at him.

"Are we having company?" Thomas asked, appearing in the doorway with a mug of coffee. His silver hair was tied back in its usual ponytail, and he'd already dressed for the day in work clothes, ready for whatever orchard tasks awaited.

"No," Beth replied, placing a sprig of rosemary for garnish. "Just breakfast."

Thomas raised an eyebrow. "Quite the elaborate breakfast for a regular Sunday morning."

Beth felt a blush creep up her neck. "Gabriel and I are trying something new. A dedicated time each week just for us, no orchard business allowed."

Understanding dawned on Thomas's face. "Ah. Smart move." He took a sip of his coffee, then added, "I'll make myself scarce."

"You don't have to leave the house or anything," Beth assured him, though she was grateful for his sensitivity. "We're just going to have breakfast on the porch. Talk. Reconnect."

"Still, I think I'll head into town. There's a farmers' market I've been meaning to check out." Thomas smiled. "Besides, it'll give me a chance to introduce myself to some of the other local growers. Make connections for the co-op idea I mentioned. Mind if I take the truck?"

Beth felt a rush of gratitude for her father-in-law's intuitive understanding. Since his arrival, Thomas had been unfailingly helpful with the orchard but had also displayed a surprising awareness of the need for boundaries. It was a trait Gabriel hadn't inherited in full measure.

"Not at all. Have a good time," she said.

Thomas nodded and turned to leave, then paused. "You know, Tori and I used to do something similar." His voice softened at the mention of his late wife. "Sunday evenings. We'd sit on the back deck with wine and watch the sunset over the orchard. No matter what else was happening—harvest, financial stress, Gabriel or James' teenage dramas—those hours were sacred."

"Did it help?" Beth asked, genuinely curious.

"Thirty-eight years of marriage before Alzheimer's took her," Thomas replied quietly. "So yes, I'd say it helped." With a gentle smile, he disappeared down the hallway.

Beth finished arranging the breakfast platter, adding honey in a small ceramic pot and freshly baked sourdough bread still warm from the oven. She'd risen early, unable to sleep with nervous energy about this planned time with Gabriel. The idea had seemed so straightforward when Christopher suggested it— set aside protected time to reconnect. But now, with the actual moment approaching, she found herself oddly anxious.

What if they had nothing to talk about besides work? What if the strain of recent months had created a distance they couldn't bridge with a simple breakfast ritual?

The sound of the shower turning off upstairs indicated Gabriel would be down soon. Beth took a deep breath, reminding herself that this wasn't a performance or a test. It was simply time—intentional, protected time to be together as husband and wife rather than business partners.

She carried the platter and a carafe of coffee out to the porch, where she'd already set the small table with linen napkins and the blue pottery dishes that had been a wedding gift from her mother. The morning air was cool but promised warmth later—a perfect early summer day in New England.

Gabriel appeared in the doorway, his light brown hair still damp from the shower, wearing jeans and a faded t-shirt Beth recognized as one of his favorites. His expression shifted from sleepy to surprised as he took in the arranged breakfast.

"What's all this?" he asked, gesturing to the spread.

"Breakfast," Beth replied, suddenly feeling awkward. "I thought... maybe we could eat out here. Together."

Gabriel smiled, the genuine smile that still made her heart skip even after almost four years together. "It looks amazing."

He settled into the chair across from her, reaching immediately for the coffee. Beth watched as he poured a cup, added a splash of cream, and took a long, appreciative sip before properly turning his attention to the food.

"So," he said, selecting a slice of apple and a piece of cheddar, "is this a special occasion I've forgotten?"

Beth shook her head. "Not exactly. I've been thinking about something Chris said when I visited last week."

"About the baby? How is little Eloise doing?"

"She's doing great," Beth assured him. "Getting stronger every day. But that's not what I wanted to talk about." She took a deep breath. "Chris mentioned how he and Becca make sure to set aside dedicated time for each other—not for baby care or practical matters, just to connect. And it made me realize that we haven't done that."

Gabriel's expression grew more serious. "You think we're disconnected?"

"I think we're busy," Beth clarified. "The orchard, your furniture commissions, my family obligations—we're constantly passing each other like ships in the night. When was the last time we had a real conversation that wasn't about irrigation systems, pest control or harvest projections?"

Gabriel was quiet for a moment, considering. "Fair point," he conceded, reaching for a piece of apple. "So this is...?"

"A start," Beth said. "I thought maybe we could make this a regular thing. Sunday mornings, just for us. No orchard talk allowed, no furniture deadlines, no family drama. Just... us."

Gabriel studied her face, his expression softening. "I'd like that."

Relief washed through Beth—she hadn't realized how tense she'd been about his reaction until she felt the knot in her chest loosen. "Really?"

"Really." He reached across the table to take her hand. "I've missed you, Bethy. Even though we see each other every day, I've missed *us*."

The simple acknowledgment brought unexpected tears to Beth's eyes. "Me too."

For a few minutes, they ate in silence, the tension that had been building between them for weeks noticeably easing. Charlie wandered over to join them, settling at Beth's feet with a contented sigh.

"So," Gabriel said eventually, "if we can't talk about the orchard or work, what should we talk about?"

Beth laughed. "Anything else. Books you're reading, things you're thinking about, places you'd like to visit someday."

"Places like where?" Gabriel asked, refilling their coffee cups.

"I don't know. Anywhere. We used to talk about traveling in the winter off-season. Remember when we first lived together, how we'd plan tips?"

Gabriel's face lit with recognition. "New Zealand. You wanted to go there during our winter, which would be their summer season."

"Exactly." Beth nodded, pleased he remembered. "Somewhere along the way, we got so caught up in the day-to-day struggles that we stopped talking about the bigger picture—about why we're doing all this in the first place."

"I'd still like to go to New Zealand," Gabriel said thoughtfully. "Maybe not this year, but eventually. Once we have the systems in place for someone else to manage things for a few weeks."

"Someone like your dad?" Beth suggested, then immediately regretted bringing Thomas into their protected conversation space.

Gabriel didn't seem to mind, though. "Maybe. He's certainly been a godsend these past couple of weeks." He paused, then asked carefully, "How are you feeling about having him here? Honestly?"

Beth considered the question, grateful for her husband's direct approach. "Better than I expected," she admitted. "When he first arrived, I worried he'd take over completely, or that you two would form this impenetrable father-son orchard alliance that left no room for my input."

"And now?" Gabriel prompted.

"Now I see that he's actually creating space for us rather than limiting it. He handles problems that would have consumed our entire evening. He steps back when decisions need to be made by us as owners." She smiled ruefully. "And he has an uncanny knack for making himself scarce when we need privacy."

"Like today." Gabriel nodded, glancing toward the empty driveway where his truck had been parked earlier.

"He mentioned that he and your mother used to do something similar," Beth said. "Sunday evenings, watching the sunset together. He said it was 'sacred time.'"

Gabriel's expression shifted, surprise and something like wonder crossing his features. "He talked about Mom?"

"Just briefly," Beth replied, understanding the significance.

Gabriel felt his father rarely spoke of her in the months following her death, as if the pain of her loss were still too raw to voice.

"Dad doesn't usually..." Gabriel trailed off, clearly moved. "That's good. That he could share that with you."

Beth reached across the table to take his hand again. "I think he approves of what we're trying to do here. Not just with the orchard, but with protecting our relationship in the midst of all the chaos."

Gabriel squeezed her fingers, his thumb tracing small circles on her palm—a familiar, intimate gesture that had been absent in recent weeks. "I'm sorry I've been so distant," he said quietly. "The financial pressure, the orchard concerns—I've been carrying it all like it was solely my responsibility, forgetting that we're supposed to be partners in this."

"It would help if you could get your brother to carry more of the load. Everything has been falling to us, which is normal since we live on the property, but…"

"I hear you. I've been thinking the same thing."

Gabriel studied their linked hands, then met her gaze directly. "I need to get better at listening to you, especially when we disagree. You bring perspective I don't have—the financial and business sense that balances my emotional attachment."

"And I need to find my role here," Beth replied. "Not trying to compete with you, James and your father in areas where you have expertise, but creating something that's distinctly mine."

Gabriel's eyebrows lifted in interest. "Like what?"

Beth hesitated. She'd been turning an idea over in her mind for weeks but hadn't voiced it, uncertain of Gabriel's reaction. "I've been thinking about the farm stand," she said finally. "Right now it's just a seasonal wooden booth at the end of the drive, open only during the spring when I sell cut flowers. But what if we expanded it? Created a year-round market space that sold not just our apples but products made from them—cider, preserves, baked goods. Maybe even feature other local producers. We also should have a better sign for the woodworking shop."

Gabriel's expression grew thoughtful. "A proper farm store? Like what the Millers have over in Andover?"

"Similar, but with our own identity," Beth nodded, warming to her topic now that it was out in the open. "I've been researching what permits we'd need, what equipment. We could start small, with apple butter and hard cider, then expand as we see what sells. It would create income streams outside of harvest season."

"We'd need help, Beth. There's no way you can do it all. Running a functioning farm is work from early morning until late in the evening. If you think we're busy now..."

She nodded. "I understand what you're saying. Let's at least consider it enough to crunch the numbers and see if it's even possible."

"You've put a lot of thought into this," Gabriel observed, no dismissal in his tone, only interest.

"I have," Beth admitted. "But I wasn't sure if it aligned with your vision for the orchard, so I kept it to myself."

Gabriel shook his head, looking chagrined. "That's exactly what I don't want—you holding back ideas because you're worried about my reaction. The orchard's vision should be ours, not just mine."

"It goes both ways," Beth acknowledged. "I should have brought it up instead of silently building resentment when other suggestions were overlooked."

They were quiet for a moment, the only sounds the distant calls of birds and the occasional rustle as Charlie repositioned himself at their feet.

"I love the farm store idea," Gabriel said finally. "It utilizes your organizational strengths, your business background. And it provides a direct connection to customers that I'm not always comfortable with."

"Really?" Beth couldn't keep the surprise from her voice. "You're not just saying that?"

"Really," Gabriel confirmed. "In fact, the old carriage house might be the perfect space for it, with some renovation. It's structurally sound, according to Dad, and it would give you a year-round indoor location."

The easy acceptance of her idea—not just acceptance but enthusiastic support—made Beth's chest tighten with emotion. This was what partnership was supposed to feel like.

"We could start planning this fall," she suggested, already mentally listing what they'd need.

"Perfect timing," Gabriel agreed. "And there's grant money available for agricultural diversification projects. Dad mentioned a few programs we might qualify for."

The conversation flowed from there, moving from the farm store idea to other aspects of their life together—a book Gabriel had been reading about sustainable forestry, Beth's thoughts on visiting her mother in Florida before Lauren's move, a documentary they'd both been wanting to watch. The easy back-and-forth reminded Beth of their early days together, before the weight of the orchard's challenges had made every conversation feel freighted with practical urgency.

As they finished the last of the coffee, Gabriel looked around at their property—the farmhouse that still needed work, the orchard spreading out beyond the lawn, the workshop where he created custom furniture when time allowed. "We're building something special here," he said quietly. "Sometimes I get so caught up in the day-to-day struggles that I forget the bigger picture."

"Me too," Beth agreed. "That's why we need this—regular time to remind each other what we're working toward, not just what we're working on."

Gabriel stood, moving around the table to pull Beth to her

feet and into his arms. "Thank you for this," he murmured against her hair. "For not giving up on us even when I've been difficult."

"Impossible, you mean," Beth teased, but she wrapped her arms around his waist, savoring the solid warmth of him.

"That too," he conceded with a laugh.

They stood like that for a long moment, the morning sun warming their shoulders, the faint scent of apple blossoms still lingering in the air from the late-blooming trees. Whatever challenges lay ahead—and there would be many—at least they would face them together, their partnership renewed and strengthened by this simple commitment to protected time.

Inside the house, the phone rang—the landline they kept for business calls—but neither moved to answer it. Whatever it was, it could wait. This moment, this reconnection, was sacred, and theirs alone.

CHAPTER 26

"Are you sure three days is enough time?" Lauren asked, scrolling through property listings on her laptop. The kitchen table was covered with printouts, sticky notes, and two coffee mugs that had long since gone cold. "There are at least twenty properties that match our criteria in the Tampa area. We've got some in Tampa and a few in Sarasota."

Jeff leaned over her shoulder, studying the screen. "Three days is what we've got. Michael and Brea are saints for taking the kids, but five days total including travel is pushing it with Daniel still being so young."

Lauren sighed, knowing he was right. Their youngest was just nine months old, still nursing, and though she'd been pumping milk to leave behind, the separation anxiety was hitting her harder than she'd anticipated—and they hadn't even left yet.

"Maybe we should narrow the search area more?" Jeff suggested. "Focus on just Tampa and the neighborhoods with the best schools for the girls?"

"That's what I've been trying to do, but there are three school districts that all seem promising." Lauren ran a hand through her hair, a gesture of familiar frustration. "And they need to be within reasonable distance to the tennis academy for Olivia."

"And within two hours of your mom on Captiva," Jeff added with a knowing smile.

Lauren looked up, caught. "Is it that obvious?"

"Only to someone who's known you for fifteen years," he replied, kissing the top of her head. "It's okay to admit that being close to your mother is a factor. It's part of why we're making this move."

"Not the only reason," Lauren clarified quickly. "Olivia's opportunity comes first. Besides, if I can get to Mom in four hours by flying, what's the point of picking a new house so far away from Captiva?"

"Of course," Jeff agreed. "Family connections are important. Finding a place that puts us within reach of Tampa for Olivia's training and Captiva for family time makes sense."

The sound of footsteps on the stairs announced Lily's approach before the eight-year-old appeared in the kitchen door-way, clutching her favorite stuffed rabbit. Despite the July heat, she wore flannel pajamas—a security choice rather than a seasonal one.

"Is Uncle Michael going to let me bring Hoppy to his house?" she asked, her voice small.

Lauren beckoned her daughter over. "Of course he will, sweetie. Uncle Michael loves Hoppy, remember? And Aunt Brea said they've set up the guest room especially for you. But I'm guessing you're going to have so much fun with their dog, Willa, you'll forget all about Hoppy."

"Never!" she insisted. "What about my nightlight? And my special pillow?" Lily's anxiety had been mounting as the trip approached, manifesting in a growing list of concerns about what would and wouldn't be available at her uncle's home.

"We're packing everything you need," Jeff assured her,

kneeling to her level. "And you'll have so much fun with your cousins that you might not even miss us."

Lily's face crumpled slightly. "I will too miss you."

"And we'll miss you, sweetie" Lauren said, pulling her daughter into a hug. "It's only for a few days, though. And when we get back, we'll have pictures of houses to show you—maybe even our new house in Florida."

At the mention of Florida, Lily's expression grew more troubled. Unlike Olivia, who had embraced the move with unbridled enthusiasm, Lily had received the news with quiet dismay. The prospect of leaving her friends, her school, and the only home she'd ever known weighed heavily on her eight-year-old shoulders.

"Will there be palm trees?" she asked finally, a question that seemed to stand in for a hundred others she couldn't articulate.

"Lots of palm trees," Jeff confirmed. "And beaches, and maybe even a pool in our new backyard."

This earned a flicker of interest. "A real pool? Just for us?"

"That's on our wish list," Lauren said, grateful for any positive engagement from her middle child. "Along with a room just for you, to decorate however you want."

"Could it be purple?" Lily asked, a touch of excitement finally breaking through her worry.

"The purplest purple that ever purpled," Jeff declared, earning a small giggle.

"Go finish getting dressed, sweetie," Lauren said. "We need to leave for Uncle Michael's in about an hour."

As Lily trudged back upstairs, Jeff turned to Lauren with a raised eyebrow. "A pool, huh? That wasn't on the official requirements list."

"It is now," Lauren replied, adding it to her notes. "Anything that gets Lily on board with this move is worth considering. Besides, I've always wanted one."

Jeff nodded, understanding. "She'll adjust once we're there. Kids are resilient. But the transition is going to be hardest on her."

"I know." Lauren sighed. "Olivia has the academy to focus on, Daniel's too young to care, but Lily... she's at that age where friends and routine are everything."

"Which is why finding the right neighborhood with good schools is so important," Jeff reminded her. "Now, back to these listings. What about this one?" He pointed to a property in a development called Lakewood Ranch. "Four bedrooms, office space for you, community pool if we can't find a house with one, and it says the schools are highly rated."

Lauren studied the listing. "It's at the top of our budget."

"Everything in Florida seems to be," Jeff noted wryly. "But if this is a long-term move, it makes sense to get it right the first time."

The baby monitor crackled to life with Daniel's morning babbling, signaling the end of his nap and their planning session.

"I'll get him," Jeff offered, already heading for the stairs. "You finish narrowing down the list. Just think—in a few days, we'll be standing in these houses instead of just looking at pictures."

Lauren watched him go, then turned back to her laptop. The reality of their move was finally hitting home. With their house on the market, in just a few weeks they would leave Massachusetts—the only home she'd ever known, except for her college years. The practical details had consumed her attention until now: selling the house, arranging Olivia's academy enrollment, planning this house-hunting trip. But underneath it all ran a current of emotion she'd been carefully avoiding.

Excitement, yes. Anticipation of being near her mother and grandmother again, of Sarah and her children becoming a regular part of their lives rather than occasional visitors. But also grief for what they were leaving behind—Beth and Gabriel, Becca and Christopher, their established community, the business she'd built from scratch.

Her phone chimed with a text from her real estate agent: *House just listed in Turtle Rock. Checks all your boxes. Added to your tour schedule for Thursday.*

Reality kept marching forward, regardless of her emotional readiness. Lauren took a deep breath and typed back a quick acknowledgment, then returned to the property listings. They had appointments with a real estate agent, twelve houses to tour, and three days to make decisions that would shape their family's future.

No pressure at all.

"You're sure the breast milk is labeled clearly in the freezer?" Lauren asked for the third time, hovering in Michael and Brea's kitchen doorway. "The morning bottles need to be slightly warmer than the evening ones, and—"

"Lauren," Michael interrupted, his expression a mixture of amusement and exasperation. "We've got this. Brea and I have raised three children, remember? Daniel will be fine."

"I know, I know." Lauren sighed. "I'm being ridiculous."

"You're being a mom," Brea corrected kindly, bouncing Daniel on her hip. The baby seemed perfectly content, fascinated by Brea's dangling earrings. "It's normal to worry. But we'll follow all your instructions to the letter, and we'll call if we have any questions."

Outside, Jeff loaded the last of their luggage into the car, with Olivia's enthusiastic but not particularly helpful assistance. Through the window, Lauren could see Lily sitting quietly on the front steps, clutching Hoppy and watching the proceedings with a solemn expression.

"Maybe this trip is too soon," Lauren murmured, her eyes on her middle child. "Lily's still so anxious about the whole thing."

Michael followed her gaze. "Which is exactly why you need to go now, find a great house, and start giving her concrete details to look forward to. The unknown is what's scary for her."

"When did you get so wise about children?" Lauren asked, nudging her brother with her shoulder.

"Around the third sleepless night with Quinn," Michael replied dryly. "Nothing like total exhaustion to bring clarity."

Lauren laughed, feeling some of her tension ease. Michael was right—Lily needed specifics to help her visualize their new life. And the sooner they found a house, the sooner they could all start picturing themselves in it.

"We'll send lots of pictures," she promised. "And we'll Face-Time every night."

"They're going to have a blast here," Brea assured her. "We've got the pool inflated in the backyard, a movie night planned with popcorn, and Michael took Friday off so we can take them to that new adventure park."

"You've thought of everything," Lauren said gratefully.

"That's what family does," Michael replied simply. "Now go. Your flight leaves in three hours, and you still have to get through security."

After a final round of hugs, kisses, and instructions—most of which Michael and Brea already knew—Lauren finally made her way to the car. Lily allowed herself to be hugged, but remained quiet, her small shoulders rigid with emotion.

"We'll be back before you know it, Lil-bug," Lauren promised, using the childhood nickname that had become Lily's official name at home. "And we'll find a house with room for all your stuffed animals and maybe even that pool you wanted."

"Okay," Lily whispered, not meeting her mother's eyes.

Lauren's heart ached, but she forced herself to straighten up and move toward the car. Prolonging the goodbye would only make it harder for all of them.

"Ready?" Jeff asked as she slid into the passenger seat.

"As I'll ever be," Lauren replied, fastening her seatbelt with slightly trembling hands.

As they pulled away from the curb, she watched through the rearview mirror as her children grew smaller in the distance—Olivia waving enthusiastically, Daniel oblivious in Brea's arms, and Lily, a small, still figure clutching her rabbit. Michael stood behind his niece, one hand resting protectively on her shoulder.

"They're going to be fine," Jeff said, correctly reading her thoughts. "Michael and Brea are great with them."

"I know," Lauren agreed, though she couldn't quite shake the knot of worry in her stomach. "It's not just that, though. It's... everything. Leaving the kids for the first time since Daniel was born. Potentially buying a house in a place we've barely visited. Uprooting our entire life."

Jeff reached across the console to take her hand. "Having second thoughts?"

"No," Lauren said after a moment's consideration. "Not second thoughts, just... reality thoughts. Until now, moving to Florida has been a someday plan, a dream. Now we're actually doing it, and it's terrifying and exciting in equal measure."

"That's how you know it's the right move," Jeff said. "The best decisions are often the scariest ones. Remember how nervous you were about starting Phillips Realty?"

Lauren smiled at the memory. "I threw up the morning of our grand opening."

"And now look—you've built it into a successful business with a team that can carry on even after you relocate." Jeff squeezed her hand. "You'll do the same thing with this move. Build something strong, create a new home for our family."

"With your help," Lauren added, squeezing back.

"Always," Jeff agreed.

As they merged onto the highway toward Boston's Logan Airport, Lauren felt a curious lightening in her chest. The anxiety was still there, but underneath it ran a current of excitement that grew stronger with each mile. They were heading south—not just for a house-hunting trip, but toward a new chapter of their lives.

Whatever waited for them in Florida, they would face it as a family, and with love.

CHAPTER 27

"Oh. My. Gosh." Lauren stood in the center of a sun-drenched kitchen, her mouth slightly open as she took in the expanse of quartz countertops, custom cabinetry, and floor-to-ceiling windows that overlooked a lanai and pool area. Beyond that, a small lake glittered in the afternoon sun, surrounded by swaying palm trees. "This is..."

"Perfect?" Jeff suggested, coming to stand beside her.

"Ridiculous," Lauren corrected, though she couldn't keep the wonder from her voice. "We can't possibly afford this."

Diane Mueller, the Sarasota real estate agent recommended by Nell, smiled knowingly. "Actually, it's within your budget. Barely, but within. The owners are relocating to Arizona for health reasons and need to close quickly. They're motivated."

"But it's so... much," Lauren gestured to the soaring ceilings, the open floor plan, the gleaming fixtures that all looked fresh from a design magazine.

"It's Florida." Diane shrugged. "You get more house for your money here than in Massachusetts. And Turtle Rock is one of the best neighborhoods in Sarasota for families. The schools are excellent, there's a community center with tennis courts that would be perfect for Olivia to practice on, and you're less than fifteen minutes from the interstate for her academy commute."

Jeff wandered into what appeared to be an office space just off the kitchen—a light-filled room with built-in shelving and views of the garden. "Is that a Meyer lemon tree?" he asked, pointing to a small tree laden with fruit.

"It is," Diane confirmed. "The current owners are quite proud of their garden. Mango trees in the back as well, and an herb garden just outside the kitchen door."

Lauren joined Jeff at the window, trying to imagine herself working from this sun-drenched office, picking fresh herbs for dinner, watching the children splash in the pool. It seemed too perfect, too far removed from their modest colonial in Massachusetts with its small backyard and tired kitchen.

"What's the catch?" she asked, turning to Diane. "There's always a catch."

Diane laughed. "Observant. Well, the HOA fees are not inconsiderable. And hurricane insurance is a must, which adds to your monthly expenses. Florida has its challenges—humidity, the occasional tropical storm. But for most transplants, the benefits far outweigh the drawbacks."

"Let's see the rest," Jeff suggested, his arm slipping around Lauren's waist. She could tell he was already smitten with the property, his practical objections weakening with each new feature they discovered. They'd already looked at several houses and this one excited them both.

The tour continued through four spacious bedrooms, three bathrooms, a bonus room that could serve as a playroom or media space, and finally out to the lanai and pool area. The screened enclosure kept bugs at bay while still providing panoramic views of the lake and surrounding greenery.

"The pool has a child safety fence that can be installed," Diane pointed out, clearly noting Lauren's concerned assessment of the water feature. "And the shallow end is very gradual, perfect for little ones learning to swim."

Lauren nodded, mentally calculating how many swimming lessons Daniel would need before she'd feel comfortable with a backyard pool. Lily, on the other hand, would be in heaven—the child who had to be practically dragged out of the water at the end of every beach day.

"What do you think?" Jeff asked quietly as Diane stepped away to take a phone call. "Be honest."

Lauren took a deep breath, trying to separate her practical assessment from the emotional whiplash of seeing a house so different from their current home. "It's beautiful," she admitted. "More than I ever thought we could afford. The location seems perfect for schools and Olivia's commute. And my mother will faint when she sees it."

Jeff laughed. "Is that a pro or a con?"

"A pro, definitely." Lauren smiled. "She's been telling me for years that we should upgrade from our 'starter home.' The fact that we've been in that starter home for much longer than we planned is beside the point."

"But?" Jeff prompted, sensing her hesitation.

"But it's so... Florida. So different from what we're used to. Part of me wonders if we'd feel like we were living in a vacation rental rather than a real home."

Jeff considered this, looking out over the serene lake view. "I think a home becomes real when you live in it. When Lily's artwork is taped to the refrigerator and Olivia's tennis gear is cluttering the hallway and Daniel's taking his first steps on that fancy tile."

Lauren leaned against him, the image he painted settling something within her. "You're right. And it does check every box on our list—and then some."

"Plus," Jeff added with a grin, "think of the guest rooms. Your family can visit anytime, stay comfortably. Beth and Gabriel could escape those New England winters for a week."

The mention of Beth sent a pang through Lauren. Her sister had been supportive of their decision to move, but Lauren knew how much Beth would miss them—especially since Christopher and Becca were also contemplating an eventual move to Florida.

"We should take some pictures for Lily," Lauren said, pulling out her phone. "Show her the pool, that bedroom with the bay window that would be perfect for her."

"Already on it," Jeff replied, his own phone in hand as he snapped photos of the backyard. "I took a video of the entire upstairs earlier while you were talking to Diane about the schools."

Diane returned, tucking her phone into her pocket. "So, what do we think of this one? It just hit the market yesterday, and I already have another showing scheduled for this evening."

Lauren and Jeff exchanged a look—that married-couple communication that needed no words. They'd seen seven houses over the past two days, and none had felt right until this one. Despite her initial shock at the grandeur, Lauren could easily picture their family here, building a new life in this sun-drenched space.

"We'd like to make an offer," Jeff said, a note of finality in his voice.

Diane's professional composure cracked slightly with genuine pleasure. "I was hoping you'd say that. This property really does check all your boxes, and I think you'll be very happy here." She gestured toward the house. "Shall we go inside and discuss the details?"

As they followed her back through the lanai doors, Lauren's phone chimed with a text from Michael: *Everything fine here. Lily helping make cookies. Daniel napped well. Olivia watching a tennis match on tv. How's it going?*

Lauren smiled, typing back quickly: *Found a house! Pictures coming soon. Home day after tomorrow.*

Within seconds, three responses appeared in succession:

From Michael: *That was fast! Congrats!*

From Beth: *Can't wait to see it! Call me when you can.*

From her mother: *FINALLY! Send pictures immediately!*

The chorus of support from her family, spread across states but connected by invisible bonds of love and shared history, settled the last of Lauren's doubts. This move—this adventure—wasn't taking her away from family. In many ways, it was bringing her back to it.

"Lauren?" Jeff called from inside. "Diane needs your input on the offer letter."

"Coming," she replied, taking one last look at the backyard that might soon be theirs. The Florida sunshine glinted off the pool water, palm fronds swayed in the gentle breeze, and somewhere in the distance, a mockingbird sang its complex melody.

Different from Massachusetts in every possible way, but beautiful in its own right. A new place to put down roots, to create memories, to build a foundation for their family's next chapter.

Taking a deep breath of the flower-scented air, Lauren turned and walked inside to sign the papers that would set their future in motion.

With their offer accepted, Lauren and Jeff returned home and the following days were organized chaos. It didn't take long for the bidding war to start on the sale of their Andover home, but Lauren knew it would sell fast. Her real estate experience meant they could sell their home without hiring a real estate agent.

Once the closing date was firmly set, Lauren tackled the next thing on her list—making sure her real estate business was in good hands.

Nell set the stack of résumés on Lauren's desk with a decisive thump. "I've narrowed it down to these five. Brian agrees they're the strongest candidates."

Lauren looked up from her laptop, where she'd been reviewing the photos Jeff had sent of the Turtle Rock house. "Perfect. Looks like you two have been busy."

"We work efficiently when the boss is away," Nell replied with a smirk. "Besides, you were very clear about the timeline. If we're going to have two new agents trained by the time you leave for Florida, we needed to move quickly."

Lauren picked up the top résumé, scanning the qualifications. "Jennifer Hathaway. Five years in commercial real estate, moving to residential. Strong sales background."

"She's my top pick," Nell confirmed. "Professional, poised, and hungry to prove herself in a new market segment."

"And the others?"

"All solid in different ways. Brian's favorite is the former teacher—he thinks her communication skills would translate well to client management. My second choice is the young guy from Boston University's real estate program. Less experience but impressive recommendations and very tech-savvy."

Lauren nodded, impressed with Nell's thoroughness. "Set up interviews for next week. I want to meet all five before we make any decisions."

"Already scheduled," Nell replied, sliding a printed itinerary across the desk. "Tuesday and Wednesday. Brian and I will sit in if you want a consensus opinion."

"Definitely," Lauren agreed. "These people will be representing Phillips Realty long after I'm settled in Florida. We all need to be comfortable with them."

Nell's professional demeanor softened slightly. "Are you getting excited?"

Lauren couldn't suppress her smile. "I am. The house is gorgeous. It's... well, it's nothing like what we have here. Much more elaborate, very 'Florida' with a pool and palm trees and ridiculous amounts of natural light."

"Sounds perfect," Nell said. "The kids must be thrilled."

"Olivia's over the moon. Lily's still processing, I think. She liked the room we picked out for her—it has a window seat, which she's always wanted—but she's the one I'm most worried about with this transition."

"She'll adapt," Nell said confidently. "Kids are resilient. And she'll make new friends quickly—she's such a sweet girl."

"I hope so." Lauren sighed. "There are moments when I wonder if we're doing the right thing, uprooting everyone for Olivia's opportunity. Is it fair to the other two?"

Nell settled into the chair across from Lauren's desk. "Can I be honest?"

"Always."

"You're not just moving for Olivia. You're moving for yourself too—to be closer to your mom, Sarah and your grandmother. There is family that your children don't get to see often. I think having their other cousins to play with will make all the difference. But, it's important for you and Jeff as well. I know how much you miss your mother. Ever since she moved to Captiva, you've had a sadness. I don't think you've ever been able to accept the distance between you two."

Lauren felt a flush of guilt at having her private motivations so accurately named. "Is it that obvious?"

"Only to someone who's worked alongside you for a decade," Nell replied with a gentle smile. "I've heard you talk about Captiva, seen how you light up when your mom visits here. This move isn't a sacrifice you're making solely for your daughter's tennis career. It's also a homecoming of sorts for you."

"Does that make me selfish?" Lauren asked, the question that had been lingering at the edges of her consciousness finally given voice.

"It makes you human," Nell countered. "And honest enough to recognize your own desires alongside your family's needs. There's nothing wrong with that."

Lauren nodded, not entirely convinced but grateful for Nell's perspective. "I'm going to miss this," she said, gesturing between them. "Our talks, your insights. Working with you every day."

"We'll still have video calls," Nell reminded her. "Probably more than you'll want once I'm running the show up here and need your advice on a daily basis."

"You won't need my advice," Lauren assured her. "You're more than ready to take the reins."

Nell's expression turned unexpectedly serious. "Ready or not, it won't be the same without you. But I understand why you're going. Family first—that's always been your mantra, and you're living it now."

"Family first," Lauren echoed softly. The phrase had been one of her mother's favorite sayings throughout Lauren's childhood, a constant reminder of what mattered most. Now she was orienting her entire life around that principle, bringing her children closer to their extended family, creating new connections while strengthening old ones.

Put in those terms, the decision felt not just right but inevitable—the natural progression of a journey that had begun the moment her mother moved to Captiva five years earlier.

"Enough sentimentality," Nell declared, standing up. "We have three contracts to review before the end of day, and Brian's waiting for your sign-off on the Henderson listing."

Lauren smiled, grateful to return to the practical tasks that had defined her professional life for so many years. "Let's get to it, then. I'm here for another month—might as well make the most of it."

As Nell left to retrieve the contracts, Lauren's gaze fell on the photos of the Turtle Rock house still open on her laptop. The spacious kitchen with its expansive views, the pool glittering in the sunlight, the room that would soon be Lily's with its perfect window seat.

Lauren laughed, imagining her mother's excitement. Maggie Wheeler Moretti had been waiting for this moment since the day she left Massachusetts for Captiva. Now her patience was finally being rewarded—another daughter returning to the fold, another set of grandchildren within easy reach.

"Wheeler women together again," Lauren murmured, echoing her mother's text. Not all of them—Beth would remain in Massachusetts, firmly rooted to her chosen path. But enough to recreate the close-knit female support system that had defined Lauren's childhood.

A support system her own children would now experience firsthand as they built their new life on Florida soil.

She would miss her morning conversations with Nell, but she smiled when she remembered there would be many intimate conversations with her mother that would most definitely take place watching either the sunrise or sunset over a freshly brewed pot of tea.

CHAPTER 28

The summer sun beat down on Beth's shoulders as she moved between rows of apple trees, clipboard in hand, all the while avoiding a yellow jacket who wanted a taste of whatever it could get.

The July heat had settled over the orchard like a heavy blanket, making even the simplest tasks feel like monumental efforts. But Beth persisted, methodically checking each tree in the commercial section, noting growth patterns, pest evidence, and fruit development with the precision that had once made her an exceptional attorney.

"You're being awfully thorough," Thomas observed, appearing at the end of the row. He carried two bottles of water, offering one to Beth as she straightened from examining a young Honeycrisp.

"Just documenting everything for our records," Beth replied, accepting the water gratefully. "If we're going to make this orchard profitable, we need data."

Thomas nodded, though something in his expression gave Beth pause. "Data is good," he agreed, taking a sip from his own bottle. "Though apple trees don't always follow spreadsheet projections."

Beth wiped sweat from her forehead with the back of her hand. "Maybe not, but financial institutions do. We'll need to show productivity metrics when we apply for that expansion loan in the fall."

Thomas was quiet for a moment, studying the trees around them with the practiced eye of someone who had spent decades in their company. "Beth," he said finally, his tone careful, "I think we need to have a conversation about timeline expectations."

Something in his voice made Beth's stomach tighten. "What do you mean?"

Thomas gestured to the surrounding trees—young saplings they'd planted three months earlier, alongside more established trees that had been part of the property when Beth and Gabriel purchased it. "When did you and Gabriel expect this section to produce marketable fruit?"

"Well, not a large harvest of course, but maybe something this fall," Beth replied, the answer automatic. "These older trees should be ready for harvest by September, and while the new plantings won't produce this year, they should start bearing fruit next season."

Thomas sighed, removing his hat to wipe his brow. "That might have been true if the orchard had been properly maintained over the past decade. But these trees..." He moved to the nearest mature specimen, pointing to the trunk. "See this scarring? And the irregular branch growth? Years of neglect, followed by improper pruning."

"Gabriel pruned them this spring," Beth said, defensive on her husband's behalf.

"He did," Thomas acknowledged. "And he did a good job with what he had to work with. But it takes more than one season of proper care to rehabilitate trees that have been neglected for so long. The underlying root systems, the branch structure—these need time to recover."

Beth felt a cold weight settling in her chest despite the summer heat. "What are you saying, exactly?"

Thomas met her gaze directly, his expression compassionate but firm. "I'm saying that this section won't be producing marketable fruit this fall. Or in significant quantities next year either. You're looking at a minimum of two years before you'll see the kind of harvest that could start turning a profit."

The clipboard slipped from Beth's fingers, landing in the grass with a soft thud. "Two years? But we've already invested so much —the irrigation system, the pest management program, Gabriel's time away from furniture commissions..."

"I know," Thomas said gently. "I should have been clearer when I first arrived. I thought Gabriel understood the timeline, but I see now that he might have been...optimistic in his projections to you."

"Optimistic," Beth repeated flatly. "That's one word for it." She bent to retrieve her clipboard, her mind racing with financial calculations. They had budgeted based on at least some income from the orchard this year, with increasing returns in subsequent seasons. Two years with nothing but expenses would drain their savings completely.

"The heritage section might produce some fruit this fall," Thomas offered. "Not commercial quantities, but enough for small-batch cider perhaps, or preserves."

"The heritage section," Beth echoed, unable to keep the bitterness from her voice. "The section I wanted to de-prioritize while we focused on the commercial varieties that actually had a chance of turning a profit."

Thomas winced slightly. "You weren't wrong about the commercial varieties being the long-term profit center. You just didn't have all the information about the recovery timeline."

"Information Gabriel should have shared with me," Beth said, her hurt and anger rising to the surface. "Information that would have affected every financial decision we've made in the past year."

Thomas didn't immediately respond, seemingly weighing his words carefully. "I think," he said finally, "that Gabriel sees this orchard through a different lens than you do."

"Clearly," Beth replied, her tone sharper than she intended. "He sees it as a passion project. I see it as a business that needs to eventually support our family."

"That's not entirely fair," Thomas countered gently. "Gabriel cares deeply about making this work financially. But he also has an emotional connection to this land that sometimes...colors his perspective."

Beth took a deep breath, trying to rein in her frustration. It wasn't Thomas's fault that they were facing a far longer road to profitability than she'd anticipated. If anything, she was grateful for his honesty now, however difficult the news might be.

"I need to think about what this means for our plans," she said finally. "For the farm store idea, for everything."

"The farm store might actually be more important now," Thomas suggested. "It provides an avenue for monetizing smaller harvests, for creating value-added products that can command premium prices."

Beth nodded absently, her mind already racing ahead to difficult conversations with their bank, adjustments to their business plan, the potential need for Gabriel to take on even more furniture commissions to make up the shortfall.

"I should find Gabriel," she said, tucking the clipboard under her arm. "We need to talk about this."

Thomas laid a gentle hand on her shoulder, stopping her. "Before you go charging into what I suspect might be a heated discussion, walk with me a bit longer?"

Beth hesitated, torn between the urgency she felt to confront Gabriel and the genuine concern in Thomas's eyes.

"All right," she agreed finally. "But I do need to talk to him today."

"Understood," Thomas said, gesturing toward a footpath that cut between the orchard and a small, wooded area on their property. "This way."

They walked in silence for a few minutes, Beth's thoughts churning with implications and contingency plans. The path wound along the edge of a stream that marked the property boundary, the water running low after several weeks of minimal rainfall.

"You know," Thomas said eventually, "when Tori and I first took over this orchard from my father, we faced a similar situation."

Beth glanced at him in surprise. "You did?"

Thomas nodded, his expression distant with memory. "The trees had been neglected during my father's illness. The irrigation system was outdated. We had hardly any capital to invest in improvements. And Tori was pregnant with Gabriel."

This detail caught Beth's attention. "What did you do?"

"Panicked, initially," Thomas admitted with a rueful smile. "Then argued. A lot. Tori wanted to sell portions of the land to fund improvements to the rest. I refused—this property had been in my family for generations, and I couldn't bear to part with any of it."

"That sounds familiar," Beth murmured.

"I imagine it does," Thomas agreed. "The thing is, we were both right. Tori was practical, focused on the financial viability. I was emotional, connected to the history and legacy. It took us months to find a middle path."

"Which was?"

"Patience," Thomas said simply. "We decided to give the orchard three years. Not expecting miracles in the first season, or even the second, but committing to steady progress. Meanwhile, I took construction jobs in the off-season. Tori started a small jam and jelly business using what fruit we could harvest, selling at farmers' markets."

They reached a fallen log beside the stream, and Thomas gestured for Beth to sit.

"The parallels to your situation aren't exact," Thomas continued, settling beside her. "But I see the same fundamental dynamic —one partner connected to the land through emotion and legacy, the other bringing necessary practical perspective. Both viewpoints are valid, both are essential. But they create tension when they're seen as opposing forces rather than complementary strengths."

"It's hard not to see them as opposing when they lead to such different decisions," Beth pointed out. "If I'd known last year that the orchard wouldn't produce meaningful income for this long, I might have advocated for selling portions of the property, just like Tori did."

"Perhaps," Thomas acknowledged. "But consider this—would selling immediately have been the right long-term decision? Or would it have been a reaction based on incomplete understanding of orcharding?"

Beth was quiet, considering his point.

"An apple orchard and a marriage have something in common," Thomas continued. "Both require patience to bear the sweetest fruit. Both involve seasons of growth, pruning, sometimes even apparent dormancy. And both can fail if you try to force production before the foundation is strong enough to support it."

"That's very poetic," Beth said, though the edge in her voice had softened. "But poetry doesn't pay the mortgage."

Thomas laughed, surprising her. "No, it certainly doesn't. I'm not suggesting blind faith or magical thinking here. What I am suggesting is that you and Gabriel approach this setback as partners—acknowledging the reality while also remembering why you chose this path together in the first place."

Beth stared at the stream, watching the water navigate around stones and fallen branches. Tears started to form. "I feel like he wasn't honest with me," she admitted, giving voice to the hurt beneath her anger. "He must have known the trees wouldn't produce this year."

"I think," Thomas said carefully, "that Gabriel sees possibilities more clearly than limitations. It's not dishonesty so much as a different relationship with hope." He paused, then added, "It's what made him an exceptional furniture maker—the ability to see what could be rather than what is."

"But we're not talking about a dining table," Beth countered. "We're talking about our financial future, our family's security."

"Which is why he needs your perspective as much as you need his," Thomas replied. "Your practical concerns aren't wrong, Beth. They're essential. But so is his vision of what this place could become with time and care."

Beth sighed, feeling her anger gradually subside, replaced by a more complex mixture of concern and reluctant understanding. "So what do I do now? Just accept that we're looking at years of financial strain without the outcome we planned for?"

"Not at all," Thomas said. "You adapt. You and Gabriel sit down together and create a new plan that acknowledges the reality while preserving the dream. Maybe that means he takes on more furniture commissions. Maybe it means developing the farm store concept more quickly to capitalize on what harvests you do have and working with other farmers in the area."

"All of the above, probably," Beth said, the problem-solving part of her mind already activating despite her emotional turmoil.

"Most likely," Thomas agreed with a smile. "But whatever path you choose, choose it together. Not as adversaries with competing priorities, but as partners with complementary strengths."

Beth was quiet for a long moment, absorbing his words. For

all her frustration about the orchard timeline, she couldn't deny the wisdom in what Thomas was saying. She and Gabriel had always been stronger together than apart, their different perspectives creating balance rather than conflict when they were working as true partners.

"Thank you," she said finally, meeting Thomas's gaze. "For being honest about the orchard. And for the perspective on marriage."

"I've had some practice with both," Thomas replied with a gentle smile. "Made plenty of mistakes along the way, too. If I can help you and Gabriel avoid some of them, I'll consider my time here well spent."

Beth studied his face, noting the genuine care in his expression. "You know," she said, "when you first arrived, I was worried you'd take over, that Gabriel and I would lose our authority over our own property. But you've been... really respectful of our ownership while still offering your expertise. I want to apologize if I've been less than welcoming."

"No need, it's your orchard now," Thomas said simply. "I'm just passing along what I've learned so you don't have to make all the same mistakes I did."

"I appreciate that," Beth said. She stood, brushing off her jeans. "I should still find Gabriel. We need to talk about this—calmly and constructively, but soon."

"He's in the barn," Thomas told her.

Beth nodded, then hesitated. "Will you be home for dinner tonight?"

"Actually," Thomas said, rising to stand beside her, "I've been meaning to talk to you about that. James and his family have invited me to stay with them for a while. They have that larger guest house on their property, and with Julia expecting their second child, they could use an extra pair of hands around the place."

Beth blinked in surprise. "You're moving out? But you've been so helpful with the orchard, and we have plenty of room—"

Thomas smiled, his eyes crinkling at the corners. "I'm not abandoning the orchard work. I'll still be here most days. But I think you and Gabriel could use some space—to be a couple, not just business partners with a houseguest."

The thoughtfulness of the gesture touched Beth deeply. "That's very considerate of you."

"Just practical," Thomas demurred. "Besides, I've barely spent any time with my other son since arriving. It's time to balance the scales a bit."

They walked back toward the orchard together, the afternoon sun casting long shadows across the neat rows of trees. Despite the disappointing news about the harvest timeline, Beth felt oddly lighter. There was something freeing in facing reality squarely, in having concrete information to work with rather than optimistic assumptions.

As they reached the barn, Thomas gave her a gentle nudge. "Go on. Talk to him. Remember—partners, not adversaries."

Beth nodded, squared her shoulders, and set off to find her husband, but then suddenly stopped and turned to face Thomas. She ran back to him and wrapped her arms around his waist squeezing tight. "Thank you, Thomas," she whispered.

Overcome with emotion, Beth felt the warmth of his embrace as Thomas's arms encircled her. In that moment, memories of her father Daniel washed over her. Not since his passing had she felt this sense of paternal comfort, of being protected and understood by someone she could truly call family. As Thomas's gentle hands patted her back, Beth closed her eyes and allowed herself, just briefly, to feel like someone's daughter again.

CHAPTER 29

$\mathcal{G}$abriel ran his hand along the edge of the maple tabletop, feeling for imperfections in the wood's surface. His touch was both analytical and reverent, fingers tracing the subtle grain patterns unique to this particular tree. The dining room table was nearly finished, its sturdy farmhouse design a blend of traditional craftsmanship and clean contemporary lines that had become his signature style.

The barn workshop smelled of sawdust and linseed oil, sunlight filtering through high windows to cast geometric patterns across the wooden floor. Gabriel reached for his burnishing cloth, preparing for the final polishing when he heard the distinctive sound of the barn door opening.

He knew it was Beth before he turned—the deliberate cadence of her footsteps, the slight creak of the floorboards beneath her boots. When he looked up to greet her, the expression on her face told him immediately that something was wrong.

"I talked to your father," she said.

Gabriel's heart sank. He'd been meaning to have this conversation with Beth for weeks, searching for the right moment, the right words. Evidently, his father had found them first.

"About the harvest timeline," he guessed, watching her nod in confirmation. "Beth, I was going to tell you. I just—"

"Didn't want to disappoint me?" she supplied, her tone more tired than angry. "Didn't want to admit that we're looking at two more years of investment without significant return?"

Gabriel sighed, setting down his polishing cloth and straightening from his work. Wood shavings clung to his apron as he removed his safety glasses.

"Something like that. I kept hoping that with the care we've been giving them, the trees might surprise us. Show more vigorous recovery than expected."

"Hope isn't a business strategy," Beth said, though the words lacked the sharpness he'd anticipated. "We need reality, Gabriel. However disappointing it might be."

"I know," he acknowledged. "And I should have been more forthcoming about what that reality might look like. I'm sorry."

His straightforward apology seemed to catch Beth off guard. Perhaps she'd been preparing for a more defensive response, for the need to argue her point more forcefully. Instead, she looked momentarily lost for words.

"Well," she said finally, "at least now we know where we stand. We need to recalibrate our entire financial plan, rethink the timeline for the farm store, probably increase your furniture commissions—"

"Beth," Gabriel interrupted gently, wiping his hands on a clean rag and removing his work apron. "Can we pause the planning for just a minute? I'd like to show you something first."

She looked skeptical but nodded reluctantly. "All right."

Gabriel guided her out of the workshop and into the late afternoon sunlight. He took her hand and they walked across the property, past the main orchard rows toward the heritage section where the oldest trees grew.

They stopped before a tree smaller than its neighbors, with slender branches reaching skyward.

"This is a Baldwin," Gabriel explained. "One of the oldest apple varieties in New England, first discovered in Massachusetts around 1740. My great-grandfather planted this particular tree."

Beth looked at it without speaking, and Gabriel wondered if she was really seeing what he wanted to show her or just humoring him before returning to practical concerns.

"Five years ago, before you and I met, this tree was barely alive," he continued. "Most people would have taken it out, replaced it with something new. But look at it now."

He guided her around the trunk, pointing to the new growth visible along the branches, the small apples developing amid healthy leaves.

"This tree has survived more than a century of New England weather," Gabriel said. "Blizzards, droughts, pests, changing climate patterns. It's been neglected, over-pruned, and undervalued. But given proper care and time, it's coming back stronger than anyone expected."

Beth's expression softened slightly as she traced a finger along one of the lower branches. "It's a beautiful tree," she acknowledged. "But I'm not sure what point you're trying to make with this particular horticultural history lesson."

Gabriel smiled, recognizing the subtle shift in her tone that indicated she was open to hearing him out, despite her lingering frustration.

"My point is that some things can't be rushed," he said. "Not because they're stubborn or difficult, but because deep, lasting growth takes time. This orchard—our dream for it—is like that. The timeline is longer than we hoped, but what we're building will be stronger for the patience required."

"That's a lovely sentiment," Beth replied, "but sentiment doesn't pay bills."

"Fair enough," Gabriel conceded. "So let's talk practically. Yes, we need to adjust our plans. James and I will take on more furniture commissions. And yes, your farm store idea becomes even more important now as a way to maximize value from limited harvests. Heck, the huge pumpkin patch could supply enough for months of pumpkin pies," he teased.

Beth studied him, seeming to weigh his words. "You're being very reasonable about this," she noted, a hint of suspicion in her voice. "I expected more resistance to changing our approach."

Gabriel laughed softly. "Maybe I'm growing," he suggested. "Or maybe I just had a good talk with my father a few days ago about the importance of balancing vision with practicality. About the value you bring to this partnership that I sometimes fail to fully appreciate."

"Your father said that?" Beth asked, genuine surprise in her voice.

"He did," Gabriel confirmed. "He also mentioned that he and my mother went through something similar in their early years running the orchard. That they had to find a middle path between his emotional attachment to the land and her practical concerns about viability."

Beth's expression shifted, understanding dawning, and she started to laugh. "He told me the same story today."

"Sounds like my father has been doing some relationship management on both sides," Gabriel observed with a rueful smile. "Though I can't say I mind. He's not wrong."

The tension that had been visible in Beth's shoulders since her arrival began to ease. "No," she agreed. "He's not wrong. We do need to find that middle path—acknowledging the reality while preserving the dream, as he put it to me."

"I like that," Gabriel said softly. He reached for her hand, encouraged when she didn't pull away. "I am sorry I wasn't more transparent about the harvest timeline. I think I was afraid that if you knew how long it might really take, you'd regret this whole enterprise."

"I might have," Beth admitted. "If you'd told me last year that we were looking at three to four years before meaningful profit, I might have balked. But now..."

"Now?" Gabriel prompted when she trailed off.

Beth looked around at the heritage section, at the rows of trees stretching toward the farmhouse in the distance, at the land that had become their home and their future. "Now I'm invested in more than just the financial outcome," she said. "I'm invested in what we're building here together. In the legacy we're creating, not just preserving."

Gabriel felt a surge of emotion at her words—relief, gratitude, love so intense it nearly took his breath away. "So we adjust," he said. "We create a new plan that reflects reality while still moving us toward our goals. Partners, not adversaries."

"Partners," Beth echoed, squeezing his hand. "Though I reserve the right to be occasionally adversarial when you withhold important financial information."

"Fair enough." Gabriel laughed. "I reserve the right to be occasionally impractical when it comes to heritage trees with historical significance."

"Deal," Beth said, a genuine smile finally breaking through her serious expression.

They stood together beneath the Baldwin apple tree, hands clasped, the summer light filtering through leaves overhead. Gabriel was struck, not for the first time, by how perfectly Beth fit into this landscape—her strength and resilience a match for the land they were nurturing together.

"I almost forgot to mention," he said. "Dad's moving to James's place for a while. He says they could use help with Julia's pregnancy, but I think he's trying to give us space."

Beth's eyebrows rose in surprise. "He mentioned it to me too. I was going to tell you." She hesitated, then added, "Do you think that's necessary? He's been so helpful with the orchard."

"He'll still be here during the days," Gabriel assured her. "But I think he's right about the space. We've been so focused on the orchard, on practical concerns, on daily logistics... we haven't had much time to just be us."

"That's true," Beth acknowledged, her expression softening further. "And our Sunday morning tradition is wonderful, but it's just a few hours each week."

"Exactly," Gabriel agreed. "I think Dad's giving us the gift of privacy, of quiet evenings without a third person in the house. Time to reconnect beyond just orchard business."

Something shifted in Beth's gaze, a warmth kindling there that made Gabriel's heart beat faster. "That sounds nice," she said, her voice lower than before. "When is he planning to move?"

"This weekend," Gabriel replied. "He's packing up this evening."

Beth nodded, seeming to contemplate this information. Then, to Gabriel's surprise, she stepped closer, her free hand coming to rest against his chest. "So by Sunday, we'll have the house to ourselves."

"We will," he confirmed, his arm circling her waist. "Any particular plans for this newfound privacy?"

"I might have a few ideas," Beth murmured, her fingers playing with the top button of his shirt. "None of them involving orchard business or financial planning."

Gabriel laughed softly, drawing her closer. "I like the sound of that."

"I thought you might," Beth replied. Then, more seriously, "We're going to be okay, aren't we? The orchard, our finances, us —we'll figure it out?"

"We will," Gabriel assured her, absolute certainty in his voice. "It might take longer than we hoped, and the path might look different than we expected, but we'll get there. Together."

Beth studied his face, seeming to find the reassurance she needed in his expression. "Together," she agreed.

The afternoon sun had begun its descent toward the western

hills. In a few hours, they would need to return to practical matters—dinner preparations, evening chores, the endless list of tasks that came with running a farm. But for now, in this moment between work and responsibility, they allowed themselves to simply be together beneath the heritage apple tree, its branches a living reminder of patience rewarded and promises kept.

Gabriel bent to kiss her, feeling Beth respond immediately, her body melting against his as naturally as it had since their first kiss years ago. Whatever challenges lay ahead—financial setbacks, delayed harvests, the inevitable complications of building a life and business together—they would face them as they faced everything.

Partners, not adversaries. Complementary strengths rather than competing priorities. A balance of vision and practicality, of passion and patience, of roots and wings.

Gabriel hugged his wife and could see his father in the distance.

Thomas Walker watched his son and daughter-in-law embrace beneath the old Baldwin tree. A smile of satisfaction crossed his weathered face as he turned and walked quietly back toward the farmhouse, leaving them to their private moment.

Gabriel held his hand up to thank his father. Thomas nodded and continued to the farmhouse.

Some things, after all, couldn't be rushed. But with proper care and patience, they grew stronger than anyone might have expected.

Including love, especially love, taking root in fertile ground.

CHAPTER 30

*M*aggie was in the middle of explaining the upcoming week's reservation schedule to Iris when the rumble of a large engine turning into the driveway caught her attention. She glanced out the front window of the Key Lime Garden Inn, expecting to see the delivery truck from their produce supplier.

Instead, a gleaming white Dodge Ram camper van with custom blue striping along the sides rolled to a stop in the circular driveway, taking up nearly twice the space of a normal vehicle. Sunlight glinted off the solar panels mounted on its roof.

"Who on earth is that?" Maggie wondered aloud, squinting to see through the tinted windshield. "Did you book a van life travel blogger or something I don't know about?"

Iris shook her head, equally perplexed. "Not that I recall. Though it would make for good publicity."

The driver's door swung open, and a slender leg wearing bright turquoise capris and a fashionable white sneaker extended toward the ground. Then, with surprising agility for a woman of eighty-one, Grandma Sarah hopped down from the driver's seat, adjusting her straw sun hat and oversized sunglasses.

"It's your mother," Chelsea said, putting her coffee cup down.

Maggie ran outside with Chelsea following closely behind. By the time they reached the driveway, Grandma Sarah was ceremoniously running her hand along the van's side, looking for all the world like a proud new parent.

"Mother," Maggie said, her voice deliberately controlled. "What is this?"

"This," Grandma Sarah announced with unmistakable pride, "is Garrison's Getaway, my new home on wheels." She patted the van's side affectionately. "Isn't she magnificent?"

"Your new what?" Maggie sputtered.

"My new home," Grandma Sarah repeated patiently, as if explaining to a particularly slow child. "Well, my part-time home, anyway. I'll still keep my condo, of course. But the Getaway here gives me freedom."

Chelsea stepped forward, trying not to laugh at the expression of utter bewilderment on Maggie's face. "It's certainly... impressive, Grandma Sarah. When did you decide to join the van life movement?"

"After my third YouTube interview with Silver Solo Sisters," Grandma Sarah replied, as if this explained everything. "Meredith—she's the one who converted a Mercedes Sprinter all by herself, you remember—she convinced me that at my age, there's no time to waste waiting for adventure."

"Your YouTube channel," Maggie said faintly. "The one I thought was just a harmless hobby interviewing eccentric people?"

"Harmless?" Grandma Sarah sniffed indignantly. "I'll have you know I have over twenty thousand subscribers now. My interview with Nomadic Nora got thirty-seven thousand views. People are inspired by seniors reclaiming their independence."

"And you've decided to... reclaim your independence... by buying a camper van?" Maggie clarified, clearly struggling to process this development.

"It's not just any camper van," Grandma Sarah corrected, opening the side door with a flourish. "Come see!"

Against her better judgment, Maggie followed her mother into the vehicle, with Chelsea trailing behind, biting her lip to keep from laughing out loud.

The interior of the van was a marvel of compact efficiency. A small but functional kitchen area featured a two-burner stove, a mini refrigerator, and a sink with a retractable faucet. Beyond that, a dining area with a small table and cushioned bench could clearly convert into a bed. At the rear, storage compartments lined the walls, and a tiny bathroom cubicle occupied one corner.

"It has everything I need," Grandma Sarah declared, demonstrating how various components folded away to create more space. "Solar power, a composting toilet, even a little outdoor shower for when I'm boondocking in the wilderness."

"Boondocking?" Maggie repeated weakly. "Mother, you can't possibly be planning to sleep in Walmart parking lots at your age."

Grandma Sarah's eyes narrowed dangerously. "My age? May I remind you, Margaret Wheeler Moretti, that I am in excellent health. My blood pressure is better than yours, my cholesterol is perfect, and I can still touch my toes without bending my knees, which is more than I can say for you."

Chelsea choked back a laugh at Maggie's offended expression.

"That's not the point," Maggie protested. "The point is safety. Security. What if something happens while you're out in the middle of nowhere?"

"I have a satellite phone, a medical alert bracelet, and the Silver Solo Sisters convoy meets up twice a month for safety check-ins," Grandma Sarah replied, clearly having anticipated this objection. "Besides, I'm not planning to camp in dangerous areas. Just national parks, beach campgrounds, the occasional beautiful overlook."

"But why?" Maggie asked, genuine confusion in her voice.

"You have a lovely condo. You have family nearby. Why would you want to live in a van?"

Grandma Sarah's expression softened slightly. "Because there's still so much I want to see, Maggie. So many sunrises over mountains I've never climbed, so many starry skies above deserts I've never crossed." She gestured around the compact space. "The Garrison Getaway here gives me the chance to have those experiences while I still can, without giving up my home base."

"But—" Maggie began.

"No buts," Grandma Sarah interrupted firmly. "I've made my decision. The van is purchased, my route is planned, and my YouTube followers are expecting a series of videos documenting my adventures."

"YouTube followers," Maggie muttered. "When did my mother become an influencer?"

"Around the same time you started saying things like 'when did my mother become an influencer?'" Chelsea suggested helpfully, earning a glare from Maggie.

"I don't expect you to understand," Grandma Sarah continued. "But I do expect you to support me. I'm not asking permission, Maggie. I'm eighty-one years old. I'm telling you how it's going to be."

Something in her tone—the unmistakable echo of the woman who had raised three children largely on her own after being widowed relatively young—made Maggie pause. She looked around the van again, taking in the thoughtful design, the safety features, the small touches that made the space uniquely her mother's—a favorite throw pillow embroidered with "Not All Who Wander Are Lost," a small, framed photo of her late husband, a stack of well-worn travel guides.

"You've really thought this through, haven't you?" Maggie asked, her resistance beginning to crumble.

"Of course I have," Grandma Sarah replied, adjusting a decorative succulent plant on the tiny countertop. "I'm spontaneous, not reckless. There's a whole community of nomads like me. I'm not going to be alone."

Chelsea, who had been examining the van's features with genuine interest, looked up. "So what's your first destination, Grandma Sarah?"

"The Great Smoky Mountains," she replied promptly. "I've always wanted to see the fireflies synchronize in early summer. Then up to Maine for the fall colors, before heading back here for the winter. I'll be back on Captiva by Thanksgiving, of course."

"Of course," Maggie echoed faintly.

"Did I mention I'll be picking up Esther Jenkins next week?" Grandma Sarah added casually. "She's joining me for the first leg of the journey."

"Esther Jenkins? Your bridge partner? The one who can barely see over the steering wheel of her Buick?" Maggie's voice had risen again.

"The very same," Grandma Sarah confirmed cheerfully. "She's bringing her Yorkie, Napoleon. Don't worry, I've installed pet safety restraints."

Maggie looked to Chelsea for support, but her friend merely shrugged, clearly entertained by the entire situation. "She seems to have thought of everything," Chelsea pointed out.

"That's not helpful," Maggie muttered.

Grandma Sarah checked her watch—a high-tech fitness tracker that looked incongruous on her slender wrist. "Now, if you'll excuse me, I need to film my 'New Van Tour' video for my channel while the lighting is good. Chelsea, would you mind holding the camera?"

"I would be delighted," Chelsea replied, accepting the surprisingly professional-looking camera Grandma Sarah extracted from a storage compartment.

"Mother," Maggie tried one last time, "don't you think we should discuss this further? Maybe have Paolo take a look at the van's mechanics? Or at least go over your itinerary in detail?"

"No need," Grandma Sarah said breezily. "I had it thoroughly inspected before purchase, and my itinerary is designed to be flexible. That's the whole point of van life, Maggie—freedom to change course when the spirit moves you."

"When the spirit moves you," Maggie repeated weakly.

"Now, for the video, I'm thinking of starting with an exterior shot, then a slow reveal of the interior features," Grandma Sarah continued, directing Chelsea on camera angles. "My viewers love a good transition. Oh, and we'll need to get a shot of me looking contemplatively at the horizon. That always gets good engagement."

Maggie stood in stunned silence as her octogenarian mother proceeded to transform into a polished content creator before her eyes, delivering a practiced introduction to the camera: "Hello, Silver Wanderers! It's Grandma Sarah here with the moment you've all been waiting for—the grand reveal of the Garrison Getaway, my new home on wheels!"

"Did she just say, 'Silver Wanderers'?" Maggie whispered to no one in particular.

"It's her audience demographic," Chelsea explained between takes.

"I see," Maggie said, the reality of the situation finally sinking in. "My eighty-one-year-old mother has bought a camper van, named it the Garrison Getaway, and is about to drive across the country making YouTube videos with her half-blind bridge partner and a Yorkie named Napoleon."

"When you put it like that, it does sound like the premise for a sitcom," Chelsea agreed, adjusting the camera as Grandma Sarah demonstrated the van's convertible bed/dining area.

"This isn't funny," Maggie insisted, though a reluctant smile was beginning to tug at her lips.

"It's a little funny," Chelsea countered. "And also kind of

inspiring, if you think about it. How many people her age are still embracing new adventures?"

Before Maggie could respond, Grandma Sarah called out from inside the van, "Maggie, come do a cameo for my viewers! They'll want to meet my daughter."

"I am not appearing on your van life channel, Mother," Maggie called back.

"Don't be difficult, Margaret," Grandma Sarah replied, using the tone that had compelled obedience from Wheeler children for decades. "It will take thirty seconds. Your hair looks fine."

With a resigned sigh, Maggie climbed back into the van, Chelsea following with the camera, now barely containing her laughter.

"And here's my daughter, Maggie," Grandma Sarah announced to the camera, pulling a reluctant Maggie into the frame. "She's a bit concerned about her mother taking to the open road, but I'm sure my Silver Wanderers understand that sometimes we need to show our children that life doesn't end at retirement."

"Mother," Maggie protested weakly.

"Say hello to my viewers, dear," Grandma Sarah prompted.

Maggie looked directly into the camera, her expression a complex mixture of exasperation, grudging admiration, and unmistakable love. "Hello, Silver Wanderers," she said finally. "If any of you have advice on how to deal with a mother who's more adventurous at eighty-one than she allows her children to be, I'm all ears."

Grandma Sarah beamed, clearly delighted with this participation. "And that's why Maggie runs an inn while I'm free to roam the country," she told the camera with a wink. "Different strokes for different folks, as they say."

Chelsea had to lower the camera, her shoulders shaking with suppressed laughter.

"I'm going inside to tell Paolo about this development,"

Maggie announced, making her escape from the van. "He, at least, might have some practical input about van maintenance."

"Excellent idea," Grandma Sarah agreed cheerfully. "Ask Iris to bring out some of those almond cookies she made yesterday. I'll need provisions for the road."

As Maggie retreated toward the inn, shaking her head, Chelsea captured one last shot of Grandma Sarah standing proudly beside her van, the Florida sunshine glinting off the solar panels and her silver hair alike.

"And that, my Silver Wanderers, is the beginning of a new chapter," Grandma Sarah declared to the camera. "Because life isn't about how many years you have left—it's about how much life you put into those years. This is Grandma Sarah, signing off from Captiva Island. Next stop: adventure!"

Chelsea lowered the camera, genuinely impressed. "That was quite the closing line, Grandma Sarah."

"Thank you, dear," she replied with a satisfied smile. "I've been practicing it for days. Do you think it will get a lot of likes?"

"I think it'll go viral," Chelsea assured her. "Especially when Maggie tells the story about how she nearly fainted when you rolled up in this beast."

Grandma Sarah laughed, the sound as youthful and vibrant as a woman half her age. "That's my Maggie. Always worrying about the wrong things." She patted the van's side affectionately. "She'll come around. They always do."

"They always do," Chelsea agreed, helping Grandma Sarah gather her camera equipment. "Though I wouldn't count on her joining you for any road trips in the near future."

"Oh, I don't know about that," Grandma Sarah replied with a mysterious smile. "I've got plenty of surprises left in me yet. The van is just the beginning."

Chelsea didn't doubt it for a second. If there was one thing she'd learned about the women in Maggie's family, it was that they were full of surprises—and Grandma Sarah most of all.

Inside the inn, Maggie poured herself a much-needed cup of coffee and wondered where, exactly, she had lost control of her seemingly sensible mother.

She looked through the window and watched her mother talking to Chelsea.

She shook her head and smiled, because out in the driveway, in the sunshine, beside a van named the Garrison Getaway, her mother looked more alive than ever, her eyes bright with the promise of open roads and new horizons.

Age, it seemed, really was just a number. And in her mother's case, eighty-one looked an awful lot like twenty-one—just with better judgment and more comfortable shoes.

CHAPTER 31

Beth stood in the bathroom of the farmhouse, staring at the pregnancy test on the counter. Two pink lines, unmistakable in their clarity. She picked it up, examining it from different angles as if the result might somehow change, though she'd known the answer even before taking the test.

Six days late. Tender breasts. A strange new awareness of smells that had never bothered her before. And most telling of all, a bone-deep exhaustion that sleep couldn't seem to touch.

"Beth?" Gabriel's voice came from the hallway. "Have you seen my blue notebook? The one with the furniture sketches?"

She took a deep breath, setting the test back on the counter. "In the kitchen, next to the coffee machine," she called back, her voice steadier than she expected.

"Found it, thanks!" he replied. Then, after a pause, "Are you okay in there? You've been in the bathroom for a while."

Beth looked at her reflection in the mirror—same dark hair, same determined eyes, same face she'd known all her life. Yet something had shifted, a subtle change visible perhaps only to herself. She was still Beth, but she was also something new. Someone new.

"I'm fine," she answered. "Be out in a minute."

She wrapped the test in tissue paper and tucked it into her pocket, not quite ready to leave the evidence in the bathroom trash. One last look in the mirror, a deep breath, and she opened the door.

Gabriel was sitting at the kitchen table when she emerged, sketching furniture designs in his notebook. He looked up as she entered, his expression warming.

"There you are. I was thinking we could drive into town later, maybe have lunch at that new place Michael recommended. Dad won't be back from James's until tomorrow, so we've got time to ourselves."

Beth nodded absently, her hand touching the pocket where the test rested. "Sounds nice," she said, moving to sit across from him at the table.

Gabriel's pencil stilled, his brow furrowing slightly as he studied her face. "What's wrong? You look... strange."

"Not wrong," Beth corrected, meeting his gaze directly. "Just... unexpected."

Setting his pencil down, Gabriel gave her his full attention. "What's unexpected?"

Beth took a deep breath, her hand slipping into her pocket to retrieve the wrapped test. "This," she said simply, placing it on the table between them.

Gabriel looked confused for a moment, then understanding dawned as he carefully unwrapped the tissue paper. His eyes widened at the sight of the two pink lines, his gaze darting up to meet hers with a mixture of shock and wonder.

"You're pregnant?" he asked, his voice barely above a whisper.

Beth nodded, watching his face carefully for his reaction. "I took the test this morning, but I've suspected for about a week. I think it's why I've been so stressed."

"We're having a baby?" Gabriel said, the question transforming into a statement as comprehension settled in. "We're having a baby."

"We are," Beth confirmed, tension she hadn't realized she was carrying beginning to ease at his wondering tone. "Are you... happy about it?"

Gabriel's face broke into a smile so radiant it seemed to illuminate the kitchen. "Happy doesn't begin to cover it," he said, rising from his chair to crouch beside hers, taking both her hands in his. "Beth, this is... I don't even have words. A baby. Our baby."

Relief and joy mingled in Beth's chest, bringing unexpected tears to her eyes. "I know the timing isn't ideal," she began. "With the orchard work, and the financial strain we're already under—"

"No," Gabriel interrupted gently, squeezing her hands. "Don't go there. The timing is perfect because it's happening now. We'll figure out the rest."

"But—"

"Do you remember what Dad told us?" Gabriel reminded her. "About the orchard and our marriage requiring the same things— patience, care, belief in the future? This baby is part of that future. The most important part."

Beth smiled through her tears, recognizing the truth in his words. "I'm scared," she admitted. "Not just about the practical aspects, but about... all of it. Being someone's mother. The responsibility."

"Me too," Gabriel confessed, his honesty reassuring her. "But we'll figure it out together. Like we do everything else."

He pulled her into his arms, holding her close against his chest. Beth felt his heart beating, strong and steady, against her cheek.

"When?" he asked after a moment, his voice rumbling in his chest beneath her ear. "When will the baby come?"

"March, based on my calculations," Beth replied. "A spring baby."

Gabriel laughed softly. "Perfect for orchard folk. The trees will be blooming right around the time our baby arrives."

They stayed like that, wrapped in each other's arms in the sunlit kitchen, the magnitude of the change ahead settling over them like a blanket—daunting in its weight but also providing a new kind of warmth and protection.

"We should call my father," Gabriel said eventually. "And your mother. And your sisters. And—"

Beth laughed, placing a finger against his lips to halt the growing list. "Let's take it one step at a time. I'd like to wait a few weeks before telling everyone. Except maybe my mom and Paolo. And Thomas and your brother."

"Whatever you want," Gabriel agreed, pressing a kiss to her forehead. "I'm just... I can't believe it. A baby, Beth. We're going to be parents."

Gabriel's hand moved to rest gently on her still-flat stomach, his touch reverent. "Hello in there," he whispered. "I'm your dad. And I already love you more than I thought possible."

The simple declaration undid her completely. Beth felt tears spill over, streaming down her cheeks as she covered his hand with her own.

"I love you," she said, looking up at Gabriel through her tears. "Both of you."

Gabriel smiled, using his free hand to brush away her tears. "Both of us," he repeated softly. "I love the sound of that."

That evening, Beth sat on the porch swing with her phone in hand. The sun was beginning its descent toward the western hills. A gentle breeze carried the scent of freshly cut grass, a quintessential New England summer evening.

She'd rehearsed this conversation in her head several times throughout the day, imagining her mother's reaction to the news.

"Just make the call," Beth muttered to herself, scrolling to her mother's number.

Taking a deep breath, she pressed the call button and listened to the ring tone, her heart beating a little faster with each electronic pulse.

"Beth!" Maggie's voice came through, warm and slightly surprised. "What a lovely coincidence. I was just thinking about you. How are things?"

"Good," Beth replied, smiling at her mother's familiar enthusiasm. "We're making progress."

"That's wonderful, honey. And how are you and Gabriel?"

"We're great," Beth confirmed, her hand unconsciously drifting to rest on her abdomen. "Actually, that's why I'm calling. I have some news to share."

There was a brief pause on the line. "Good news, I hope?" Maggie asked, a note of concern creeping into her voice.

"Very good news," Beth assured her. "Mom, I'm pregnant."

The squeal that came through the phone was so loud that Beth had to hold it away from her ear, laughing despite herself at her mother's unrestrained reaction.

"A baby! Oh, Beth! When? How far along are you? How are you feeling? Does Gabriel know? Have you told the rest of the family? Maybe I should call a Code Red and get everyone's attention that way. This is wonderful news!"

The questions tumbled out in rapid succession, giving Beth no chance to answer one before the next arrived. It was so typically Maggie that Beth felt a rush of affection for her mother's enthusiasm.

"Mom, breathe." She laughed. "Yes, of course Gabriel knows—he was the first person. I'm about six weeks along, due in early March. I'm feeling okay—a little tired, but nothing too dramatic yet. And no, I haven't told Lauren or Sarah. I wanted you and Paolo to know first."

"March," Maggie repeated, clearly already calculating dates and plans in her head. "A spring baby. That's perfect. And how's Gabriel taking the news?"

"He's over the moon," Beth said, unable to keep the smile from her voice. "You should have seen his face when I showed him the test. He's wanted a baby for a while as you know. I wasn't so sure, but life has a way of happening when you're planning other things."

Maggie laughed, the sound warm with understanding. "Of course he is. Let me get Paolo. He'll want to hear this too. Paolo!" Her voice became distant as she presumably turned away from the phone. "Paolo, come quickly! Beth's on the phone with wonderful news!"

Beth heard muffled conversation, then Paolo's voice came through. "Beth! Maggie says you have news that cannot wait. What is happening?"

"I'm pregnant, Paolo," Beth replied, smiling at her stepfather's characteristic enthusiasm. "You and Mom are going to be grand-parents again."

"Magnifico!" Paolo exclaimed. "This is wonderful news! The best news! When will the piccolo arrive?"

"In March," Beth repeated, touched by his genuine joy. "A spring baby."

"Perfect timing," Paolo declared. "The winter will be behind us, the world coming back to life just as your little one joins it."

Beth laughed. "That's almost exactly what Gabriel said."

"He is a smart man, your Gabriel," Paolo said approvingly. "How is he taking the news?"

"Ecstatically," Beth replied. "Though I think we're both a little terrified too. It's a big change, especially with the orchard still finding its footing."

Maggie's voice returned, apparently having reclaimed the phone. "Don't worry about that, sweetheart. Babies and new businesses have coexisted since the beginning of time. You'll find your rhythm."

"I hope so," Beth said, some of her underlying anxiety surfacing despite her joy. "The timing isn't exactly what we planned, but..."

"Life rarely follows our carefully laid plans," Maggie observed, her voice softening with maternal understanding. "But some of the best things come from those unexpected detours. Look at me and Paolo—I certainly wasn't planning to fall in love again at my age, but here we are."

"And look how well that turned out," Beth acknowledged, feeling some of her anxiety ease at her mother's perspective.

"Exactly," Maggie agreed. "Besides, babies don't need nearly as much as the baby industry tries to convince new parents they do. A safe place to sleep, food, diapers, and most importantly, love. You and Gabriel have plenty of that last one to go around."

"Thanks, Mom," Beth said, genuinely grateful for her mother's practical reassurance. "I needed to hear that today."

"That's what mothers are for," Maggie replied warmly. "And speaking of mothers, have you told Thomas yet? He's going to be a grandfather again!"

"We'll tell him tomorrow. We're going out to dinner to celebrate, just the two of us."

"That's wonderful. I won't say a word to anyone and let you tell the rest of the family when you're ready. I can tell you, though, everyone will be very excited."

The conviction in her mother's voice was reassuring. "I hope you're right."

"I'm always right," Maggie declared with mock seriousness. "It's one of my more annoying qualities, according to your brothers."

Beth laughed, feeling lighter than she had all day. This was what she'd needed—her mother's particular blend of enthusiasm, practical wisdom, and humor.

"Beth, honey. I've been worried about you."

"What? Why?"

"I thought you might be upset about Lauren moving down here."

"Oh, that. Well, I guess I was at first, but the truth is that I've somehow always known that Lauren wouldn't stay too far away from you. Out of all of your children, she's the one most like you. I think the two of you will never be too far from one another for the rest of your lives. Just like you and Grandma."

Maggie laughed. "Don't let me get started about your grandmother. That's a conversation for another day. In the meantime, I'm glad you're not too upset. You know how much I want all my children living down here. What's it going to take to get you and Gabriel to move to Florida?"

"Mom, let's not go there again."

"Oh, I'm just teasing you... sort of."

Beth could hear Paolo's muffled laugh in the background, followed by his voice coming closer to the phone. "Beth, your mother is indeed glowing with grandmother joy. It is quite something to see."

The conversation continued for several more minutes, with Maggie offering advice on morning sickness remedies and Paolo suggesting traditional Italian foods particularly beneficial for pregnant women. By the time they said their goodbyes, Beth felt wrapped in the warm embrace of family support, despite the physical distance separating them.

As she ended the call, she looked out toward the barn, where Gabriel was visible in the distance, sweeping the sawdust-filled floor.

Life was changing, growing in unexpected ways—much like the heritage apple trees that had surprised them all with their resilience and renewal. Beth placed a hand on her stomach, still flat but now containing the greatest promise of new life, of future harvests both literal and metaphorical.

"Your family can't wait to meet you," she whispered to the child growing within. "Every single one of them, near and far."

The breeze picked up, rustling through the orchard leaves in what sounded almost like a response—patient, like the trees themselves, but filled with the quiet certainty of time unfolding exactly as it should.

CHAPTER 32

"If you give my dog one more treat, I'm going to have to put her on a diet," Maggie complained, as Chelsea handed Maggie's dog another cookie.

Lexie jumped and twirled and obeyed every one of Chelsea's commands, but when Maggie admonished her friend, she put the dog cookies away in her beach bag. "Sorry, Lexie, your mean mother said no."

"Nice. Now she'll hate me."

When Lexie finally understood the cookies were gone, she circled on the blanket and finally settled into a relaxed position.

The setting sun painted the sky in spectacular shades of orange and pink. Chelsea and Maggie joined the crowd of people gathered in front of The Mucky Duck to see the sun set.

"We should do this more often," Chelsea said. "I think living here makes us forget how special this is."

"I'm glad we got down here before this crowd. I'm always surprised at how many people do this every night."

"Perfect timing," Maggie observed, settled into her chair and gesturing toward the horizon where the sun was beginning its dramatic descent. "Twenty minutes until sunset, just enough time to get properly settled."

Chelsea uncorked the wine bottle with practiced ease and poured two generous glasses, handing one to Maggie. The pale golden liquid caught the light, seeming to glow from within.

"To surviving another Captiva summer," Chelsea said, raising her glass in a toast.

"And what a summer it's been," Maggie replied with a smile, clinking her glass against Chelsea's. "I'm not sure I've ever experienced so many family dramas compressed into such a short time."

Chelsea laughed, taking a sip of her wine. "Between your mother's van life revelation, Becca's early delivery, Lauren's move, Isabelle and Gretchen's café adventure, and now Beth's pregnancy news, I'd say this qualifies as the summer of surprises."

A family of sandpipers scurried past, their thin legs a blur as they chased the receding wavelets. A short distance away, a young couple walked hand in hand along the water's edge, leaving paired footprints that disappeared moments later under the gentle assault of the incoming tide.

"Gabriel must be over the moon," Chelsea observed. "He's had that 'future father' look in his eyes since they got married."

"Beth says he's already talking to her stomach, telling the baby all about life on the farm," Maggie confirmed with a fond smile. "Apparently, the little one needs to know the difference between a McIntosh and a Northern Spy before even developing ears," she said and then switched subjects. "I still can't quite believe Lauren is really moving to Florida. After all these years of hoping, it's finally happening."

Chelsea studied her friend's face, noting the subtle glow of happiness that seemed to emanate from within. "You're over the moon about this, aren't you?"

"Is it that obvious?" Maggie laughed. "I'm trying not to be too smug about it. Beth already thinks I orchestrated the whole thing somehow."

"Didn't you?"

"I wish I had that much power! But no, this was all Olivia's talent and Lauren and Jeff making the right decision for their family." Maggie sipped her wine, then added more softly, "Though I won't pretend I'm not thrilled to have them close. Lauren has always struggled with the distance more than she admits."

"She has," Chelsea agreed. "She's never fully accepted you moving here. Not the way Beth, Christopher and Michael have."

A comfortable silence fell between them as they watched a pelican dive into the water, emerging moments later with a fish wriggling in its beak.

"Have you heard from your mother lately?" Chelsea asked, unable to keep the amusement from her voice. "How's the Garrison Getaway adventure progressing?"

Maggie groaned, though her expression was more fond than truly exasperated. "She's on her way to the Smoky Mountains with Esther Jenkins and that ridiculous Yorkie. Apparently, Napoleon has his own Instagram account now. My mother is managing social media for a dog while driving across the country in a camper van. This is what my life has become."

Chelsea burst out laughing. "I've started following her YouTube channel. The synchronized firefly video was surprisingly moving."

"Of course you're following her." Maggie sighed. "Everyone is. Paolo showed me her subscriber count yesterday—it's nearly doubled since she hit the road. She's becoming a genuine senior influencer."

"Speaking of surprising living arrangements," Chelsea said, refilling their wine glasses, "Gretchen mentioned something interesting this morning. Apparently, Isabelle has offered to let her move in until she finds her own place."

Maggie's eyebrows shot up. "Seriously? Isabelle and Gretchen living under the same roof? Working together AND living together?"

"That's exactly what I said!" Chelsea laughed. "They'll either kill each other or the Captiva Café and the team of Isabelle and Gretchen might be the best thing to hit the island in years."

"My money's on the latter, actually," Maggie said thoughtfully. "They have an odd chemistry together. Isabelle keeps Gretchen focused, and Gretchen brings out a lighter side of Isabelle that's been missing since Sebastian died."

"True," Chelsea agreed. "Though I'm not sure Isabelle fully understands what she's getting into. Gretchen's personal organization system makes a hurricane look orderly. My house hasn't been the same since she moved in. As far as your mother is concerned, does it really surprise you, though?" Chelsea asked. "Your mother has never been one to fade quietly into the background. The van life suits her independent spirit."

"No, it doesn't surprise me," Maggie admitted. "It worries me, but it doesn't surprise me. She's always been fearless—much more so than I am."

"Says the woman who uprooted her entire life to start an inn on Captiva Island in her fifties," Chelsea pointed out. "I'd say fearlessness runs in the family."

Maggie smiled at that. "Perhaps. Though moving to Captiva felt less like a leap of faith and more like coming home. This has always been where I belonged."

"And now your children are finding their way here too. Well, most of them."

"Two out of four isn't bad," Maggie said. "Though I haven't completely given up hope for Beth and Christopher eventually. And, Michael, being a Boston police officer, will never move out of Boston."

"One miracle at a time," Chelsea advised. "Let's celebrate Lauren's move before you start plotting to lure the rest of your brood south."

"Speaking of which," Maggie said, digging into the beach bag at her feet, "Lauren sent a picture of the new house today. It's practically a palace compared to what they have in Massachusetts."

She handed her phone to Chelsea, who let out a low whistle as she swiped through the photos.

"Goodness, is that the master bathroom? It's bigger than my first apartment," Chelsea marveled. "And that pool! Daniel's going to be swimming like a fish within a month."

"Lily is thrilled about the window seat in her room," Maggie said. "And Olivia's already planning how to organize her tennis trophies in the built-in shelving. Jeff seems relieved they found something so perfect so quickly."

"Has the reality of the move hit Lauren yet?" Chelsea asked, handing the phone back. "Moving is stressful even when it's a positive change."

Maggie nodded, tucking the phone away. "She's in that strange in-between phase—excited about the future but a little melancholy about what they're leaving behind. Twenty years in one place creates deep roots. Plus, she has plans to build her real estate business down here. We'll see, one step at a time."

They refilled their wine glasses as the sun dipped lower on the horizon. A group of dolphins appeared in the distance, their dorsal fins breaking the surface in a synchronized dance that drew delighted cries from the few remaining beachgoers.

"How's Isabelle doing?" Maggie asked, her tone growing more solemn. "I saw her at the café site yesterday with your sister, but we didn't get a chance to really talk."

Chelsea considered the question carefully. "She has good days and harder days. The café project has been a blessing—it gives her purpose, a future to work toward. But I still catch her sometimes with that faraway look."

"Grief isn't linear," Maggie observed softly. "It comes in waves, retreating and advancing when you least expect it."

"She told me something interesting last week," Chelsea said. "We were discussing paint colors for the café, and somehow the conversation turned to Sebastian. She said she's realized that grief isn't just sadness or loss—it's love with nowhere to go."

"That's beautiful," Maggie murmured. "And true."

"She's finding places to channel that love, though. The café. Her friendships with us. Even my chaotic sister seems to bring out something positive in her."

"Your chaotic sister has been surprisingly grounded lately," Maggie pointed out. "Maybe they're good for each other."

Chelsea nodded thoughtfully. "They balance each other in an unexpected way. Isabelle provides structure and refinement; Gretchen brings enthusiasm and spontaneity. Their differences complement rather than clash."

"The way all the best partnerships do," Maggie agreed. "Like you and Steven."

"Or you and Paolo," Chelsea added with a smile. "They're lucky, you know," Chelsea said more seriously. "Your children. Having a stepfather who embraces them and their children so completely."

"I know," Maggie replied softly. "I'm the lucky one, though. Finding Paolo when I did, having this second chapter that's turned out to be more beautiful than I could have imagined." She glanced at Chelsea. "Just like you with Steven."

"Just like me with Steven," Chelsea echoed. "Though I still maintain Sebastian did me a favor by introducing us, even if his motives were questionable at the time."

"The universe works in mysterious ways," Maggie agreed. "Sometimes the paths we think are leading us to one destination are actually taking us somewhere much better."

"I'm going to miss Sebastian. He was a special person," Chelsea added.

Maggie placed her hand on Chelsea's arm and smiled. "Me too."

They watched as the sun finally touched the horizon, the sky ablaze with color as day prepared to surrender to evening. The water reflected the fiery display, turning the gentle waves into ribbons of gold and crimson.

"Do you remember what Isabelle said that night at my house, after Sebastian's memorial?" Chelsea asked, her voice growing softer as the moment called for reverence. "About sisters?"

Maggie nodded, her eyes on the sunset. "I've practically memorized it and even shared it with Beth. 'Sisters, whether born of the same blood or found in the journey of life, are like the different threads in a tapestry. Alone, each is beautiful—but woven together, they create something far more magnificent.'"

"Captiva Sisters," Chelsea said softly. "That's what we've become, haven't we? You, me, Isabelle. All of us here. Different threads in the same tapestry."

"I like that," Maggie replied, reaching over to squeeze Chelsea's hand. "Captiva Sisters. Different paths that somehow led us all to this same stretch of beach, to these shared sunsets and intertwined lives."

"I wouldn't want it any other way," Chelsea said.

"Neither would I," Maggie agreed.

They sat in silence as the sun disappeared below the horizon, leaving behind a sky painted in deepening shades of purple and blue. Stars began to appear, one by one, while the restless Gulf waters continued their eternal conversation with the shore.

Family dramas would come and go. Children would move closer or further away. Mothers would embark on surprising new adventures. Friends would face loss and renewal. Through it all, the island remained—a constant in the changing tides of their lives, a place where threads of different colors and textures could weave together into something stronger and more beautiful than any could create alone.

The Captiva Sisters raised their glasses one more time as

darkness settled fully over the beach, a toast to everything that had been and everything yet to come.

"To us," Chelsea said simply.

"To us," Maggie echoed. "And to all the chapters yet to be written."

THE END

Thank you for reading Captiva Sisters. The characters in this series have become family to me, and I hope you feel the same.

If you haven't read the other books in this series, I've listed them all as well as other books I've written on the next two pages.

ALSO BY ANNIE CABOT

THE PERIWINKLE SHORES SERIES
Book One: CHRISTMAS ON THE CAPE
Book Two: THE SEA GLASS GIRLS
Book Three: ON CLIFF ROAD

THE SEASIDE PALMS SERIES
Book One: KEY WEST PROMISES

THE CAPTIVA ISLAND SERIES
Book One: KEY LIME GARDEN INN
Book Two: A CAPTIVA WEDDING
Book Three: CAPTIVA MEMORIES
Book Four: CAPTIVA CHRISTMAS
Book Five: CAPTIVA NIGHTS
Book Six: CAPTIVA HEARTS
Book Seven: CAPTIVA EVER AFTER
Book Eight: CAPTIVA HIDEAWAY
Book Nine: RETURN TO CAPTIVA
Book Ten: CAPTIVA CABANA
Book Eleven: CAPTIVA COTTAGE
Book Twelve: CAPTIVA MOONLIGHT
Book Thirteen: CAPTIVA BOOK CLUB
Book Fourteen: SLEIGH. BELLS ON CAPTIVA

For a free copy of the prequel to the Captiva Island Series -
Captiva Sunset- please sign up for my newsletter here: https://dl.
bookfunnel.com/1k2zenybuw

ABOUT THE AUTHOR

Annie Cabot is the author of contemporary women's fiction and family sagas. Annie writes about friendships and family relationships, that bring inspiration and hope to others.

With a focus on women's fiction, Annie feels that she writes best when she writes from experience. "Every woman's journey is a relatable story. I want to capture those stories, let others know they are not alone, and bring a bit of joy to my readers."

Annie Cabot is the pen name for the writer Patricia Pauletti. A lover of all things happily ever after, it was only a matter of time before she began to write what was in her heart, and so, the pen name Annie Cabot was born.

When she's not writing, Annie and her husband like to travel. Winters always involve time away on Captiva Island, Florida where she continues to get inspiration for her novels.

ACKNOWLEDGMENTS

With each book I continue to be grateful to the people who support my work. I couldn't do what I do without this team. Thank you all so much.

Cover Design: Marianne Nowicki
Premade Ebook Cover Shop
https://www.premadeebookcovershop.com/

Editor: Lisa Lee of Lisa Lee Proofreading and Editing
https://www.facebook.com/EditorLisaLee/
Beta Readers:
John Battaglino
Nancy Burgess
Michele Connolly
Anne Marie Page Cooke